ON SINAI'S LOFTY MOUNTAIN

Other Works by Sidney Du Broff

Woe to the Rebellious Children

Black Fuse

Shooting, Fishing and Gun Book

Fishing the English Lakes

Fly Fishing on Still Water

Sid Du Broff's Field Sports Diary

Still Water Fly Fishing for Young People

Sidney Du Broff

ON SINAI'S LOFTY MOUNTAIN

Geiser Productions
London

First published in the United Kingdom in 1997
by Geiser Productions
7 The Corner, Grange Road, London W5 3PQ
Tel: 0181 579 4653, Fax: 0181 567 6593

ISBN 0 9503262 4

Typeset in 11/13pt Nebraska by
Ann Buchan (Typesetters), Middlesex
Printed byAthenaeum Press, Newcastle-upon-Tyne

For Nedra

Who reaches for the stars in the sky –
and gives them as her gift to me

1

M ark Spaulding sits at a table in Dario's with several others, near the door, in the process of finishing lunch.

Dario's is a small, intimate restaurant where Washington insiders gather to exchange thoughts, some ideas, some information, some relevant gossip.

Mark is a lawyer, a partner in the Washington-based think-tank, the United States Center for World Study. He is more than six and a half feet tall, with broad shoulders, an imposing man in his early forties, as much inclined to listen as to speak.

Ruggedly good-looking, people cannot help but take notice of him, though he is not particularly aware of his exceptional looks. His eyes are brown, his hair, cut short – but not too short – is auburn. His face is clean-shaven, open and inquisitive. There is an air of quiet confidence about him. His physical power is obvious, too, which he appears – not consciously – to try to minimize, concerned that it might be intimidating.

The door bursts open at Dario's. George Warton explodes into the restaurant, seething with anger and indignation, a newspaper in his hand. A man in his forties, biggish, going to fat, hair cropped short; Mark knows him as someone fairly high up in the Defense Department, whom he does not particularly like, rather overbearing like those frequently encountered at Defense.

Warton stops in front of Mark's table. He holds up the paper, which has obviously just appeared, in both of his trembling hands. The headline screams: ALAN BRADY CAUGHT SPYING FOR ISRAEL.

In a voice filled with rage, Warton says, "He's that rotten little Jew-bastard over at Naval Intelligence. All those rotten Jews are traitors. They'll sell out to Israel every day of the week. Too bad Hitler didn't get them all!"

Only by chance has Warton stopped at Mark's table. Now Mark

stands up, and confronts Warton, towering over him. Warton looks surprised, and annoyed, that someone is about to interfere with his important disclosures.

Mark takes a slow and deliberate step toward Warton. With the same deliberation, he gathers up Warton by the shirt front with his left hand, and smashes him hard in the face with his right hand, the sound of fist against flesh audible throughout most of the restaurant.

The diners gasp in stunned silence as Warton falls against the not-yet-cleared table opposite. Most of those present who are witness to the entire scenario feel immense satisfaction; those not in sympathy find it expedient to stay silent, and seated.

Warton remains immobile on the table, blood spurting from an obviously broken nose. He looks up at Mark, who is standing over him, with a mixture of terror and hatred, too frightened to move, too frightened to offer a defense. "I'll get you," Warton says. "I'll get you if it's the last thing I ever do."

Mark is in no mood to be threatened. He jerks Warton from the table, and holds him up with both hands. He looks hard into Warton's eyes and says, "Get me! Get me now, you son of a bitch!"

Now is not the time. Warton remains limp, like a rag doll, held up only by Mark's powerful hands. Warton makes no reply, aware that his immediate future is highly dubious.

Mark flings him down hard against the table. The table collapses. The dishes fall on him. The gravy stains his suit, and his white shirt, now turned red with his own blood.

Dario, having observed the whole scene, rushes over to Mark. "Are you all right, Mr. Spaulding," he asks, concern in his voice.

"I'm fine, Dario, just fine."

Dario turns to Warton, still on the floor. "Get out of my restaurant," he screams at him. "Get out of my restaurant and don't ever come back, you scum of the earth." He signals for his waiters, who are standing nearby. "Get this man out of here. Throw him in the gutter."

Before they can comply two men appear from the back of the restaurant, perhaps colleagues whom Warton had come here to meet, if their close-cropped heads are any clue. "We'll deal with him," one of them says.

Distastefully they lean down to retrieve Warton, who moves his elbows slightly so that the two men can pick him up. Clumsily they get him to his feet, half carrying him, half dragging him out of the door.

Most of the diners break into spontaneous applause. "Good for you," some of them call. "Well done."

Mark reddens. He feels suddenly embarrassed. He returns to his chair and sips his coffee, and rubs his bruised hand.

This is Washington D.C. – District of Columbia – the capital of the United States of America, where the laws are made, essentially a small town, where news travels fast. In a very short time most people in Washington will have heard about the incident at Dario's. Before the day is out it will also be common knowledge in the bedroom suburbs around Washington. Mobile phones have their uses.

Mark returns to his office. His partner, Bill Cooper, knows about it. So does his assistant, Claire Alderson. Mark sits down at his desk. Claire is immediately aware of his bruised hand, taking it in both of hers to comfort and minister to it. "It's terrible," she says.

He withdraws the hand, unwilling to let her have it. "I'm all right," he says.

"You're not. That hand needs attention."

Claire goes to get the first aid kit. She is in her beginning thirties, highly attractive, highly competent, like the thousands of girls who come to Washington every year to pursue a career – with a congressman from back home, in law offices, with lobbyists, in governmental institutions, with think tanks. She returns with the first aid kit and sits down in the chair next to Mark. She takes his hand. He gives it, but with a certain amount of reluctance, not looking at her. If he had been watching her, he would have noticed the tears coming into her blue eyes. She is tall and thin and smart looking, with darkish shoulder-length hair.

Bill Cooper takes the chair on the other side of Mark, and sits down. He is in his early fifties, a one-time university professor, of political science. His gentle face shows deep concern.

"Mark, why don't you go home," Cooper advises.

"What for?"

"You must be shaken up."

"I feel remarkably good, Bill. Now I'm sorry I didn't hit him again."

"Mark, this could be serious."

9

"Very serious. I made that plain enough."

"What about repercussions?"

"I don't think the Defense Department will want to become directly involved. They wouldn't want to appear too obvious."

"But they will be there – along with Warton."

Mark shrugged. "Probably."

"What are you going to do about it?"

With his left hand Mark opens the bottom drawer of his desk. A 9mm Israeli-made Jericho auto-loading pistol rests in a shoulder holster. "I'll stop off at the range and get in some target practice."

Claire, seeing the gun, and hearing Mark's words, begins to tremble. With her shaking hands she clutches Mark's injured hand, which she causes to gyrate. He turns to look at her disapprovingly. The tears are running down her cheeks. "I'm sorry," she says, laying Mark's hand down in her lap.

"Are you finished?" he asks her rather curtly.

She shakes her head. "No."

"Claire, please hurry up. I've got a lot of work to do."

"I can't help it."

To Bill, Mark says, "I thought I had escaped the perils of a Jewish mother. And this one isn't even Jewish."

"Please don't make fun of me, Mark."

Mark, feeling contrite, says, "It's my bad sense of humor. I apologize."

The tears flow. There is the occasional sob. Mark pretends not to hear nor to see. He leaves his hand with her, to do with as she likes, a kind of peace offering. This is not the usual Claire, who hardly ever flaps, who can deal effectively and efficiently with most situations – who has been doing it for Mark here at the United States Center for World Study for the past eight years.

Bill, also embarrassed, pretends not to notice. "I'm not saying there's anything wrong with being able to hit the target. But under the circumstances you may very well be the target. They will get in the first salvo – and there won't be any opportunity for you to reply."

"I'll have to take my chances, Bill. Won't I."

Claire reacts to his words with a repressed sob. Mark wants to tell her to go back to her own office, and to leave his arm behind. But he says nothing; only his arm stiffens in reaction.

Bill, deeply concerned, says, "We know the Defense Department occupies an inordinately high place in this country. Too much so. They are the tail that wags the American dog."

"It's going into the current report, Bill." The project on which Mark and Claire are working at USCWS is the examination of America's state and condition.

"I think we should lodge a protest."

"With whom?"

"The Defense Department."

"Do you think it will be of any value?"

"It will serve notice on them that we are taking the behavior of one of their employees with the utmost gravity. We are the ones issuing the complaint. And it might be useful to notify the press. We have nothing to hide. And I think that it could be useful protection for you."

"You have a point."

"I also think that this Brady thing has some very deep implications. The Defense Department knows something we don't know – a lot. Warton probably reflected that."

2

Mark reaches home that evening after work. His son David, almost thirteen, is there to greet him, opens the door before Mark does. He throws his arms around his father. "I'm glad you got that son of a bitch."

Mark gives his son a hug, and looks at him disapprovingly.

David says, "I'm just quoting – you."

Mark looks down at his son and smiles with pleasure. "How was I ever lucky enough to have a son like you?"

"Because I was lucky enough to have a father like you."

Mark hugs his son warmly.

David, tall for his age, has blond hair and blue eyes. He does not resemble his father at all, but it is not hard to see that David is Mark's son, mainly by the way David recreates in himself, consciously or otherwise, his father's movements and gestures.

Gently David picks up Mark's bandaged hand and examines it, suffering his own pain. "You must have hit him pretty hard."

11

"I probably did. But don't be deceived by the bandage. It doesn't reflect the wound. Claire was playing nurse."

"I like Claire. She's nice."

"Except when she plays nurse. What have you been doing today?"

"Answering the phone a lot. All the papers have been calling – the Washington Post was the last one. I told them all about it. I told them how you punched in the face of that son of a bitch."

"Maybe I ought to let you handle my public relations."

"All the kids at school know about it. I was really proud of you, Dad."

"Thanks. Besides dealing with the press what else have you been doing?"

"I had a very interesting experience. I think it was spiritual. I went with Aaron to his Bar Mitzvah class – with Rabbi Moreheim."

"Doesn't that compromise your atheist principles?"

"I don't know. I was wondering if they're not just yours," David replies slowly, thoughtfully.

"Are you going to abandon them then?"

"If we as Jews created God, then there must be one – if not in the flesh, then in our souls and in our hearts."

"I can't argue with that."

"You always said that man created God, and not the other way around. All right, so man did create God. And when he finished – he had God. If you make a book shelf, then you got a book shelf. It's real. It's there. And the same with God. You make God. You got God."

"If you want God. Do you?"

David thinks about it for a moment. "I don't know. I'm not sure. Aaron doesn't have any problems with it. He says it's comfortable. And he just leaves it there. He's a Jew, and I'm a Jew, but we don't seem to be in the same place. Aaron speaks Hebrew. His father speaks Hebrew. It's supposed to be our holy language. I don't speak a word of it – just 'Shalom'. When we were in Israel I said 'Shalom', and they said 'Shalom' back. And when it was Saturday they said 'Shalom Shabbat'. And I didn't know enough to say 'Shabbat Shalom'."

Mark nods "I understand what you're saying, David."

"I'm a Jew – but why? What do I do with it? I know Grandpa was in the war – and he fought for Israel – and Grandma, too.

Grandpa's friend was killed in the War of Independence – and he wasn't even Jewish. And Grandpa and Grandma planted a forest for him in Israel. And I'm named after him. But what have I done? What am I? Mom doesn't even light the candles on Friday night."

"Would you want her to?"

"Sure. But it's not just that. It's a lot of things. There are a lot of things I don't understand, Dad. Maybe you can explain them to me. We'll talk about it. I want to get my thoughts together."

"Any time you're ready, David."

"I always felt something was missing. I don't know what exactly. But today, with Aaron, and Rabbi Moreheim, I felt, maybe, here it was."

Mark puts his arm around his son. "Maybe. We'll explore it further."

"Okay, Dad. I'd like that."

"Your mother is home?"

"She's in the den. I think she's kind of worried."

"What about?"

"You."

"I'd better have a word with her and tell her there's nothing to worry about."

Mark tousles David's hair and walks across the large living room, his limp, slight, but easily perceptible, in the direction of the den, and down the few stairs. The door is closed. Mark opens it and enters.

Sandy is sitting near the fireplace, making notes on a clip board. When she sees Mark she takes off her glasses and stands up. "Come on over and give me a big hug," she says, in her soft Georgia drawl. "I've been looking forward to it the whole day."

Her eyes shine, the same blue eyes that she had given her son. It is easy to see that she is David's mother. The room seems to take on a new glow. Mark hugs her and holds her close, and kisses both of her eyes. And then her lips.

"That's just what I needed," she says. "You had a hard day."

"But a rewarding one."

She holds up his bandaged hand. "So I understand."

"It's Claire's work. If it was up to her I'd be in splints. I can take most of it off now – now that she's not around."

"She's in love with you, Mark. Don't be too hard on her."

"I don't believe it. She must have loads of boy friends. She's a remarkable woman. I don't know what I'd do without her. She's as involved with this report on the American condition as I am."

Sandy is a lawyer, a partner in the law firm of Draycott Webber Warner and Fraser. About two years younger than Mark, she remains the gracious southern lady. Her presence can be felt. The warmth that she generates touches those who come close. Her blonde hair, tied in a bun at the back of her head, is allowed to fall over her shoulders at bedtime.

She puts her glasses back on, used for reading, sits down on the black leather chair and looks at her clip board. Mark sits on the big leather hassock in front of her. "I won't pretend I'm not concerned," Sandy says. "I am. I don't believe the Department of Defense is very happy at the moment. I expect they're going to try and retaliate. The best thing we can do is get all the publicity we can. If the press wants to talk to you, you sure do want to talk to them. The way I see it, it's a kind of insurance policy."

"I'm not sure the Department of Defense wouldn't prefer to ignore the whole thing."

"Maybe. But will Warton? I don't think he will. And I think he'll involve Defense as much as he's able. which brings me to the second point. There's something going on here. Defense is involved. But it's bigger than that. And it smells worse than any skunk that's been hit on the road. Mark, it's to do with Alan Brady. There are a lot of things they're not telling us here. Why was he spying for Israel?"

"I assume Israel has spies around – just like we do."

"But why did Israel need to? That's my point. I would have assumed that Israel and the United States has some sort of mutual arrangement regarding the pooling of information. Don't they? Did they ever have? Did it come unstuck?"

"It's obviously an incident that's embarrassing to both sides. My guess is that they will both choose to ignore it."

"Except that it wouldn't have made the headlines. Washington would have waved a finger at Israel and said, 'Don't do it again'. And we wouldn't know anything about Alan Brady if they were prepared to overlook it."

"Presuming you're right, how do you read it?"

"An overt shift in policy regarding Israel – and an attack on American Jews."

"I wouldn't like to think so."

"Jews have a way of ignoring unpleasant facts – in the hope that they will go away – but they never do."

"Then what do we do? Shout 'Fire!'?"

"Could be the incident today has a lot to do with it. And you sure as heck shouted 'Fire!'. Not that I'm saying there's anything wrong with what you did. That bastard really got what he deserved."

There is silence for a moment. Mark wants to say something. Something related to this, and unrelated. He isn't sure how to say it, or how it will be received. Say it directly, he thinks. Say it how it is.

"Sandy," he says at last, "there's something I want to talk to you about."

She leans back in the leather armchair, takes off her glasses, puts them on the rug near her, and looks up at Mark attentively.

"I want you to convert," he says simply.

Sandy breaths out slowly. It is a few moments before she replies.

"Because of today?"

"I suppose that might have something to do with it."

"You're feeling isolated – as a Jew – and the person closest to you is a gentile."

"I haven't analysed it, but if I did, I'd probably reach that conclusion."

"I understand."

"Do you?"

"Of course. I'm part of you, my love. You are Jewish, I am Jewish. What you are, I am. It's never been any other way. I wouldn't want it any other way. We've been through this before – a long time ago. I thought it was settled."

"Maybe it was just in abeyance. Maybe it was dormant, because it didn't matter so much then. Now I feel it's imperative."

"Why is a formal conversion necessary?"

"Because it's a statement – a commitment."

"Don't you have that commitment already, Mark?"

"Logically, yes. There's never been any doubt. Emotionally, I don't think so. I feel that you're holding back something – something you won't give all the way."

"I would sooner die than hurt you. Do you believe that?"

"Yes."

"I can't be apart of your history and your culture. No matter

15

how much I study and understand it. If we were religious people, perhaps I would see it differently. But we have always shared our non-religious faith. We have always had that in common. Christianity is not my religion any more than Judaism is yours."

"Judaism isn't my religion, but it's my life – what I am – all that has gone before."

"No one is denying that. Your son is Jewish. It's his culture and his history. I come from the outside. I have joined up with you. I am your ally in life, in everything that you do. I would like to be Jewish. I would like your history to be mine, your culture to be ours. I am the one who has been deprived in many ways. Perhaps in a Jewish milieu, where I was part of it, working with it, and in it, I would have a different perspective. But we never have lived in that milieu. Your commitment is historical and cultural and perhaps for you that is sufficient. But for me – I founder. It can't mean the same thing for me that it does for you. I think that someone in my position has to be involved in it – has to earn the right to be Jewish."

"I take your point, Sandy."

"But you're not convinced."

Mark shakes his head. "I'm convinced by your arguments. They're perfectly reasonable."

"But the isolation remains. At least a part of me, you feel, remains in the enemy camp."

Mark doesn't reply. His silence is agreement. He stands up and walks from the den.

Sandy bites her lip. Tears come into her eyes. It would be easy to covert. That is what he wants. Is she being a fool, she asks herself, to deny him that? She has hurt him deeply. She could not bear the thought of bringing him pain. Yet conversion meant giving up a part of herself – all that went before in her life. Admittedly it isn't all that much to get excited about, that much to want to retain. But it was hers. Certainly it could be in addition. But Judaism isn't an extension of her life, because a Jewish world hardly touches them. For her it is in the abstract. Mark could just take it for granted, and not have to think about it most of the time, except when he had to hit someone. Too bad it wasn't going to solve all the problems – or any of them – and could well make more.

Their life together was good. Why did this thing have to intrude now? Maybe Mark was right, and it was always there, more or less

16

dormant. This is what she could not fathom, the complexities of Judaism, of his Judaism, or even the Judaism that was hers. She had read, and learned and studied, and she knew something about it, but from books, and not from inside of her, because it wasn't hers. They would resolve this issue, she thought to herself, ultimately. She knew that she would not let it stand between them. Nothing would ever come between them. But how did she remain herself, when the most important person in her life demanded alterations?

She looks about the den. It was a wonderful room, a symbol of their lives. Deer heads protruded from the walls, good white tail bucks that Mark and David had taken, as well as David's first pheasant, and his first good size trout. There was a covey of bob white quail – from a hunt down in Georgia. Her father had had them mounted – his present to them – so that they could remember it always. Photographs and paintings of dogs and game lined the wall. And the gun cabinet was filled with rifles and shotguns that belonged to Mark and David.

Father and son – friends, companions. She could make a child, and give it as a gift to this man, whom she loved, all without complexity. But this – it had the profoundest implications – and without obvious solutions.

3

Mark returned to Berkeley after his war. He was glad to be back, glad to still be alive. Most people took being alive for granted. He never would again.

Not all that much had changed at Berkeley, except that now there were even more posters, more banners, more graffiti denouncing the war in Vietnam, which he viewed with satisfaction. This was the University named for George Berkeley, the Irish-born philosopher, dedicated to man's highest ideals.

Here at Berkeley they were quick to perceive that the war in Vietnam was the wrong war, and made their feelings apparent. And they inspired the rest to stand up and state their objections. The awareness of the war was real here, but the reality, far removed from the killing grounds. Young men and women walked in peace on this beautiful autumn day, carrying books, which soon many of those young men would be exchanging for guns, unless they could bring this war to an end.

It was the first day of class. Mark was resuming his law studies. He entered the large lecture hall. Sandy was already there, standing, waiting, as if for him. Their eyes meet for the first time. Perhaps their souls too. They are transfixed. For them the earth stops rotating. There is no one else on the earth except for them. It all takes place in the space of a moment.

Reluctantly Mark forces himself to break the spell, to move away. Sandy remains standing where she is, unable, unwilling to let this moment end.

Mark takes a place at the back of the lecture hall. He needs to be able to stretch out his leg. It has been bothering him. It is throbbing, his souvenir from Vietnam.

Sandy sits at the front. He watches her take her seat, relieved that she has allowed for a separation between them. But at the same time, he wishes that she were sitting next to him. Inside he is churning. The law professor is saying something. Obviously something important. Mark does not know what. Mark does not hear a word. His eyes take him to where Sandy sits. He watches the back of her, her blonde hair. Could this have really happened? Or is it just imagination. He attributes it to Vietnam, but knows deep down that he has run away from this girl, frightened by what he feels.

Sandy does not hear the professor, either. She knows that this has happened to her, relives the moment, makes it a part of her. He is behind her, sitting there somewhere at the back. She wants to turn, and see him there, affirm what she knows. But she waits, waits, savors the instant when she will turn. Did it really happen? She knows that it did. Does he know it, too?

She swivels around swiftly, a part of her afraid that unless she moves quickly, he won't be there, only the shell of her imagination. But he is there. His eyes have been on her. Theirs meet for a tiny part of a second, before he consciously turns them away.

She knows. And he knows. But there seems a certain reticence, a reluctance to acknowledge what had taken place between them. He is frightened – though he does not look as if he would be frightened of anything. He is. Of her. She senses this of him. Too fast. Too fast. For him.

She waits for him after the lecture. He seems reluctant to leave his seat. Don't wait. Don't wait. Go. He stands up, but does not move until he can think of no reason for continuing to stand there. Someone else will be using this room soon. Maybe he could stay for the next lecture. He wonders what the topic is.

She waits. But he does not appear. He obviously does not wish for their meeting of eyes to be further consummated. She walks on. He won't go away. And neither will she. There is tomorrow, and tomorrow. Perhaps it is too sudden for him, too difficult to assimilate all that their eyes said to each other, their souls and their hearts.

In the real world there is a war to be fought, the war against the war – the war America will ultimately lose. Mark presents himself at the anti-war office, volunteers his services wherever they might be of value. She is there. Their eyes acknowledge each other, and he turns away. Her smile is barely perceptible, a smile of satisfaction: He is here. He would come here. She has been here for some time. His presence here confirms what she knows. It does not come as a surprise.

They work together in the fight against the war. They talk – strictly about the war: how many posters they need, how many envelopes. Nothing personal. Nothing revealing about how they feel. It has already been said, if not spoken. She accepts it for that. He does not want to encourage what he knows is there.

In the lecture hall his eyes fall upon her. She turns, aware of him, and he turns away quickly. She smiles to herself. With others he is easy, and talks and jokes. He has an infectious personality. So has she; people are drawn to her. She laughs easily. She touches people, physically, unconsciously, wanting to know them, to understand what they feel. Sandy and Mark do not touch, do not see each other socially, only in the war office, in class, at demonstrations. But they are regarded as a couple. No one thinks to question it. It is there, demonstrably obvious, yet there is no evidence that this is so. Perhaps it is the way she looks at him when he speaks at anti-war rallies, the way she looks at him when he is close by.

There is a big anti-war rally on campus. It is Saturday afternoon. Mark is the main speaker. He sits on the platform with the others, a long row of medals attached to his jacket, presented to him for extraordinary service, by a grateful nation. From time to time

19

Sandy studies his face, lets her eyes fall on his medals, then returns to his face. There is a look of quiet satisfaction about her; perhaps it is that look that makes it apparent that they are one.

The crowds are enormous. Many carry placards demanding an end to the war. They shout anti-war slogans. Sandy sees only Mark. The press is there in large numbers – the San Francisco Chronicle, the Bay papers, the Los Angeles Times, as well as the wire and press services.

It is Mark's turn to speak. He goes to the microphone and raises it up. He speaks without notes, spontaneously, off the top of his head. He is not at a loss for words. "It is up to us to save our country," he says. "It is up to us to extricate ourselves from this disgraceful war we have inflicted on millions of innocent people in Vietnam . . . and on ourselves. They are our victims, and we are our own victims – self-imposed and self-inflicted, by a government that places no value on your life, intent on fostering its erroneous concepts on a mainly resisting world. It is for us, who will be asked to pay the price, to resist, to make our feelings unmistakably clear, to stand up to this government and say NO!" There is tumultuous applause and cheering. Mark waits until there is silence again. He talks. They listen. They agree with every word. This is them, this is their country. They want to fight to save it.

"I was there," Mark says. "I was in the wrong place, doing the wrong thing. And for that they gave me some medals" – amongst them the Distinguished Service Cross, awarded for exceptional heroism; the Congressional Medal of Honor, for risking life above and beyond the call of duty; the Purple Heart, for shedding blood for his country.

Mark removes the medals from his chest and drops them at his feet. "I do not want these," he says. "They do me no credit. Nor are they any credit to my country."

He steps on them and crushes them under his foot.

The crowd goes wild, shouting and applauding. The press photographers record the event, delaying their shock until after they have done their work.

The rally ends. Sandy goes up to Mark. She puts her hand on his arm. "You were wonderful," she says.

"Thanks," he replies.

Their eyes meet.

"Let's talk, Mark."

He turns away, in the direction of his crushed medals. He does not say anything for a moment, as if searching for a way to avoid what now appears inevitable.

"All right," he says at last.

They walk on the campus. She takes his arm, as if it were her natural right. She feels the arm stiffen.

"Is there anything wrong with me?" she asks.

"No. Of course not."

"Then why do you avoid me?"

Mark stops. Her hand remains on his arm.

"Because I can't handle the situation."

"I wouldn't have thought it was all that difficult. In fact, I would have said it was pretty straight forward. Would you like to tell me why?"

"There are two thousand reasons."

"That sounds like a lot of reasons. Things look pretty bad. Could you explain that a bit better, so I can understand."

"Two thousand years of Christianity."

"Oh, that," she says, relief in her voice, easily dismissing those two thousand years. "I thought it was something important."

"It is, Sandy, for me."

"Are you talking about the past," she asks him, "or the present?"

"The present is as a result of the past."

"Let's sit down, Mark."

They find a bench. She sits close to him, both of her hands on his arm, as if she needs to hold on to him, frightened that he will flee.

"We didn't make the past, Mark. It isn't our responsibility."

"For some of us it is."

"If we choose it that way."

"I have chosen, Sandy. I like it that way. I want it that way. It is my history – my culture. I was born with the responsibility of that history and culture."

"That isn't a problem for me, Mark."

"But it is for me – the problem of who you are. My culture may have been a burden at times, but only as a result of those who wanted to take it away from us – one way or another. A Christian world out there seems determined to either kill us or convert us."

"I'm not trying to convert you, Mark."

"What frightens me – about us – is that you are a threat to who

I am."

She leans her head against his shoulder. "I present no threat to you, Mark, now or ever."

"A relationship like this – it tends to dilute that culture – until it disappears."

"I see no reason why it should. Don't let it exclude me, Mark." She looks deep into his eyes. "What you are, I am."

He holds her eyes with his, then looks away. "That's a very big commitment."

"I'm prepared to make it."

"I have no right to ask."

"I have the right to offer – to make the choice."

Mark does not speak. He is obviously shaken by this encounter.

"You think very hard with your head," she tells him.

"I'm trying."

"There isn't any need. Just remember, your life is mine. I want to share it with you."

"You barely know me, Sandy."

"I know all I need to know. Do you know me?"

"Yes."

"Then there's your answer. I heard your heart say it. Let's not throw this away. It's too good."

He does not reply. They stand up. She takes his arm, and they walk on, as if it is all settled between them.

"Let's go home, Mark," she says. "Let's go home."

They touch. They make love. They come to know each other fully and completely.

Afterwards, she says to him, "You're not obligated to marry me, you know."

"I'm relieved to hear that."

"My Daddy has a shotgun," she says with an exaggerated Georgian drawl, "but he ain't going to come looking for you with it and make you walk down that there church aisle with me."

He kisses her forehead. "It wouldn't be so bad if it were a synagogue."

"I don't think he'd go for that."

He kisses her eyes. "I'm not too concerned about your 'pappy'," he tells her with mock earnestness. "It's my 'mammy' you want to worry about. She's got a German Luger, and if she'd put an X on the handle every time she'd ever shot anybody, she'd need a box of extra handles."

"There must have been a lot of women in your life."

"Just giving you fair warning."

"I sure do appreciate that. And I'll bear it in mind."

"Does that put you off?"

"A bit. But I'll just have to take my chances. I'm sure your 'mammy' is a very protective lady."

"Very."

She leans over him and buries her head in his hairy chest. "I think your 'mammy' and I are going to get on real well." She looks up at him. "Mark, there isn't any point in living separate. Why don't you just get your things and move in here with me."

Georgia was the thirteenth colony. It was meant to be a haven for those who might safely be released from debtors' prison. They had to be sober, and convince a panel of judges in London that they were otherwise reliable and dependable. They got some land and some tools and could start life anew. Others followed, not all of them debtors, and not all of them total abstainers. Georgia is Sandy's state, Albany her hometown. The house in which she was brought up, Ashleigh, is big and comfortable. Her father is a judge – Jack Fraser. Ella May is her mother. She is an older version of Sandy, but of the generation who had not yet liberated themselves, nor even tried. They were generally strong and determined women – yet very feminine.

Ella May is preparing the guest room, filled with excitement and anticipation. Sandy is coming home to visit, and she's bringing Mark. Sandy will stay in her old room, Mark in the guest room. She hopes he'll like it. She can hardly wait to meet him. She has seen pictures of him. He's gorgeous. She can understand that Sandy could become involved with him.

Judge Fraser comes into the house then. He wears an old buckskin jacket, with fringes on the sleeves. It comes from the eight-point white tail deer, the head of which is attached to the wall. There are also fish on this wall – bass – their mouths wide open. Sometimes Judge Fraser wears a cowboy hat. But most of the time he wears a peaked hat, a baseball-type hat, known more generally as a redneck hat.

Judge Fraser is wearing one now. It is maroon. He thinks it is a dignified color. It says on it, in big yellow letters, I'M FOR JUDGE FRASER. Judge Fraser isn't a redneck, but he likes to give the impression that he is, that that is from where he comes. He says "ain't" a lot, and gives away his Judge Fraser hats as a gesture of good will.

"I'm worried," the judge says, "about this friend Sandy's bringing home."

"He looks all right to me," Ella May replies, "at least from his picture."

"You can't tell nothing from a picture. She ain't never brought anyone home before – at least, not a man. It must be serious."

"She's a girl with a lot of good judgement."

"In most things, yeah. I'd agree with that. But you know, when it comes to men, a girl can sometimes do some pretty foolish things. The man says some sweet sounding words, and next thing you know, the poor girl thinks she's in love."

"You mean like you and me."

"Now Ella May, you know what I mean. If I said 'em, I meant 'em."

"And maybe if he said them, he meant them, too."

"All right, so he does mean 'em. That ain't the big problem, though. What worries me is, he's a Jew."

Ella May shrugs.

"That doesn't worry you, woman?"

"Not especially. He probably doesn't have horns. If Sandy likes him, she must have some pretty good reasons."

"He ain't of our religion, or our way of life."

"He got his on Mount Sinai . . . On Sinai's lofty mountain."

"And what's even worse – he probably hasn't even got no religion – Jewish or otherwise. Sandy just threw away hers, like it was some worn out old shoes. It didn't suit her no more, and she didn't want it. I knew that was going to happen when she went away to that there school in California. I should've never let her go. They're all a bunch of radicals out there. And now my daughter's one of 'em. I guess we didn't bring her up so good, Ella May."

Ella May kisses the judge on the cheek. "We brought her up just fine. You know you're just as proud of her as I am."

"Well, I used to be – no use sayin' different. But then there was that there picture in the paper – right there in the Atlanta Journal

24

– of him stepping on his medals. And who's standing there right next to him – Sandy. I could've died when I saw that picture – him doing that to his medals – and her lookin' so pleased about it. Folks kept asking if it was Sandy in that picture. I kept sayin', 'No, of course not. That's just somebody who looks like Sandy.' I don't know if anybody believed me. Everybody knows what Sandy looks like. People all over the State probably sayin' 'Poor old Judge Fraser, got a radical daughter going to Berkeley'."

"They were his medals, Jack. He earned them – the hard way."

"Steppin' on the Congressional Medal of Honor? That's steppin' on your country. What kind of lack of patriotism is that? That don't go down very well with me."

"Maybe that's how he expresses his patriotism."

"Woman, I think you are as big and bad a radical as your daughter. You don't mind Jews. You don't mind people steppin' on their country. My family – and yours – they always fought for what they believed in – in every war this country had to fight. Only thing I got regrets about is that we didn't succeed – we didn't need to be in no union anyway. We had the Confederate States of America. And that's what makes me proud."

He points to the large Confederate flag that decorates the wall, said to have been carried into battle at Gettysburg. "That is my flag. Our ancestors – yours and mine, fought for that flag."

"And they were rebels, Jack, fighting against the Federal Government of the United States of America. So they weren't so patriotic after all."

The judge is taken aback for the moment. "They had their own patriotism – to their own cause."

"Just like the people at Berkeley."

"Ella May, you sure don't give a man no comfort. My daughter is bringing home a Jew, a Northerner – and you know what they think of us Southerners – a radical, probably an atheist – who wants to overthrow the government. And you don't think I have something to worry about? The least you could be doing is worrying alongside me."

Judge Fraser takes the bayonet-tipped Civil War percussion rifle down from the wall, one of many arms decorating the walls. He cradles the rifle in his arms fondly, then brings it up to his shoulder and aims it at the eight point buck. Sure that he has scored a hit, he lowers the rifle, turns to Ella May and says, "Too bad we didn't win that war. We wouldn't be having none of these problems now."

Mark and Sandy come to visit Ashleigh. Ella May hugs Mark warmly and kisses him on the cheek. And he kisses her. He is Sandy's choice, so he is hers, too. Sandy loves him, so she too loves him. Mark feels her warmth, is immediately comfortable with her.

Mark and Judge Fraser shake hands. The judge is somewhat overwhelmed by Mark's physical presence. He wants not to like him. Yet, now that they have encountered, he is even more disturbed, because there appears to be no apparent reason for antipathy. But of course, all the other reasons – they are still there – like cannon balls, piled up neatly, to be fired when expedient. However, if this man is his daughter's choice – for now anyway – firing cannon balls, no matter how accurate, will not make him go away. He knows he will not do anything that will alienate him from his daughter, assumes, at least hopes, that being a sensible girl, she will see things in their true light.

Sandy spends the night in her old room. Mark is in the guest room. In the morning Sandy, barefooted, goes down the hall to the guest room. Quietly she opens the door and enters. Getting into bed besides Mark, she says, "Move over."

He puts his arms around her and kisses her.

"Did you miss me?" she asks.

"No," he replies.

She pokes him in the ribs. "Pig. I missed you," she tells him. "It was horrible without you there. I slept in that bed almost my whole life. And now, suddenly, the part of my life that was without you was only half a life. I can't imagine a future without you lying close to me and holding me tight. I wouldn't want to. I think I'd sooner be dead."

Their lips touch gently.

"We've worked out well together, Mark, haven't we?"

His nod is barely perceptible.

"But you still have reservations." It is a statement, not a question. "I am Jewish, Mark," she says.

He sits up in bed, and leans against the backboard. "You don't just say 'I am Jewish' – and you are. The Inquisition has to be yours, and the pogroms, and Auschwitz, and the establishment of Israel as the homeland for the Jewish people."

"And if I converted, then Auschwitz would suddenly become mine, more so than it is now?"

"It's a declaration that says you want it to be."

"I make that declaration, Mark, every moment that you are with me – and every moment that we are apart. I make it when you hold me in your arms – because I am a part of you. Do you deny that?"

He shakes his head. "No."

"Would you want this never to have been? Would you want it to end?"

He moves close to her and buries his head on her chest. She has her answer, and his.

Over breakfast the judge says to Mark, "You ever been fishin'?"

"Yeah, quite a bit. But I haven't been for a long time."

"Hows come? Don't you like it no more?"

"I used to go with my father. When he died, it didn't seem the same after that. I tried going a couple of times on my own, but without him there I just couldn't come to terms with it. I remember, I took this good trout. I started walking back up stream – I wanted to show it to him. Then suddenly I remembered, he wouldn't be there. I never went again."

The judge nods sympathetically. "I understand. Where'd you do all this fishin'?"

"Alaska. British Columbia, the Eel, some of the other rivers in northern California. Sometimes we would go up to the High Sierras and pack in."

"That's a lot of fishin'. That was for trout and salmon and such like?"

Mark nods.

The judge is impressed. "What did you take 'em on mostly?"

"Flies."

The judge moves his head up and down slowly. There is awe in his voice. "You must be a pretty good fly caster."

"Not bad."

"You ever fish for bass?"

"Fairly often. We lived in Los Angeles and there were some warm water lakes not too far away, with a lot of good bass in them."

"You take them on a fly, too?"

"That's how we liked to fish."

The judge's eyes narrow, and he looks at Mark as if he wanted to confirm the veracity of someone in court who might appear before him. "You ever get any big ones?"

"My father had one that went over fourteen pounds, and several others over ten. I had a couple ten pounders."

"Good God. They sure must grow 'em big out there in California. I never had a ten pounder. I been trying my whole life. It ain't that we don't have none. I know they exist over in my lake at Ashmere. I just never caught none. I got me this here clerk over at the court house. He got hisself a ten pound bass. He prayed to the good Lord for one. He did a lot of prayin', that fella. He said 'Lord, you give me a ten pound bass, and I'll quit fishin'.' And sure enough, the Lord heard his prayers, and give him that fish."

"Did he stop fishing after that?"

"Had to. He made a deal with the Lord. You can't go back on no deal you make with the Lord.

"Maybe there is a lot of power in prayer."

"It didn't work with me. Of course I didn't make no deals. I didn't want to stop fishin'. But I did offer to make a very substantial donation to our church. That didn't work neither. I would've thought the Lord would've seen that as a lot better arrangement. Something like that can shake a man's faith . . . Listen, I got me a fly rod. It was a couple of years back. I seen it on television. This here fella was fly fishin' for bass, and when he done it, it sure did look easy. But when I tried, there was nothing easy about it. The dang-busted line kept winding itself around the tip of the rod. And when it didn't do that, it came and hooked me twice. I couldn't get the line out no how. I had the most miserable day of my whole life fishin'. I put that fly rod away and I ain't touched it since. Do you reckon you could teach me how to use it?"

"I think there's a pretty good chance."

"I'd be mighty grateful to you. What do you say we have a try after breakfast."

Sandy and her mother exchange knowing glances with each other.

In the large garden Mark gives instruction, while the judge holds the rod firmly in his hand, at the same time betraying his fear of it. "That line is near to human – and it's got the devil in it."

"You have to show it who's boss, Judge."

Mark is a good teacher.

The judge is a good pupil. "I'm getting the hang of it," he says excitedly after a time. "Come on, let's go out to the lake and try it for real. It ain't far to Ashmere."

The judge gives Mark one of his Judge Fraser hats.

Ella May packs some sandwiches and they go off. The women stay at home and talk.

"You love him," Ella May says. It's a statement, not a question.

"He's my life."

"I can see it. You don't take your eyes off him. It's nice, Sandy. What is there better than love. You figure there's going to be problems?"

"None that we can't handle"

"Religious differences?"

"There aren't any, since neither of us have a religion, or want one. In some respects it would be easier if we did. Then I could convert, and that problem would be solved. It's harder when the differences are more abstract – and his involvement is so deep. There is so much I can't share, I can't be a part of. I would like to. I've read great mountains of books about Jews, and I understand – but I can't feel it the way he does – because it isn't mine. We never had anybody die in Auschwitz."

"Nor did we ever make any serious effort to keep anybody from dying there."

"You have been reading the books I recommended."

"With great interest. They are a very complex people, the Jews. We tend to think of them as a homogeneous entity. But they're not, are they. They represent so many different and differing points of view. I find it fascinating. Your father has been having something of a look into those books himself – a book disappears for a while, then it suddenly reappears again. He doesn't say anything to me about it. We don't discuss the books. The first time one disappeared, I asked him if he knew where it was. 'Never seen it,' he said. 'I didn't even know you was readin' a book.' It can't hurt him any."

"Mark has a very deep involvement with Israel. His father fought in the War of Independence. He was wounded. His mother fought in the war, too."

"She must be quite a lady."

"I haven't met her yet. I think Mark is afraid. They feel very strongly about things in that family. They have always had a very deep involvement with Israel – a political involvement, not a religious one. The family was left-wing Zionist – they supported the kibbutz movement – the left wing of the kibbutz movement."

"Hashomer Hatzair," Ella May says, pleased with herself. "Mapam, I think, is the name of the political party."

"You are doing well, Mother."

"I've been enjoying it. I got more than just a passing interest."

"Do you like him?"

"I love him."

"So do I."

On the lake at Ashmere, the family plantation, Mark rows the boat. Judge Fraser casts from the back, toward the shore.

"You're doing great," Mark says.

"Not bad, not bad. I got me a good instructor. I never thought I'd be able to do it."

Just then a bass grabs the popper a little way from the lily pad. It makes skyward and then plunges into the depths.

"Hell's bells!" The judge shouts, "I got me a fish on! What do I do now?"

"Play it, Judge, like you always do. Just stay calm."

The judge takes hold of the line. The bass comes up and this time dances on its tail – breaks the monofilament – and disappears back into the depths.

The judge sits on the back seat, deeply despondent. "I neared to have him. Maybe it ain't never going to happen again."

"Aren't there any more fish in this lake?"

"Hell, yes. Plenty."

"Then let's tie on another fly and see if we can't get some of them."

Mark rows. The judge casts.

Just then something takes the judge's fly, and tries to make off with it. His reel shrieks as the line tears off it.

"Hey, we ain't got no alligators in this here lake," the judge cries out in delight. "At least none that eats no flies."

His rod bends almost double.

"Man, it sure does feel like an alligator," the judge shouts as more line strips off. "I can't hold the bugger no-how."

"Take back some of that line, Judge."

"He ain't lettin' me have none."

"Stay calm."

"Calm, hell. I got my heart comin' out of my mouth."

They fight. The judge manages to get some line, but then the fish takes it back again. The judge thinks he is winning, but the fish has too much to lose to give that impression.

"Oh, Lord," the judge cries out in anguish, "don't let me lose this here fish. You hear me Lord. I want this fish!"

The Lord must be listening. The fish is losing. The judge is winning.

Ultimately Mark puts the landing net under the giant fish and scoops it up.

"He's mine," the judge shouts. "Thank you, Lord." The judge is shaking with excitement. "He's over ten, ain't he, Mark."

"He's over ten, Judge."

"I knew it. I knew we had 'em in here. I done it, son. You wait till I tell 'em down at the court house. And I done it on a fly. I'm sure as hell going to have this one mounted – maybe give him a whole wall."

They return home. The judge holds up his bass. "I got 'em," he shouts. "Ten pounds, nine ounces."

Ella May kisses her husband. "Congratulations."

Sandy kisses her father. "I'm pleased for you, Dad."

"It is the greatest day of my entire life."

Ella May is annoyed. "I would have thought that our wedding day was also a great day in your life – and the day our daughter was born."

"They was. They was. But how often do you get a ten pound bass in your life – maybe never – even after spending a whole lifetime trying. The Lord was sure good to me today. And this here young fella – I would nevera' done it without him." He turns to Mark. "Listen, son, I don't mean to pry. It's your life and you know how you want to live it, but tell me something – you goin' to be stayin' around, or are you just passin' through on your way to somewhere else?"

Ella May is horrified. "That's not a question you want to be asking!"

Sandy cries out, "Dad!"

"Like I say, I don't mean to be prying. But this here sure was a

good day. I got me the best daughter in this here whole world."
He speaks to Mark. "She used to go fishin' with me – and huntin',
too. But when she growed up a bit, she didn't have much interest
in it no more. But she kept comin' anyway – because she knew it
pleased me to have her along. Then I said to her one day, 'Honey,
ain't no need for you to be comin' along. I know'd you'd a lot
rather be somewhere else.' I sure missed her. I never did have a
son." He turns to Ella May to explain. "Now all of a sudden,
there's one being dangled in front of me, and I don't know if he's
going to be stayin', or if he's going to be snatched away. That's
why I'm askin'."

All eyes turn to Mark. It is a moment before he speaks. For
Sandy and Ella May and the judge it feels like an eternity.

"I'm staying," Mark says. "I'll be staying around."

Sandy puts her arms around him. Ella May stands on her tiptoes
to kiss him. The judge offers his hand. Mark takes it.

"Welcome to this here family," the judge says. Then he hugs
Mark, too. "And you know something, we got great quail hunting
over at Ashmere. You'll love them bob whites."

Mark smiles, rather overwhelmed by the commitment that he
has just made. "I'm sure I will, Judge."

"And did you know, son, Judah P. Benjamin was the Secretary of
State of the Confederacy? – the second highest office, next to Jeff
Davis. And he was a Jew, you know. We had about 1200 Jews in the
Confederate Army. And there was Major Moreheim – First Georgia
Cavalry – two of my ancestors served under him in the War Between
the States – one of the finest officers there was in the whole of the
Confederacy – and he was a Jew, too. A couple of more like him, and
we would've won the war, no trouble at all. You know, son, I was just
readin' about Judah P. Benjamin – had to escape over there to
England – or else they would've hung 'im – the Yankees."

Ella May says to the judge, "It's a great day for all of us. And I'm
almost as excited as you are, but give the poor boy a chance."

"Of course I'm excited, woman. Why shouldn't I be? All in one
day I got me a ten pound bass and a son." He speaks to Sandy.
"When you fixin' to get wed?"

"We don't know. Until two minutes ago we didn't know we were
getting married."

"You don't want to be waitin' too long. Now you listen here:
We'll have us this wedding down home. It'll be big, I can promise

you. And then you'll be wanting a honeymoon – say up in northern California. You have the first week on your own. And then we'll join you for the second week – maybe have some fishing together – go after them steelheads on the Eel, or the Russian."

Ella May says, "Maybe they'd like to plan their own honeymoon – without us tagging along. Going on your daughter's honeymoon isn't exactly the way things are done."

"Don't be silly, woman. They'd be havin' a week all by theirselves. We wouldn't be coming along until the second week."

4

Alan J. Brady opened the door to his Washington D.C. apartment and stepped inside.

Alan's wife, Leah, sitting on the sofa, reading a book and listening to Swan Lake, smiled with pleasure at her husband's entrance and stood up to greet him. They came together in the center of the room and held each other close.

"I missed you," she said.

"How could that be? You just saw me this morning."

"Because I love you. Whenever you're not with me I miss you." They embraced again.

"And I missed you," Alan J. Brady said. "And I love you very much."

Alan walked over to the window and stood there for a time, scanning the street below. His face showed his concern. It was a highly intelligent, sensitive face, with a mustache that made him look somewhat older than his thirty-one years.

Leah, two years younger, with long strawberry blond hair, was tall and erect. She noticed Alan's concern. Her blue eyes became grave.

"What is it, Alan?"

"The FBI, I assume."

"The FBI? Why? What? I don't understand," Leah said, completely confused. "What have they got to do with us?"

Alan sat down on the sofa, leaned back into it, and exhaled slowly.

Leah sat rigidly on the edge. She took Alan's hands in both of hers.

"I've been spying for Israel," Alan said simply.

For a moment no words came from her. "I heard what you said, Alan. But I can't comprehend. You have been spying for Israel. What does that mean? Why does Israel need you to spy for them? Is that why the FBI is here? Does that mean they know about you?"

Alan smiled sardonically. "They suspect."

"Will they come bursting in here, and arrest us?"

"I don't think so. Not yet."

"Start from the beginning, Alan," she cried in anguish.

Alan put his hand on hers. "The American Administration is trying to destroy Israel," he said simply.

Leah struggled to regain her calm. "We know they're not overly friendly. None of them have been."

"For some time American intelligence has been withholding vital information from Israel. I provided it."

"Alan, shouldn't you have told me what you were doing?"

"I didn't want to involve you – in case I got caught."

"I am involved. I'm involved in whatever you do. Of course I'm glad you have been helping Israel. But this – to come out suddenly -"

"I'm sorry, honey. A part of me wanted to share this with you – right from the start. Maybe I should have. I knew you'd approve. But if they caught me – and you knew – they could make you an accessory."

"I would want to be."

"No. I had to protect you. I couldn't bear it if anything happened to you. I couldn't live with it. I couldn't live with myself. All this information was coming through – vital for Israel's survival. The United States has an agreement to exchange intelligence with Israel. But we were not living up to our part of the arrangement. When they did send information – it was misinformation – meant to confuse, to misinform. I contacted the Israeli Embassy – and told them everything."

"It was the right thing, Alan," she cried out. "You had to do it. There wasn't any other way. I'm scared. But it was right. I have no question."

Gently he stroked her hair with his hand. "Thank you, my sweet . . . The trouble is, Israel's existence is seen as inhibiting

34

better relations with the Arab and Moslem countries. American oil interests determine policy – they always have. The oil companies don't want an Israel – because the Arabs don't. And they do exactly what the Arabs tell them to do."

"We – the United States – are in Arab hands. The oil companies put us there."

"It's not new – just more acute – as the Arabs have grown more powerful. They make greater demands – and the United States is compelled to accede to them. But Israel didn't need me to tell them that. They already knew. It's obvious that those who control the oil can control most other things as well."

"Then what did you tell Israel?"

"That Iraq is on the verge of becoming a nuclear weapons power."

"But Israel bombed those facilities years ago."

"The Iraqis started over again. They're getting help from the United States, Germany, Britain, France, Italy. They have all contributed."

"Knowing that Iraq intends to use this kind of weaponry to destroy Israel?"

"Of course."

Leah exhaled slowly, struggling to absorb the enormous ramifications of what Alan was now revealing.

"But that's only part of it," Alan continued. "Iraq already has huge biological and chemical capacity – and a delivery system. Right at this very moment, Iraq is manufacturing poison gas – the Germans built that facility for them – it's essentially the same gas the Germans used in the concentration camps to eliminate the Jews."

"And now the Germans are at it again."

"In many case, the same ones. Iraq is now capable of introducing anthrax into Israel – as well as a number of other infectious disease that could kill all or most of the population of Israel. Syria is prepared to sacrifice 200,000 men in an effort to roll over Israel on the Golan Heights."

Leah shook her head slowly from side to side, stunned by Alan's revelations.

"And there's more. I've copied literally thousands of documents. I've had access to some of America's top-secret facilities – I did a lot of work over at the Suitland, Maryland, complex. That's where most of America's skeletons are hidden away, and it was expected that they would remain hidden . . . Leah, the Secretary of State was a traitor to America. He supported Nazi Germany before, during, and after the war. The head of the CIA, his brother, was also a Nazi. Standard shipped oil from South America to Germany by way of Spain during the whole of the war."

Leah stood up. She paced the length of the floor twice, shaking her head, the strawberry blond hair swinging. She needed to absorb what Alan was telling her, but she found it difficult to comprehend that this could be happening to ordinary people. She thought of themselves as ordinary people. But they were not – at least, not Alan. Not any more. And she was not, either. Neither of them would ever be ordinary again. This would change their lives. It had already changed the destiny of one country – probably of several.

"Britain, France and the United States financed the creation of the Nazi war machine," Alan continued. "The Vatican contributed substantially, too. After the war they were involved in protecting the Nazi war criminals – gave them asylum, and helped to get them out of Europe – to Egypt, Syria, Iraq, South America, to the United States."

"You found out all of this?"

"It's all carefully documented – some of it was misfiled – deliberately, I assume. But I kept digging away, and kept finding new revelations."

Alan, a civilian employee of U.S. Naval Intelligence, had twice received Special Commendations from the government for his outstanding analytical work.

"And to think," Alan said, "my father didn't want me to go to work for the Navy. He said they were anti-Semitic."

"But if the American government finds out that you gave this information to Israel – or if Israel ever should make it apparent – it wouldn't be a question of merely spying on an ally."

"Israel isn't likely to say anything."

"Hopefully not. But then why are they outside – the FBI, I mean?"

"It's hard to know for sure. I've been supplying information to Israel for a very long time now. As I told you long ago, I have top security clearance. I can go anywhere on a 'Need to know' basis. Maybe somebody got suspicious when I kept coming back for information that wasn't directly connected with my work. The Israelis often had specific requirements and directed me into particular areas."

"The Israelis must be very pleased with you."

"They say they are."

"I'm pleased with you, Alan. You make me very proud. What you did was right – no matter what happens." She was thoughtful for a moment. "What will they do to us, Alan?"

"It depends."

"On what?"

"Whether they catch me or not."

"You're being very calm," Leah observed, uncertain if she felt reassured by his casual approach.

"I'm an old spy by now."

"They're downstairs waiting."

"They're tailing me. They want to see where I go – to try and find out who I'm working for."

Leah nodded. "I assume you have a plan."

"Of course. We've always considered the possibility that this could happen. There are passports for us at the Israeli Embassy. We'll go there. They'll see to it that we get to Israel – presuming you want to go –"

"Was there ever any question in your mind?"

"No."

No, no question – but suddenly this life was ending, and where and how was the next one beginning?

"Where you go, Alan, I go too."

"We'll start a new life in Israel."

"It sounds very exciting. You will be a hero there. The whole country will be able to express their gratitude."

"I don't want gratitude. I did my duty. That's all."

They were silent for a moment, each contemplating the future, not absolutely certain that there would be one.

They embraced, each clinging tightly to the other.

Then Leah said, hesitantly, "We're going tonight?"

"Yes. Tonight. Now," Alan said positively. "We'll each take an overnight bag."

Leah looked around the room, resigned. "It was such a nice apartment," she said.

"I know."

"But I won't miss it. In Jerusalem we'll have nice apartments, too."

"And your gown – the one you wore to the inauguration. You'll have to leave that, too."

"That old thing – I wouldn't want to wear that again – after the way the president has behaved." The tears had welled up in her eyes. "Besides, who needs a gown like that in Jerusalem? Maybe I'll get a Yemenite gown – long, and black and sleek, all the way down to the ground."

"You'll look stunning in it."

"With a slit up the side – so I can dance the hora."

"That's my girl."

"And that old dinner jacket of yours – frankly, Alan, I thought you looked rather stuffy in it."

"Did you?"

"Yes. Definitely."

"Well, in that case, I'm very glad to be leaving it behind."

"So am I."

Alan stood up. Their moment of frivolity passed. "We'll drive around – try to lose them – and get to the Embassy."

They packed quickly and went down to the car in the underground garage. As they moved out into the street, a nondescript Chevy began tailing them. Alan drove along in the heavy Washington traffic. He made it through the light on yellow, but the Chevy didn't. He drove around the block, waited a bit and drove back in the opposite direction.

"Do you think we've shaken them?" Leah asked.

"The Chevy is gone, but I'm sure they've got friends around. It's just a question of knowing which one."

In a little while Alan spotted a blue Datsun. "I think we're back in contact. Do those guys in the blue car look like they ought to be in the FBI?"

As they stopped for a light, Leah turned around for a better look. "I'm sure of it," she said. "Not very patriotic, are they? Don't they have a 'Buy American' policy over at FBI Headquarters?"

"You would think so, wouldn't you. But if you're going to try and look like everybody else, you'd better be driving a Datsun."

They lost the Datsun, and then they couldn't tell who was tailing them – if anybody. They drove up, and around, and down.

"We'll leave the car," Alan decided. "And we'll get a cab. Even if they lose us for a while, they probably have the police monitoring the whole town."

They left the car in a "No Parking" zone and hailed a cab.

"The Israel Embassy," Alan said to the driver.

In a little while they were in front of the iron gates of the Embassy. They got out and paid, and the cab drove off.

Alan rang the bell.

A disembodied voice inquired, "Can I help you?"

"I want to speak to Chaim Springer," Alan said. "It's 'Eilat' here."

The gates opened.

They hurried inside. A guard, carrying an Uzi, let them in. He escorted them to an outer office, empty now, and withdrew.

"We made it," Alan said with relief.

"I knew we would."

The door of the inner office opened. An elderly man, white shirt open at the neck, appeared, looked at them inquiringly.

"I want to speak to Chaim Springer," Alan said again. "I'm Eilat."

Without saying a word, the man with the open shirt disappeared back behind the inner office door.

The minutes passed slowly as Alan and Leah waited, for what seemed an extraordinarily long time.

"Do you think there's a problem?" Leah asked.

"No. They're just checking. They are really very efficient. I should know."

Ten minutes passed. Fifteen. Then twenty.

On the twenty-first minute the man with the white shirt reappeared. "There is no Chaim Springer here," he said in a pronounced Israeli accent. "There must be some mistake."

"It's his code name," Alan said. "I'm 'Eilat'. That's my code name."

"They never heard of him. And they never heard of you."

"That's ridiculous," Alan said, his voice rising. "We have passports here. They told me they were here – in the name of Alan J. Brady, and Leah Brady. We're Israeli citizens."

"There are no passports. They never heard of you." The man's voice was cold and steely. "Please leave the Embassy at once."

"There's a mistake, I tell you, " Alan shouted.

The man shook his head. "There is no mistake. Leave at once," he repeated.

"But they must know who I am!"

"Nobody knows who you are." There was exasperation in the man's voice. "Please go or I'll call the guards."

"We're not going anywhere. You will get me Chaim Springer. I want to talk to him."

"There is no Chaim Springer here," the man said in a slow, deliberate voice. "No such person exists."

The man pushed the button on his desk.

The guard with the Uzi appeared, accompanied by another.

The man in the white shirt spoke to them in Hebrew. It was apparent, even to someone who didn't know Hebrew, what he said.

The guards seized Alan and Leah roughly, and dragged them toward the door.

"There's a mistake! I tell you!" Alan shouted.

The guards probably understood English. But, if they did, they made no reply.

They dragged them outside. The iron gate opened. They shoved them out into the street.

The nondescript Chevy was there – waiting.

A man got out. "Good evening, Mr. Brady. And Mrs. Brady. There are a few questions we would like to ask. Would you mind coming with us, please."

Another man got out of the back seat of the Chevy, and stood there, holding the door open.

The Bradys got into the back seat of the nondescript Chevy.

The man got in beside them, and closed the door.

5

It is in the Prime Minister's office, in the Knesset, the Israeli Parliament in Jerusalem. Prime Minister Peres sits regally behind the big desk. He would like to think that it is his – for all time – at least until the general election, after which he could claim it again. He'd give in to the Orthodox – take them into the coalition again. But the trouble was, that *momser* (bastard) sitting opposite him, the so-called Foreign Minister, Yitzhak Shamir, he was going to be Prime Minister in a very short time. That's the way they had worked it out – the deal they made. It stank. It was crazy. But there it was. You could just see him, Shamir, sitting there, squirming with eagerness to get on the other side of the desk so that he could have his turn to be Prime Minister.

Then he, Peres, would be Foreign Minister. Not that it was so bad being Foreign Minister. There was going to be a lot of work to do, work to undo all the stupid, ridiculous and dangerous things that that terrorist *momser* had already done. And then it would be the general election, and Shamir would go to the Orthodox and let them have whatever they wanted in return for their support. It was bribery – nothing but bribery. They already ran the country. They held the balance of power. They always held the balance of power. All right, he was prepared, he'd let them steal even more than what Shamir would promise. There would be no *chozzerim* (pigs) in Israel. Everybody would eat kosher – or they'd starve. Even on the kibbutzim.

Maybe not on the kibbutzim. There would be a revolution. But even if the kibbutzim, by some miracle, agreed to become kosher, where was the guarantee that he was going to head the party list at the next general election? That other *momser* – that double *momser* – Yitzhak Rabin, the Minister of Defense – was already challenging him for leadership of the Party. He could not decide whom he hated worse – Shamir or Rabin. On balance he thought it must be Rabin. Shamir was what he was – an old terrorist – an Irgun fascist terrorist who would never change. But Rabin – he presented himself like he was the only true representative of the Labor Party – close to Ben Gurion – like they were brothers.

And now there was trouble. Big trouble. It wasn't exactly Rabin's fault. But Rabin benefited. He was running that American spy, Brady – Alan Brady – the one who had access to all of America's top secrets. He told Rabin everything Rabin wanted to know, and even what Rabin didn't want to know. It was a good thing to have such a spy, but this one knew too much, too much about all of them. Of course they needed the information – that Iraq would soon be dropping nuclear bombs on them. They had let Iraq know that they could get in there first, and with more, and then there wouldn't be any more Iraq. They had made it clear to Iraq, and to the world, that they had the capacity, without actually saying so.

This man who saved Israel – Brady – everybody thought he must be the personal representative of the Messiah. But now that he was caught, it wasn't going to be so good for Israel. In fact, it was going to be very bad for Israel. It was bad any way you looked at it – bad because America and all the rest of Israel's "good friends" had supplied Iraq with the know-how to eliminate Israel one day, and that America was eager to see Israel's existence ended forever. And it was bad because America knew that Israel knew.

The people said Israel had to support Brady. He was the great hero. Already a kibbutz said they had a house for him there, waiting, for when he and Leah came to live in Israel. There were demonstrations demanding that the Government of Israel confront the United States over this incident and insist that Alan J. Brady be allowed to come "home" to Israel.

That was exactly the point: Israel didn't want a confrontation with the United States over this matter. There were enough problems with the United States – that great friend – who wanted to see Israel wiped off the map forever. What, that was something new? It didn't take Alan J. Brady to know that. There were plenty in the United States, including that so-called friend of the Jews – Franklin Roosevelt – who stood there, completely indifferent, while six million Jews got incinerated. He was in Ibn Saud's pocket right from the start.

And Mossad was angry – because they weren't running Brady, and somebody else was getting the credit. And there was a lot of credit, because Brady told them everything. He had access to where America's best-kept secrets were hidden away, and where he copied, literally, thousands of files. The Bush administration was in a panic. America didn't have any secrets left anymore. And, if it got out, there was going to be big trouble.

You try to cultivate good relations, and then somebody comes along and spoils it all. The only good thing – they were a Government of National Unity. This was national unity? Every time he thought about being national unity with that *momser* sitting opposite, the taste of bile was in his mouth. Likud, they called themselves. Why didn't they just call themselves fascists? That was their color. That was their aim.

Except that now, if they were in opposition, they would be screaming about Alan Brady – how the government let him down – this great Jewish patriot who saved Israel. And then it would be worse. But with national unity, who could blame the other? In this they could work together. Maybe there was something to be said for national unity. But not much. Just this.

The buzzer sounded on Peres' desk. A voice said, "Jacob Ben Zvi is here."

"Send him in," Peres replied.

Jacob Ben Zvi entered, a man in his fifties, high up in Intelligence, he was no stranger to this office. He and Shamir nodded to each other, just a small nod, to acknowledge the other's existence. Ben Zvi was a Labor man, had often reported on Likud, even events that had never occurred.

Unasked, Ben Zvi pulled up a chair, as far from Shamir as he could get.

"We are forming a committee," the Prime Minister said to Ben Zvi.

Ben Zvi nodded. His head went up slightly, and then immediately dropped down. He understood. High up in the Mossad, he was accustomed to dealing with difficult problems. Ben Zvi was from Afula, an uninteresting agricultural town in the Galilee, whose residents had the reputation for being slow to grasp the ways of the world, or even events as far away as Tel Aviv, though that was not the case with Ben Zvi.

"You are in charge," Peres said.

Ben Zvi nodded again. The same way. He was glad he was in charge. He often was in charge. He didn't know of what he was in charge, but he knew that ultimately he would find out.

"We are calling it the Campaign for Alan Brady," the Prime Minister said.

Jacob Ben Zvi nodded. He was a little bit confused as to why they wanted a campaign for Alan Brady, considering the damage the event was causing. Unless they knew something he didn't know. But probably he would find out if he sat here long enough.

"The Foreign Minister and I are in complete agreement in this matter."

Ben Zvi didn't know whether to be glad or sorry about that. He hated to think that there were issues on which these two men could agree. But obviously on this one they did.

"You will talk to everybody involved in this Brady business," the Prime Minister said, "everybody who wants us to go to his defense. You are the contact man. You will explain that we are negotiating."

"Behind the scenes," Shamir broke in.

"You tell them that you can't say very much at this point," Peres explained. "It's very delicate."

"And secret," Shamir added.

Shamir did not talk much. He hardly ever listened either. His mind was usually made up in advance. Then he issued orders, which he expected to be followed. Often they were. A lot of people thought, too often. He was Head of the Party, respected, not loved, perhaps not even "liked". He didn't joke. There was nothing light about him. His enemies hated him. He had a lot of those. The British found him particularly unpleasant, especially so since his objective had been to eject them from this country in which they had no legitimate business or claim. Now they had to negotiate with him. He could summon the British Ambassador and make his feelings on any topic unmistakably clear. And the British Ambassador had to listen.

"We want to make it very plain that we are doing something about Brady – helping him. Helping him in every way that we can," the Prime Minister said.

"But in fact we will be doing nothing at all," Shamir said.

Ben Zvi understood. He nodded, to let them know he understood.

"You are the official government representative," Peres said. "You will deal with the press, with the agitators. With Brady. With the Brady family. You will say, 'We are working behind the scenes.' Everybody will believe it. Because they know we work in secret – behind the scenes. Everybody will accept it. And you will form a parliamentary committee."

Parliament was very restless about Brady – all the factions; they had crossed Party lines. Particularly that Guela Cohen – she was the worst fascist of them all – she was even too right-wing for Yitzhak Shamir. She had her own party, but she voted with Likud. She was another terrorist *momser* – used to smuggle sten guns – half of one at a time – under her skirt, during British Mandatory days. Now she had already organized an all-Party committee in the Knesset to stir up support for Brady. And Edna Salidar was almost as bad – from his own party, yet.

"We want you to sound like we are doing something," the Prime Minister gave instructions. "You have to keep the lid on the agitation here. Get the Knesset to send out official letters to

America – to the President. If anybody wants to agitate, direct them toward America. Let them write letters. Let them protest. But in the direction of America. It is America's fault. It is there where they are holding Brady. It is there where they are persecuting an American Jew who helped Israel. We want the criticism directed toward America, and away from us."

"The people here will believe this?"

"Probably not. But we want to create the impression that we are doing something. That we leave up to you. In time the people here will forget – it won't seem so important. They have got other problems to think about – this one will fade into the background. Here every day it's a crisis. In a little while it will be yesterday's crisis. And how long can you dwell on yesterday's crisis when you have got a whole bunch of new ones today."

"You can be sure I will give this my best efforts."

"We want to avoid further antagonizing the United States. Things are bad enough. They asked us to give back all the documents Brady sent us."

"We're doing that?"

"Of course. With his fingerprints on them."

"They want to make a case."

"They've got a case," Shamir said.

"He'll get a year or two," Peres said casually. "We'll pay the legal fees, if we have to. Maybe Brady's father needs some help – financial help. We don't want him coming here to say it's our fault, we did it to his son. We don't need him stirring things up, maybe going to the Western Wall carrying a sign. What do we want, riots in the street? We don't have enough trouble? It isn't even along party lines. It's practically the whole population. We're telling America it was a "rogue" operation – done behind our back."

"They believe it?" Ben Zvi asked.

"Of course not," Shamir said.

"But it shows our good intentions. Like we don't want to fight about it, and we're sorry it ever happened. If we knew, we wouldn't have let it happen."

Ben Zvi nodded his head up and down several times, suggesting that while he will do his part, he thinks the Americans might find that somewhat difficult to believe.

"We're sorry we can't do more for Brady," Peres said, not

sounding sorrowful. "He came to us voluntarily. He knew the risks. He made the sacrifice. It's like a soldier killed in battle."

"And he isn't dead," Shamir observed.

"Just remember, 'Working behind the scenes'. That is the answer to everything," Peres gave instructions. "You will meet with the Knesset as often as necessary. Meet with agitators – groups and individuals. Put all your other work aside. Drop it. This is full time – 24 hours a day. This is the most important assignment you have ever had. We don't need people putting pressure on us to help Brady. Just assume it has nothing to do with us. This situation could be very dangerous for the government – can you imagine, the people in his country, and the Knesset, all lined up against the government? There could be blood in the streets."

6

Mark is in his office. He thinks about the Passover recently concluded, and about the Seder at the Halidays. They go there every year. Jim Haliday had read from the Haggadah in Hebrew, then in English: "*Blessed art Thou, Oh Lord our God, King of the Universe, Who has chosen us from all peoples, and exalted us above all languages and sanctified us by His commandments. And You have lovingly given us, Oh Lord our God, this day of the Feast of the Unleavened Bread, the season of our Freedom, a holy gathering, a memorial of the departure from Egypt.*"

David was aglow with fervor. Mark wondered about Sandy; is she really as interested as she appears? Or is it just show? He'd never thought about it before. It was a ceremony they all enjoyed together, mutually. But how mutual was it? What could she feel of this? Her ancestors had not crossed the Red Sea in their flight from Egypt. Her ancestors had not received the Ten Commandments on Mount Sinai.

Jim read on: "*This is the bread of affliction, which our fathers ate in the land of Egypt . . . Let all who are hungry enter and eat; and all who are in need, come and celebrate the Passover. This year we celebrate it here, but next year we will celebrate it in the land of Israel.*"

But then Jim's ancestors had not crossed the Red Sea either.

46

Nor had they received the Ten Commandments on Mount Sinai. Jim is a convert to Judaism. He chose to convert when he married Miriam. Jim takes his Judaism seriously. They attend Rabbi Moreheim's synagogue regularly. Their son, Aaron, will have his Bar Mitzvah soon. David has been going to the occasional Bar Mitzvah class with Aaron, which Rabbi Moreheim conducts.

In Hebrew, Aaron read from the Haggadah, asking the first of the four questions: "*Why is this night different from all other nights?*"

Jim followed his son's words in his own Haggadah. Miriam watched her two men with deepest pride.

Aaron read on: "*On all other nights we may eat either leavened or unleavened bread, but on this night only unleavened. On all other nights we may eat all kinds of –*"

Aaron faltered over the Hebrew text.

His father read the word, and Aaron continued on.

Mark is taken from his Passover memories by the telephone ringing on his desk. He picks up the receiver and speaks.

"Spaulding here."

He is sorry to leave Passover behind.

The voice at the other end of the line has an Israeli accent. A male voice. He says, "I have something that will be of interest to you. I have left it with Dario."

"Who is this?" Mark asks.

"It does not matter. I knew your father."

The line goes dead.

Somebody from the Israeli Embassy? Could be. But unlikely, after a moment of deliberation. He obviously knows the phone is being tapped – everybody's is. Something left with Dario? Mark knows only one Dario.

He puts on his coat, tells Claire he'll be right back, and rushes out of the office.

Mark enters the restaurant. Dario sees him and comes over to him quickly, speaks in a hushed tone. "I have something for you, Mr. Spaulding."

"So I understand."

"Come with me. It's in the office. In the safe."

Mark follows behind Dario. Could it be a parcel bomb? The thought crosses his mind.

In the office, Mark asks, "Who gave it to you?"

"I don't know. I never saw the man. He had an Israeli accent.

47

He said it was very important – to put it somewhere safe – not to give it to anybody except you."

"Nobody from the Israeli Embassy?"

"I don't think so. I know most of them."

Dario opens the safe. He takes out a black plastic briefcase, heavy with whatever is inside, the contents straining to break through.

It doesn't look like a parcel bomb.

He hands it to Mark.

"Thanks, Dario. I appreciate it."

"Any time. We are always at your service."

Mark clutches the briefcase close to himself, leaves the restaurant, and hurries back to the office.

Claire sees him, looks at the briefcase.

"What have you got there?" she asks.

"I don't know. But I'll tell you in a few minutes."

He goes into his office and closes the door. The briefcase is locked, but only superficially. With a pliers he breaks the lock. He feels a growing excitement within himself. He unzips the case and pulls out a fistful of papers. The heading on each one says: SUITLAND. Some of it is marked "Top Secret". Most of the rest would have required special clearance: COSMIC for NATO records; Q for the Atomic Energy Commission. And the appropriate code words for each security compartment: satellite intelligence, electronic espionage, cryptography. The list goes on.

Mark's hand trembles. His heart races. Suitland is where America's best-kept secrets are hidden away, the skeletons buried. Now somebody had dug them up. Only a very few would have access here – to these secret archives at Suitland, Maryland – that America had wished to obscure, but did not dare destroy. Now somebody had penetrated the depths, photocopied large numbers of those secrets, passed them on to who knew where. And now part, or all, or some of them rested in Mark's unsteady hand.

He scans the pages. He can hardly believe what his eyes tell him. He looks back at the heading, to confirm that these are really from Suitland.

The former Secretary of State was a traitor, supported the Nazi cause before, during and after World War II. The Head of the CIA, his brother, was equally involved. They, along with the Vatican, provided funds for the Nazi take-over in Germany, financed the war effort, and insured that money and valuables plundered by the Nazis remained in the hands of the plunderers.

They insured that there would be few prosecutions of the guilty, and again, with the assistance of the Vatican, spirited the war criminals out of Europe. America had provided oil for the German war machine, through Spain, during the whole of the war, by an oil company whose principle shareholder was the governor of New York – a presidential aspirant, who projected himself as a "liberal candidate."

There had always been rumors, but here, now, before him, was the proof.

Mark stops, thinks, wonders how all of this had come to him. From an Israeli, but apparently not connected with the Embassy, unwilling to be identified, is aware that they are the United States Center for World Study, a think-tank, and aware of their current project – the examination of America's condition. The man knew Mark's father, knows him, or of him; knows Dario, or, at least, who he is and that he can be trusted.

The phone rings. Marks picks it up. "Spaulding."

"You have the material?" the Israeli-accented voice asks.

"I do."

"Good."

The caller rings off.

Mark suddenly knows the origin of the material: These are part of the Brady Papers – the ones Alan J. Brady had copied during the time he had access to such sensitive material while employed by U.S. Naval Intelligence. They had been given to Israeli personnel here and transmitted to Israel. When Brady was caught, America demanded the return of those papers, aware that Israel would in the meantime have made many copies, about which America could do little. But on those originals, there would have been the fingerprints belonging to Alan J. Brady, irrefutable proof that Brady had been spying for Israel.

Israel had complied with America's request for the return of those papers, betraying the man who had been of such tremendous value. Perhaps they did it with reluctance; perhaps they did it with alacrity. But they did it.

So it wasn't only documents related to Iraq and Syria, and the supply of nuclear know-how, with biological and chemical weapons meant for the destruction of Israel; Brady had copied documents that revealed that Americans high up in government had betrayed their own country, that they were unrepentant Nazis, who supported a German victory, and were, without question or doubt, traitors who should have been hanged.

Further, the documents reveal, Israel herself (Mossad) has been, and apparently still is, deeply involved with U.S. intelligence – partners in the Iran-Contra events which America is trying so hard, with so little success, to obscure. And Mena, in Arkansas, where Barry Seal brings in cocaine from Colombia, and heroin, to be sold in the United States – somewhere between three and five billion dollars worth. He has U.S. Government immunity. Profits pay for the arms he is also bringing in – to be supplied to the Contras in Nicaragua. The name Oliver North comes up frequently. He works closely with Mossad. Mossad appears to be well-connected with some conduits of American intelligence – some completely unrelated to Israel's security, connections which in the end have to hurt Israel, and are contrary to Israel's own interests. Does the Government of Israel know about this? Approve? Is it Mossad who is working independently, independent of its own government? How much power does Mossad really have? Could it be that the Mossad tail is wagging the Israeli Government dog? Mark thinks about this. Is it so far fetched? No, not so far fetched at all.

Israel didn't have to return those papers. They could have denied ever having received them. Who could argue with that? Now Israel knew that America had a large supply of its own nasty little secrets. But betraying a benefactor was neither justifiable nor forgivable as far as Mark was concerned – a fact which appeared to be of little consequence to Israel, and which pained Mark deeply.

The Israeli who provided the material had not only had access to it, but also took strong issue with the way the government of Israel had dealt with the Brady affair. The man knew what he was doing.

Mark gathers up the material and takes it into the photocopy room. He stacks it into the holder and sets the dial for ten copies each.

Mark's partner, Bill Cooper, enters, surprised to see Mark at the photocopier.

"It must be especially interesting," Bill says.

"It is."

"Claire said there was something going on."

"A lot. You and Claire can start reading it as I run it off. You'll both want to take copies home tonight. Don't show them to anybody. I'm making extra copies to be put away in our bank vault."

Bill stands at the mouth of the photocopier as it gushes printed sheets. He takes one, glances through it, turns to Mark in shocked surprise. "What is this?"

"The Brady Papers."

"How did we get them?"

Mark explains.

"We're in for a busy night," Bill says. "Does anybody know we have these?"

"Just Deep Throat."

"Do you actually know this?"

"I don't. But it's what I strongly suspect. At least for now."

"They could put us all away for a long time just for mere possession of these documents."

"I know."

"It worries me, Mark."

"I'd worry more if I didn't have them."

"Is there a possibility that we're being set up?"

"There is."

"But you don't think so."

"I think it's worth the chance."

"I hope you're right."

Claire comes into the photocopy room, trying to take in the scene. Bill gives her a handful of papers. Rapidly she reads over the top copy and goes pale.

"Where did we get this?"

Mark tells her.

"And we're going to light the match that sets off the explosion?" Claire asks.

Mark reaches down for more paper, puts it in the hopper. "Is anybody against it?" He looks at Bill, then at Claire.

"We couldn't not do it," Bill says, resigned.

"I'm for it," Claire responds, not all that enthusiastically.

"Are you sure?" he asks her. "Maybe we shouldn't be involving you."

51

"I am involved. If you are, I am too. I couldn't think of it being any other way."

"Claire," Mark says earnestly, "we could all end up in prison."

"I'll take my chances," Claire replies unequivocally.

It is several days later. Mark stops off at the pistol range on his way to work. He goes through two boxes of 9 mm shells firing his Jericho at the cardboard men pointing their guns at him. He gets them before they can get him. But then they are only cardboard. Their menacing look is deceptive, their sudden appearance almost predictable. The real thing has to be harder. But this is good practice for when the real thing is real.

"Shooting as good as usual, Mr. Spaulding," the range manager says to Mark.

"Gotta keep in practice," Mark says.

"There's nothing like it," the manager assures him.

Mark arrives at the office, somewhat later than usual. "Been to the range," he explains. Claire is visibly upset. Bill follows Mark into his office.

"Are you feeling apprehensive?" Bill asks.

"About what?"

"The Brady Papers."

"No. Not especially so."

"I am. I thought that's why you went to the range."

"Just to keep in practice, Bill."

"Do you think that's the answer?"

"It's part of one. It wouldn't hurt if you were prepared, too."

"It's not my style. I can't bring myself to do it."

"I hope you'll never need to."

"I think I expect them to break in here any second and accuse us of illegal possession of classified material."

"There's nothing visible."

"They'd come with Deep Throat. We could get ten years. A gun in my pocket wouldn't be of much help, no matter how well I shot it. Maybe I should have stayed a university professor. The only real danger was getting bit in the back".

"With that poisonous lot it could be fatal."

"The worst you get is a nervous breakdown. At this stage I'm about to have one anyway. I'd like to tell Helen about it – so in case they cart me off, she'll know why."

"She'd find out about it ultimately."

"I wish I could be as easy about it as you are."

"Just think about Brady – and what he's going through."

"I do think about Brady – and about Helen, too – and what they could do to her," Bill says, shaking his head and making his way out of Mark's office.

Mark ponders the Brady Papers, now to be included in their report. Claire appears, interrupting his thoughts, a worried look on her face.

She sits down near him. "I'm scared."

"It's scary stuff."

"I mean for you."

Mark shrugs. "I don't think I have any choice."

"You know how easily they can eliminate anybody who gets in their way."

"We all have to be careful."

"And they have a special score to settle with you."

"I'm not going into hiding."

"Mark, if anything happened to you, I'd die. I wouldn't want to live."

Claire gets up and leaves.

Mark frowns. He'll have to talk to Sandy, try harder to find somebody for Claire. They'd had her around countless times – big parties, intimate dinner parties, barbecues – with men about in abundance, eminently suitable, available, and mostly interested. Claire is a very striking woman. Too bad the interest wasn't mutual.

Mark is dealing with the section on Vietnam. Even the CIA was against that one. They came to the Secretary of State and reminded him of Dien Bien Phu. If he had ever heard of it, it made no deep impression. They had only been Frenchmen, and everybody knew what kind of fighters they were. No matter that they had been there for a hundred years; one day a nationalist movement, simple folk with red flags, swept them away. The CIA said Keep Out, probably the only time they ever got it right in the whole of their existence. But the Secretary of State didn't listen. He was going to "cut off the evil head of communism wherever he found it," for he was the real power in America; the elected one was a war hero, who knew nothing of politics, and a great deal about golf, which he played much of the time. His only contribution was his farewell address to Congress, when he admonished them to be aware of the military/industrial complex that was taking over America.

America had fallen into the hands of the man who was never anything but an active supporter of Nazi Germany. He had rehabilitated the regime, provided it with a different suit, but one of the same fabric. Now he could turn his attention to destroying the "red menace". Vietnam was a good place in which to do it.

Mark was a student at Berkeley, the hot-bed of anti-Vietnam fervor. Articulate and persuasive, he drew the attention of the FBI, as did all of those who opposed the war. This in effect was a revolution, and Mark was amongst the leaders of that revolution.

The State employed its full power to put down the revolution. They came to Mark and they showed him that his exempt status, because he was a student, had been cancelled, and he was now, in effect, in the United States Army, as of this moment, under their jurisdiction, and without much chance of making it to Canada.

There was one telephone call home, but no farewells to his fellow student activists. He would be missing, and they would know why. He wouldn't have been the first, nor the last. Destroy the leadership, and the revolution would collapse, was their theory. But they got it wrong. Because there were new leaders, and the revolution could only grow. The revolutionaries were going to be the cannon fodder. The youth of the nation, those without student exemptions, were busy dying in Vietnam, and many more would follow. It was incumbent upon these protesters, at Berkeley, and throughout the nation, to stop the slaughter, and save their country.

Mark, surrounded by the men from the FBI, had little by way of choice under the circumstances, allowed himself to be led away. In a short time he wore the uniform of the United States Army while undergoing basic training. His "brothers-in-arms" kept their distance, and Mark could guess why; they had been told that this man was dangerous, unpatriotic and un-American, a subversive who was trying to destroy their freedom.

For the first time since the completion of basic training, Mark was to be allowed off the base. A black soldier, who Mark knew as Roy, moved past him, and, as he did so, whispered, "be careful when you're out."

At his locker, Roy turned and looked at Mark, to determine if he had understood. Mark nodded, almost imperceptibly, and Roy turned back to his locker.

Off the base Mark made for the nearest telephone to call his mother. "I'm sure it's Vietnam," he said. "Tell our anti-war people in Berkeley. They'll need to get our lawyers working on this."

Mark went into town – not much of a town – seedy, dilapidated. He walked along the street. It felt good to be alone. But it soon became apparent that he wasn't alone. There were three men, whom he had seen on the base, not doing a very good job of trying to make themselves inconspicuous. This was obviously what Roy had warned him about.

He went into a restaurant, ordered some food and considered his situation. The food was only slightly worse that what was served in the mess; it must have been a former army cook who did the cooking here. But then again, it wasn't a very nice restaurant, in an area that had no pretensions and few aspirations. His fellow diners looked as if they had long before departed for somewhere else, but that their bodies still remained here.

It was night, and in an area where nobody was going to pay too much attention to a bit of disturbance going on in the street, particularly if it happened quickly. At least he had been warned, and there wasn't going to be an element of surprise. He felt deeply grateful to Roy. He hoped they would meet up again some day.

He saw the faces peering into the restaurant window, aglow from the reflected light of the red neon sign that made them look like devils.

It was time to go, Mark decided, and have that confrontation. He was ready for it. The prospect did not frighten him, but in fact gave him a feeling of exhilaration.

He paid his check and left the restaurant. He stood in the doorway and looked around. They were not immediately visible. But he could sense their presence, as if they were just a few feet away. They came on strong.

He moved slowly, deliberately, looking for some strategic advantage. Here was the crux of the conflict, personal, not theoretical, not rhetorical – but actual. It was what he believed, against what they believed. They were out to get him, and this is the way they were convinced they could do it. They thought they could do what they wanted. He had to show them they were wrong.

He came to an alley and ducked into it. Pressing himself against a building, he was obscured by darkness. A street light off in the distance would announce the presence of his pursuers. He would have the advantage of surprise.

He did not have long to wait. The three appeared at the mouth of the alley. They stood there, filled with uncertainty, their quarry obscured, at least for the moment.

One stood just inches away from Mark. Mark grabbed him around the neck and twisted. The sound of breaking bones was easily audible. The second man flicked the button on his switch-blade knife and lunged. Mark, still holding onto the man with the cracked spinal column, used him as a shield, into which the man with the switch-blade plunged the blade.

Mark withdrew his own knife from his boot and slashed the man across the face, and then kicked him in the groin. The man fell to the ground in a pool of his own blood.

The third man wavered, not sure whether to attack or run. Mark used the interval to grab him and crack his head against the wall. He too fell to the ground.

Breathing hard, Mark continued down the alley, and emerged on the next block. There was blood on his clothes, happily none of his own. He knew that the military had no wish to make an issue of this, since it would expose them, and make them even more vulnerable. As soon as he could, he would write a report of the attack, noting only that the attackers had been beaten off, and send it to the Vietnam Peace Committee at Berkeley. They needed to be aware of what could happen to dissenters, and what appropriate action needed to be taken.

The consequences of the encounter were immediate. Mark was shipped off to Vietnam, which was his destination in any event.

Reading about the slaughter from the distance, and being a part of it, on the scene, were two very different things. You saw the young kids with their guts hanging out, screaming in anguish, with only death for relief. Another body to fill a bag. Another family in mourning. A boy dead, who had not yet even lived.

A fight for nothing. A death for nothing. Nowhere did they know it better than right here. Scared kids, waiting for death. Waiting to have shrapnel removed from their bodies, now cut open and spilling red American blood, the blood of its youth.

They knew it was for nothing, and to relieve the anguish of waiting to die, they took their fill of drugs. Nobody cared, nobody had any serious objection. Without the drugs, they may have rebelled, said they weren't ready to die, and announced that they were going home instead.

The enemy out there wasn't the enemy. They were people just trying to live, in their own country, in their own way. And they knew how to defend themselves. They dug holes in the ground, big and deep, and drove in sharpened stakes, pointing upward. Then they covered it all over. It looked just like any other piece of jungle, except that it wasn't. And the kids, dressed now in jungle camouflage supplied by their Uncle Sam in whom they had trusted, fell through space, and got themselves impaled on those sharpened stakes.

The officers tried to pretend that they were still in control. But they weren't, and they knew they weren't. So they showed their enthusiasm and their loyalty by killing defenseless civilians, claiming that they weren't civilians and they weren't defenseless. They had shovels – those eight year old children, and they could dig holes in the ground, and their mothers could sharpen those stakes, and their grandfathers could cover over the ground so that it looked like normal ground.

They went into action and they killed the enemy. The officers pretended to be gung ho, and maybe some still were. And maybe even some of the men still remained unreconstructed and unrepentant. But, for most, they were the victims, victims of themselves, victims of a government who could be so callous as to subject their own youth to the horrors of this war they had created. The survivors would carry the physical and mental scars forever more. No one could emerge unscathed.

Mark had been involved in several actions. He heard the bullets whiz past, and felt their closeness. He saw men – no, not men, boys – fall near him, once right next to him, dead as anyone could be. It was all so final, and so futile.

Both officers and men knew who and what Mark was, and what his feelings were about this war, which qualified him for extra patrols, in the hope that he might not return from one of them. But in the confusion that was normal, in the constant changes of personnel, his subversive role became somewhat obscured, particularly when the main objective of most of his companions-in-

57

arms was their continued survival. But he remained, generally, the outsider. His gun remained unfired, at least in the direction of the enemy, and was, along with the long knife he carried, a defense against his own side, who might not put all their faith in enemy bullets.

They were called out on patrol. A tank column was in trouble. Most of the faces around Mark were new faces, except for one, that of Roy, now a medic – the black fellow who had warned him to be careful when they were still in the States, just after finishing basic training. They greeted each other warmly. The lieutenant didn't seem too happy about that, perhaps aware of some of Mark's attitudinal problems regarding the war effort.

"Keep quiet!" he commanded. "You don't want to be callin' down no Cong on us just because you're long lost buddies, found each other again."

They moved forward cautiously. They spotted the tank column. The black sergeant whispered, "That ain't no tank column no more. Thems is just some tanks what used to be."

There were no signs of life. The Viet Cong had employed a tactic that had now become familiar when dealing with enemy tanks. They disabled the first one, and the last one. And the ones in between could go neither forward nor backward, nor maneuver on the jungle path. It was then just a clean-up operation for the Viet Cong.

Now, expecting that patrol, the Viet Cong was fully prepared, in, what was apparent, a classic ambush situation. There were suddenly a lot more names to go up on that plaque, not yet made, in Washington D.C. The live ones took cover. The jungle offered some protection. Shots rang out. They fired back, at whom, and at where, they could not tell. But the Cong knew where they were, in this little enclave, that gave only a small measure of protection. Would they storm it? Would they wait for night, and then move in, completing the job by hand?

They got Headquarters on the radio, reported their situation and position. "We need help," the lieutenant pleaded.

Help was on its way, Headquarters assured them. But help didn't come. Maybe the help got ambushed too. Or maybe it never got sent. Maybe they figured it was a mistake to send still-alive ones to try and save the ones who didn't have a chance, and just write them off as a bunch who hadn't been able to make it.

Roy did what he could for the wounded. Two died.

Mark said to Roy, "I hoped I'd get the chance to thank you."

"What for?"

"The warning."

"Oh, that. You sure did some damage. It was one good job, I can tell you. You think we're going to die here?"

"I was hoping not."

"Me too. But to tell the truth, it doesn't look so good."

Shots rang out from the Cong. Not much point in firing back – made it easier to be located.

Darkness was falling.

Some of the men were praying.

Another man died.

"I couldn't save him," Roy said. "I didn't know how. And I didn't have the stuff – even if I knew how. . . . I wanted to be a doctor. I thought maybe if I enlisted, I could get to go to college. I sure was stupid."

"They would've gotten you anyway."

"Not if I was in Canada. You believe in praying?"

"Not much."

"Me neither. I used to. We were great on praying – at least my mother was. We're from Alabama. We did a lot of praying down there. Then my mother took me up to Chicago. And we prayed there, too. It didn't do any good there either."

Mark didn't feel like he wanted to die here and now. It all seemed so useless. This was the war against which he had fought, and now that war seemed about to consume him. There was an air of unreality about the whole thing. The enemy was not out there. It was here, within, created in his own country. How did he explain that to those people out there, bent on killing him? It was a very hard thing to convey under the circumstances. Being here, he felt, giving up his life, was a terrible waste.

The black sergeant said to the white lieutenant, "We going to sit here forever, wait till the Cong decide to come over and kill us?"

"We're waiting for reinforcements."

"Ain't no reinforcements coming. It's pitch dark out here."

"And I say they're coming."

"And I say you is wrong."

"Don't you contradict me, Sergeant. I am in charge here, and don't you forget that."

59

"You being in charge ain't worth shit. You got us into this here ambush."

"I was following orders. I don't question my superior officers."

"Then you shoulda. I am asking you, how come you is a lieutenant, and I is just a sergeant."

"That's a stupid question."

"Well, I will give you the true answer, which don't happen to be stupid. Because you is white, and I is black."

"And if you were the lieutenant, we wouldn't be sitting here?"

"That's right. Any stupid muthafukka coulda' seen we was walking into a trap."

"Who you callin' a stupid muthafukka?"

"If it fits, you wear it."

"No black bastard calls me a mutherfucker and gets away with it."

The lieutenant drew his sidearm, pointed it at the sergeant, and pulled the trigger. Before the sergeant could hit the ground, someone shot the lieutenant. Then someone else shot the man who shot the lieutenant.

There were more shots, some from within the enclave, some from the Cong. It was difficult to tell exactly who was killing whom.

Then it was quiet.

Intuitively Mark, Roy and the others had fallen flat on their faces.

Roy put his head up. "We sure didn't need that."

"Does anyone know how to get us out of here?" someone asked.

Someone else said, "Ain't no getting out of here. This is the end of the road. We is dead men."

There was quiet again, as they thought about being dead.

"You think there's any way out of here?" Roy asked Mark.

"There could be. It's dark. They can't see us. We might be able to make our way back."

"You think so?"

"In theory."

"I haven't got anything against theories. Do you know which way is back?"

"I have a vague idea. But I'd need a compass."

Roy searched through the lieutenant's pockets, found his compass.

"Here's a compass, man. Maybe you can put that theory to work."

The way Mark saw it, there wasn't much to lose.

"Listen," Roy said to the others, "This here man got some theory that he could lead us out of here. I for one am willing to take the chance. And I strongly recommend that the rest of you do the same – because the way I see it, going with him is better than staying here."

The remnants appeared to agree. Slowly, quietly, they moved out, making progress in inches. They dragged out the wounded. One of them started to scream, "Sweet Jesus, save me!"

The Cong suddenly became aware of their efforts, fired at the sound, at the shadows. Mark got it in the leg. It was like they said – the descriptions he'd heard before of getting shot. He knew he wasn't going to like it. There was considerable pain.

Two men were dead. Another was wounded.

Roy got to Mark. "You got it bad?" he whispered.

"Not as bad as some."

"Ain't the best place to have it happen. But I'll fix you up. I'm the closest thing they got to a doctor for miles around."

"I got faith in you, Roy."

Roy stopped the flow of blood. He took care of Mark's leg.

"You still think you can get us out of here?" Roy asked.

"I think I'm very interested in trying."

"I'm glad to hear you say that. You put in a good word for me, say what a good medic I am. What are we waiting for, man?"

"Nothing, Roy. Let's get going."

They crawled foot by foot on their bellies.

The boy who asked for Jesus' help, asked again, screamed out, "Save me Jesus!"

The Cong weren't impressed. They'd heard about Jesus; the French had tried to tell them all about Him. But they still remained unconvinced. And here and now, He wasn't of much help to the man who called upon Him. He died along the way.

Mark led the men forward. He checked the compass from time to time. His one leg didn't seem to be of much value. But the pain had eased; Roy had given him an injection. He mused on life and death – how close they were to each other.

Mark got them back. Then he fainted.

There was surprise at the base by the appearance of this shattered remnant. They had already been written off.

61

Roy told everybody what had happened, and Mark's role in it. The Press, eager to report heroic feats, rather than the usual kind, picked up on the story, unaware of Mark's lack of support for the war effort, and projected him into the role of War Hero.

The military had no choice but to go along with it, eager to avoid having to tell the story in full.

7

David slides into his chair at the dinner table. He is aware of a coolish atmosphere between his parents, which has been going on for some time. He does not know why; if there is a problem, they did not discuss it in front of him. It makes him uncomfortable, uneasy. His parents never argued, never seemed to disagree. But there is something wrong. Not that he doesn't have his own problems.

"I went with Aaron to his Bar Mitzvah class today," David announces.

Sandy looks attentively at her son.

"You're getting rather involved," Mark observes casually.

"I *am* involved," David says. "I'd like to have a Bar Mitzvah – at the Western Wall – in Jerusalem."

"If that's what you want," Sandy says. "I have no objection."

"Thanks," David replies, his voice heavy with sarcasm.

"There haven't been many Bar Mitzvahs in our family," Mark says. "We felt that it was a religious expression we didn't want."

"I want it," David says simply. "I want it very much."

"Than there's the answer – you will have a Bar Mitzvah – and at the Western Wall in Jerusalem."

"I can't," David says. "I'm not Jewish."

"Of course you are," Sandy insists.

David shakes his head. "According to the rules, if your mother isn't Jewish, you aren't either."

"Is this true?" Sandy asks Mark in surprise.

Mark had never thought about it before. This is an expression of how far removed he is from the rules and regulations; in any event, it had never affected him.

"Rabbi Moreheim explained it all," David says. "In Orthodox and Conservative Judaism, the children are what the mother is. Unfortunately, Mother, you aren't Jewish. So I can't be Jewish."

Sandy looks at Mark, confused, as if there was something he had failed to reveal to her. To David she says, "We are a Jewish family. We have never been anything else. From the time I met your father I have considered myself Jewish."

"Considering yourself Jewish, and actually being Jewish are different things," David informs his mother.

Mark, not all that sympathetic to the idea of a Bar Mitzvah, nevertheless has a very considerable amount of sympathy for his son's plight. What, he wonders, was this revelation going to do to David? It had to have the most negative effect on him – to suddenly discover that he wasn't who he thought he was. It could undermine David's entire sense of security.

"What are we going to do?" Sandy, deeply disturbed, asks Mark.

David replies for his father. "You will have to convert, Mother," he says simply.

Mark does not speak, but has an overwhelming sense of triumph, of justification for his own earlier request. How could they be a Jewish family, if the wife, the mother, was not also Jewish?

Sandy exhales tiredly. "That seems to be a popular request in this house."

David looks at his mother, confused.

"Your father asked the same thing," Sandy reveals. "In a lot of ways it would be easier to just do it. I love you both. You are my life. But what you ask requires me to alter my personality – to be somebody different from what I am – from what I was born."

"I'll have to do that," David says. "I'll have to go from being a Jew – to being a gentile."

"You're the same as you always were."

"Except in reality."

"Whose reality?"

"In the eyes of the Jewish world."

"A part of it – in which your father has never taken part – nor your grandparents."

"But it's a world I want to be part of. Because of you I can't, and never will be able to."

"I have a point of view, David. I'm asking you to please try to understand it, and accept it."

"I don't understand it. I can't accept it. You say we are a Jewish family. But you're not Jewish. How can we be a Jewish family?"

"Because the Jewish connection in this house is cultural and not religious."

"But it isn't your culture either, Mother."

Sandy feels pained by her son's words, accentuated by the truth of them.

"Besides," David goes on, "somebody else has decided that my Judaism is only cultural. I don't necessarily see it that way. Why can't it also be religious – if that's what I feel? If that's what I want it to be?"

"I understand what you are saying, David," Sandy says. "And I understand what you are feeling. You have made your point very well. And there is no argument to the contrary. But you are not taking into consideration what I feel."

"But you keep telling us how Jewish you are."

"I feel I'm being coerced. I'm sure that that's not what either of you want. For the sake of my own integrity I feel that I have to take a strong position in this matter."

They lapse into silence. There is nothing more to say. Sandy's position is unmistakably clear, and David knows that a further assault on it would not alter that position.

After dinner David says to his father, "Can we go for a walk?"

"Sure."

Outside, David puts his arm around his father's waist. Mark puts his arm around David's shoulder, and they walk together, their closeness apparent. This is the way they usually walked, such neighborhood outings being frequent events, particularly when they wanted to talk together.

"We've got a problem, don't we, Dad?"

"We have to respect your mother's position."

"Either she's Jewish, or she isn't. If you were so happy with that position, you wouldn't have asked her to convert, either."

"We're making it very difficult for her, David."

"She's making it difficult for us. Why did you ask her to convert, Dad?"

Mark is a bit startled by the question. "Because I felt a breach had opened up between us. It had nothing to do with your mother. It was just events – circumstances."

"Like the Brady business – and you beating up that guy?"

"I suppose."

"It's the same with me."

"David, you could have a confirmation. We could enrol you in a reformed temple. It wouldn't matter about being half Jewish."

"I'm not totally against it – if I had been going to one all this time. I would have been learning a lot of things – about Judaism."

"That's my fault, David."

"A lot of kids at school go to Temple. It sounds nice. They talk about Jewish history and events and Jewish holidays. We never even had Passover at our house."

"We go to the Halidays."

"Sure. And I love Passover. I love going there. Aaron asks the Four Questions – in Hebrew. It sounds beautiful in my ears. And his father reads Hebrew – and he wasn't even born Jewish. He converted."

"Would you like us to have Passover at our house?"

"We don't know how. You don't know Hebrew. I don't know Hebrew, and Mom isn't about to learn."

"We could do it in English."

"It wouldn't be the same, would it, Dad."

"No, I suppose it wouldn't."

"That's why I want a Bar Mitzvah – at the Western Wall in Jerusalem. I want to study with Rabbi Moreheim. And then we could go to Israel. I'll carry the Torah in my arms, and face the Western Wall, and walk toward it. And you'd be there by my side. And I'd touch the Wall with my lips. I'd hold my hand to it, and thank Grandpa, and Grandma – and David – the English soldier who went to fight in Israel with Grandpa. I'm glad I'm named after him. And all the others who made it possible for me to be standing here, before the Wall, holding the Torah."

"David, you've made your case."

"But not to Mom."

"No. Not to Mom."

"Because she isn't Jewish. She doesn't understand. This is a historical ceremony. It confirms me in my Judaism. It says that, as of now, I am responsible as a Jewish person – to myself, to you, to my people. It's my entrance into the world of Judaism."

"We get that at birth."

"Maybe. But there's so much I don't understand. I know we care about Israel – a lot. And I know about the Holocaust. But how do I fit into this? Who am I? A Bar Mitzvah would say it all – to me, to you, to the whole world. Now I'm not even who I thought I was – or wanted to be."

Mark stops. He turns to his son. "David, it's my fault. I've taken my Judaism for granted, and assumed that you did, too. It's so much a part of me that I don't have to think about it. It's what I am. What I want to be. It's my comfort and my pride. It's what my parents gave me – and their parents gave them – going back thousands of years. But suddenly I see that it is not that easy. We have to learn about our culture – who we are, and why. So far I have only given you superficial glimpses."

"That's why I wanted a Bar Mitzvah. Then I'd know. I don't like being half a Jew. How do I make the division – up and down, or side to side. Which is the Jewish side? Can I cut out the non-Jewish part?"

They resume walking. "Dad, do you believe in God?"

"No, you know I don't."

"I don't, either – logically. It doesn't make sense. But what if you do in your heart?"

"Go with your heart."

"It kind of feels good – believing in God."

"Then you must belicve."

"You won't be annoyed with me?"

"Of course not. We haven't had any believers for a long time. If it makes you feel good, that's where you have to be."

"Thanks, Dad."

"For what?"

"For understanding."

"It isn't so much to ask, David. Our Judaism takes on many forms. We are articulate, and deeply involved. We all think that our solution is the best one, for ourselves, and for our people. In Russia, my grandparents lived in an Orthodox milieu. It wasn't one they particularly liked. They didn't believe in God, and they didn't think the Messiah would be coming to redeem Israel. From their very beginning they knew that it would have to be people who would do it.

"In America they worked hard and prospered. They supported this dream – this 'crazy dream', a lot of people called it – of a free and independent Israel. My father – your grandfather – was brought up in this atmosphere. He was a wonderful man. What a pity you two never met. You would have loved each other very much."

"He wouldn't have approved if he thought I believed in God."

"He would have said, 'David, whatever your beliefs are, you have them. They are yours'. And he would have given you a big hug."

"I don't think Grandma would be too happy."

"Well, I don't know, David. You'll just have to tell her, and try to make your case."

"It's harder, when your case is just in your heart."

"Maybe it's easier. It's hard to argue with the heart."

"I'm glad you didn't try to talk me out of it."

"Did you think I would?"

"Yeah."

"Well, I'm glad I didn't try."

"So am I . . . Dad, what do you believe? I know what you don't believe. But that isn't really a belief – not believing."

Mark smiles. "You're right. Sometimes it's hard to argue with your logic. I believe in the reality of Israel. Its existence sustains us. The few created it for the many. I'm very proud of my parents' contribution."

"But what about yours? What has your contribution been?"

Mark is not prepared for that and has to think about it for a moment. "Perhaps it's more abstract," he replies at last. "Today we all have to fight to sustain this gift that has been handed to us. I suppose I travel on their coattails."

"You're a war hero, except it wasn't the right war. Sure, I believe in Israel too. But what's my connection? We give some money. We give money to the Christmas fund too – maybe drop fifty cents in the collection box the guy dressed up like Santa Claus is shaking. I suppose it's nice they are giving the homeless Christmas dinner – I'm not sure what happens the rest of the year. But I don't think I want to go down and have Christmas dinner with them."

"Is that how you view your connection with Israel?"

"In a way – except there is a bit more involvement. But it's still off in the distance. Those guys eating their Christmas dinner – they're a lot closer to us than Israel. I suppose that's why I want to have a Bar Mitzvah, because it's all the time. It wouldn't be just for Christmas."

"I understand what you mean, David."

"Do you, Dad? Do you really? A lot of these things I haven't worked out – not fully."

"You want a commitment. You want to commit yourself."

"That's it. I want to be commited."

"And you feel that having a Bar Mitzvah will be that commitment."

"Yes. Exactly."

"David, I give you my word. I'll do everything I can to see that you have your Bar Mitzvah – and at the Wall."

They walk on, David's arm around his father's waist, Marks arm over David's shoulder.

8

i

It is 1944. Lieutenant Jonathan Spaulding hit Omaha Beach with his men on June 6th, and immediately came under heavy German fire. Five men were dead almost before they were out of the landing craft. Seven more were wounded. Jonathan hoped not to die here, and not yet. There was such a lot of work to do. He had looked forward to this moment for a long time, and now he would have a chance to do some paying back.

A machine gun directly ahead had them pinned down. This wasn't a very good place to be, and he hated the idea of moving backward. "Cover me," he ordered his men, as he moved forward on his belly. The bullets whizzed past, inches above his head. He managed to reach a bit of cover, then made his way slowly through an open place. The boys were doing a good job keeping the machine gun occupied.

He moved within grenade range, and lobbed two over in quick succession. The machine gun went quiet. Jonathan moved up cautiously, saw a wounded German trying to reach the machine gun. Jonathan shot him with his sidearm. The man had a surprised look on his face when the bullet hit him. Jonathan felt an enormous sense of satisfaction. It was a good start.

Lieutenant Spaulding motioned for his men to move forward. His war was just beginning. Ahead there were more Germans, with more machine guns – MG-42s that fired 12,000 rounds a minute. And the 88mm Flak 42 anti-tank gun, originally meant as an anti-aircraft weapon, but turned against the Sherman tanks with their too thin armor, it was instrumental in halting many Allied assaults.

155,000 Allied troops, on 59 miles of Normandie beach, faced 50,000 German troops. Already ten landing craft launched off Omaha Beach had been swamped by the heavy sea and about 1,000 men were drowned.

They said the first thousand yards were going to be the toughest – they were right. Jonathan looked back toward the beach. They hadn't moved anywhere near a thousand yards. Every man had his own war to fight – the one just up ahead. Even with the more than three to one advantage in manpower, progress was measured in yards, not miles.

As late as June 30th, Caen, a D-Day objective, was still in German hands. But heavy bombing made it possible for General Patton's forces to make reasonable gains by the end of July.

The Germans counter-attacked and fell into a trap at Argentan, about half the way to Paris. Ten thousand Germans were killed. 50,000 were made prisoners. Jonathan watched them crumble, watched them surrender. The prisoners fell into his hands in huge numbers, beaten, frightened, demoralized.

Jonathan acquired a 9mm Shmeisser, a German sub-machine gun that was superior to the American M3A1 "grease gun", and the preferred arm of those in the American military who could get them.

By the end of August Jonathan and his men were in Paris. He was now a captain.

In due course they crossed the Elbe. They were on German soil. It felt good. Jonathan was promoted again to major. His men had taken substantial numbers of casualties. He was hit in the left shoulder, but he killed the German who did it – an officer with a nice Lugar, which now suddenly changed hands, and sides.

Jonathan's wound was bad enough to put him out of the war for a while, and into a field hospital. But he wouldn't have it, and returned in bandages to his men.

They moved deeper into Germany. Hitler threw in the fifteen, sixteen and seventeen year olds. They got killed quickly or surrendered.

Jonathan was made a colonel, had most of the decorations his government could give, which, while providing a measure of satisfaction, was not what the war was about; for him, it was bringing Germany to its knees.

Then Jonathan and his men confronted another manifestation of what the "superior" German mind had been able to conceive and construct: one of the many concentration camps, meant for the elimination of an entire people.

Jonathan saw the dead and the dying, those who still clung to life. He had witnessed all the horrors of war, been an active participant, but nothing had prepared him for this. He found a place where he could be alone, and he broke down. He cried, sobbing audibly. And he threw up. And when there was nothing left in his stomach, he continued to retch.

Then he pulled himself together, and faced those who, barely alive, had managed to live through all of this, to have seen it happen, day by day.

Jonathan was made the camp administrator, charged with offering whatever assistance he could. On the third day there was a knock of his office door. "Come in," he called.

A girl entered shyly, and stood before him. She wore the striped garment of a camp inmate, her head shaved. She was fifteen, or sixteen, or seventeen – no one looked their age. But she looked better than most, less emaciated, and there was the suggestion that this was a beautiful young woman.

"Forgive me for troubling you," she said, in very good English. "I wanted to thank you and your men for liberating us."

Jonathan nodded his head, and tried to smile. What if they had come the day before, or the week before, how many could they have saved then? What could they have done to have kept this from ever happening? Some of the answers were obvious.

"Please sit down," he said to the girl.

She hesitated, as if she were already being too intrusive.

"Please," he said, indicating the chair.

She looked at the chair, as if there were something forbidding about it, then complied, sitting stiffly on it.

"Are you getting all the help you need?" Jonathan asked her. "Are there any specific requests?"

"We are being attended very well. Thank you." She was silent for a moment, and then made an effort to summon her courage.

"I am Milada Haskova," she said. "I speak English, German, French, and Russian. And of course Czech," she added as an after-thought. "It is possible that I could be of value to you."

"I'm sure that you can."

"I also read and write those languages."

Jonathan nodded his head. He could feel tears welling up in his eyes. Here, before him, sat one of the victims of this tragedy, a young girl, clothed in the uniform that said any form of degradation was permitted – since these people deserved this fate; and that we, the Germans, have instituted justice at last.

"I can also type," she added.

"Tell me about yourself, Milada."

He saw the number tattooed on her arm. He wanted to touch it, wipe it away, wipe away all that had happened here.

She did not speak for a moment, as if considering how to say it. "We are Czech," she said, "with a German cultural background and very assimilated. My father was a professor of German. He thought the German language and culture was the most advanced, the most superior in the world. They came and got him first. Very early on. We never saw him again."

She was silent for a time, as if remembering. "And then they came for my mother and me, and my two aunts – my mother's younger sisters. And they brought us here. We had more 'status' than the Polish Jews –" she spoke the word "Status" with irony, with bitterness. "We were considered to be a part of the 'German world'. My father was so proud of that. He and my mother used to argue – she was a Zionist. 'You do not need Zionism', he used to say. 'Germany has provided Jews with equality – and with all the opportunity one could ever want in a civilized society'."

Tears began to flow down Jonathan's cheeks. He made no attempt to conceal them or to wipe them away. He felt neither shame nor weakness in front of this girl, who in her short life had seen the full range of weakness and strength.

"My mother always said, 'We need our own Homeland. We will always be victims as long as we live in somebody else's country'. She was right. We are equal citizens one moment, but the next they change their minds, and we are not equal any more. And we end up here."

"Where is your mother?"

"She died – two weeks ago. My aunts died earlier," she explained without emotion. "They decided, between them – that I had to live. They made me take part of their food. It did not want to go down into my stomach. They said I had to. They said I had to fight for an Israel – to make a homeland for all of the Jewish people – so that we could be free."

"You want to go to Israel?"

"Yes."

He looked into her blue eyes. "I too."

She looked back at him, confused, not comprehending at first. Then slowly she began to assimilate what he had said.

"You are a Jew?" she asked.

Mark nodded.

Milada appeared to draw a great sigh of relief, and relax into her chair.

They both remained silent for a time, each responding in his and her own way to the other.

Milada was overwhelmed by the reality of a Jewish officer in charge here – a Jew from the other side of the world, who also wanted to fight for Israel. She liked him, because he could cry, and he was not ashamed.

Mark's tears did not abate. This girl, hardly more than a child, lived surrounded by death, could talk of her mother's death, just a little while ago, and that of her aunts, in an almost casual way. Yes, death was casual here, and they accepted it: this Christian legacy, another one of Christianity's Crusades – Hitler loudly proclaiming that he was doing the work of the Church.

U. S. President Franklin Roosevelt called a conference held in Evian, to consider the possibilities for resettlement of Germany's Jews, but it soon became apparent that nobody else wanted them, either – they already had a surplus. Poland was desperately searching for ways to get rid of the Jews it had, a position made obvious at the Conference. Britain attended, but only to assure the other delegates that Israel, which they then controlled, was not an option, that Jews certainly had no place there.

It was plain to Hitler that all Jews were surplus, that by and large the leaders of the world shared his position, and that their solution was his solution. And, in the end, there was virtually full agreement on the final solution.

But now there were remnants, and although the final solution had worked effectively and efficiently, many of the old problems remained. The world pretended concern, but still offered relatively few places for resettlement. Britain had not altered her position at all in regard to Jewish immigration into Israel.

It was obvious that these remnants needed to be resettled; large numbers wanted to go to Israel, others to the United States, Canada, Australia. Few countries were quick to offer haven, which meant that Jews languished in what had been concentration camps, and were now called Displaced Persons Camps, for years, while waiting for visas to somewhere.

The Displaced Persons, since their emergence, had not gained in popularity. The local population took little pleasure in their presence, suffered serious disappointment that even some of the DPs were still alive.

Later, on a visit into town, Milada and some of her fellow DPs were attacked by a group of town-folk.

"Kill the Jews!" they shouted. "Kill the Jews. What kind of stupidity was it to leave some of them alive!"

One man died of his injuries. Milada suffered severe bruising.

Milada sat in Mark's office and reported what had happened. Mark listened with growing anger, taking notes meant for a report, which he knew would be filed somewhere and ignored. He opened the bottom drawer of his desk. The Luger was there. He took it from the drawer, held it in his hand for a moment, then handed it to Milada. Now she held it, almost lovingly.

"Would you like to learn to use it?" Jonathan asked.

"I would love to," Milada replied.

Jonathan reached into the drawer and got two boxes of 9mm shells. He then found some tin cans, and together, in Jonathan's jeep, they drove some distance from the camp. Jonathan set up the cans, meant for targets. He moved off some distance, then loaded the Luger, as Milada watched. He raised his arm and fired at the cans in rapid succession, and each danced into the air as they were struck by the bullet.

"This is what you will do," Jonathan said. "Do you think you will be able?"

"I am sure of it."

Jonathan set up the cans again. He reloaded the Luger and handed it to Milada. "Line up the sights," he instructed her. "Then squeeze the trigger. Fire when you're ready."

Milada did as she was told.

The shot rang in her ears, as the can went flying through space.

"Very good," Jonathan said, impressed.

"Thank you."

"Now do it again."

And she did.

They used up both boxes of shells. The tin cans had a lot of holes in them.

As they got back into the jeep, Jonathan was aware that Milada was suddenly different, transformed, no longer a DP, but an individual who could control her own destiny and her own fate. He was aware that firing the Luger at those tin cans had altered her personality, given her a confidence that she had not had before.

"We'll do it again," Jonathan said.

"I am ready."

"Tomorrow."

"Good."

He was also aware of how attractive she was, with her high Slavic cheekbones, and the blonde hair that had grown considerably longer since that day she had first come into his office.

In due course Milada, who was seventeen, became highly efficient in the use of the Luger, could strip it down and could put it back together blindfolded. In the office, Jonathan cleaned the gun. He then handed it to her. "It's yours," he said simply.

Her eyes lit up. She smiled. He had not seen her smile often. There had been little in her recent life that provided a reason to smile.

The way she said thank you made it apparent that this was the best and most important present she had ever received in her life. "I will take very good care of it."

"I know you will. And you'll know what to do with it."

She knew exactly what to do with it. On the next visit to town, a group of Germans who did not even pretend to be "re-educated" approached Milada and her companions, with a view to bringing about the until-now-delayed – for them – final solution. Milada felt her heartbeat increase considerably. But it was born of excitement, of at last being able to strike back. She was no longer defenseless. The German who appeared to be the leader had a short club in his hand. He seemed familiar. Milada recognized him as a camp guard, now out of uniform. She pulled out the

Luger. The former camp guard looked annoyed. Milada squeezed the trigger. The shot was music in her ears. The man now looked very annoyed as he collapsed to the ground.

The others turned and started to run. Milada lined up the sights, as Jonathan had taught her to do, and squeezed the trigger. The man tried to keep running, but fell on his face, very dead.

She moved the sights onto another figure, some distance further on by now, and squeezed the trigger again. He too collapsed, only sixty seconds of life left in him, perhaps sufficient time to review his life as a good and loyal German.

She had given them the same kind of chance they had given her father, and her mother, and her aunts, and all the rest.

She reported back to Jonathan. He was delighted.

"How did you feel about it?"

"It was a good beginning – in a small way. The town has many who were employed in the camp. They are killers. They have gone unpunished."

"Why don't you deal with them."

She liked Jonathan's suggestion. "We will do exactly that."

They drew up a list: names, addresses, crimes committed against the Jews.

They visited the home of Heinrich Gebbler. It was a nice, neat, two-storey house, with a well-kept lawn, and a beech tree in front – a respectable German citizen, with Jewish blood up to his elbows. Milada rang the bell. A plain looking woman, in an apron, her hair tied in a bun, answered the door.

"We are looking for Heinrich Gebbler," Milada said.

"He's not here," the woman said, trying to push the door closed.

Milada caught a glimpse of someone upstairs taking refuge in one of the rooms. Milada and her friends pushed past the woman and raced up the stairs. The door was locked. The men shouldered it open. There was Heinrich Gebbler, cowering. At first he denied he was Heinrich Gebbler. But then everyone knew him, knew he was Heinrich Gebbler, and he said, "I was only obeying orders."

"Not a defense," Milada informed him. "We find you guilty of murder. The punishment is death."

"No, please, have mercy."

"Like you had mercy."

"I have a wife. And two children."

"You are just an ordinary man then?" Milada asked.

"Yes. That's right. An ordinary man."

"We have noticed that – those of us who are still alive . . . I will now carry out the sentence."

Which is precisely what she did.

As they left the upstairs bedroom Mrs. Gebbler stood below, a double barrel shotgun in her hands, which she now raised to fire. Milada squeezed off three shots in rapid succession. In the process of collapsing, Mrs. Gebbler pulled the trigger of her shotgun. Shot splattered against the ceiling in the hall. Bits of plaster swung back and forth, then dropped to the ground.

Mrs. Gebbler was very dead. All three shots had found their mark. On the way out they picked up the shotgun.

Milada and her fellow DPs became increasingly efficient. Jonathan provided them with a truck – for mobility, and which they also used as an execution chamber, bringing the war criminal to it, reading out the charges, and carrying out the sentence.

"You are doing very well," Jonathan complimented Milada, picking up a sheaf of papers on his desk and holding them up for her inspection, "judging by the number of complaints I'm getting." He dropped them into the waste basket.

"They are only the small vermin," Milada said. "The big ones are getting away. This is what our intelligence is telling us."

"Our intelligence tells us the same thing."

"Where have they gone? And how?"

"They are going to South America, Egypt, Syria, Iraq – to the United States. They are being issued with Vatican passports."

"There is nothing the American Government can do?"

"It's the American Government that's providing the protection."

Milada exhaled. "It disillusions one."

"It disillusions a lot of us. These are decisions that have been made at a very high level."

ii

Not long afterwards a man appeared at the DP camp and went to Jonathan's office. In his late twenties, he spoke English with a

Hebrew accent. "I'm Mordechai Gilboa," he said, offering his hand. "I'm from Israel – Kibbutz Gan Galil. We would like to offer assistance to the Displaced Persons here."

"Gan Galil," Jonathan said, taking the outstretched hand, "Garden of the Gaililee, on the road from Haifa."

Gilboa looked perplexed. "You have been there?"

"Yes, with my parents – before the war. They are very active Zionists."

"The Spaulding family!" Gilboa said excitedly. "Of course. And you are Colonel Spaulding. I did not make the association. Your family has planted a whole forest near the kibbutz. Your father planted the first tree with his own hands. I was there. I remember you."

"*Shalom*, Mordechai."

"*Shalom*, Jonathan."

The two men embraced.

"Your presence here will make everything much easier," Mordechai said.

Colonel Jonathan Spaulding replied, "You can be sure I'll do my best."

Mordechai explained the situation. "The British show no indication of relinquishing their hold on Israel. On the contrary, they appear to be more determined than ever to remain there. They maintain a virtual ban on Jewish immigration and have instituted an extremely tight blockade. We have decided to try and run that blockade – to bring in our people – 'illegally' – in an operation to be known as Aliyah Beit. Probably most will not get through. But it will bring our plight to the attention of the world. The British have warned us that illegal immigrants will be returned to their displaced persons' camps in Europe, or interned on the Island of Cyprus, which, as I understand it, is another concentration camp."

"Most of our people here want to go to Israel," Jonathan informed Mordechai.

"We can begin the process. I will meet with them and tell them of our plans – and the dangers – that they could wind up back here again, or in a British concentration camp that could be worse."

"Worse?"

"Here they are free to come and go – relatively free. In the British concentration camps in Cyprus they will be locked in. The

British have made this unmistakably clear. There won't be any gas chambers – but there will be enough horrors – just being locked in again – for who knows how many years."

After the First World War the League of Nations had mandated Great Britain to develop Israel as a homeland for the Jewish people, an undertaking the British betrayed before the ink had dried on the Balfour Declaration, which had proclaimed support for such a concept. The original mandated territory was 45,760 square miles, on both sides of the Jordan River. In 1922, without asking anyone, Britain amputated 35,222 of those square miles – the area lying east of the Jordan River – and created the Hashemite Kingdom of Jordan – an artificial entity that had no reason and no justification to exist, except as a British foothold in the Middle East.

It was plain for everybody to see that Britain had taken an unequivocal position in support of the Arabs, their cause and their oil.

Chaim Weizmann, ultimately to become Israel's first President, and David Ben Gurion, the to-be-first Prime Minister, essentially hostile towards each other, were both under the misguided impression that Britain would honor its commitments to the Jewish people. But Weizmann, a brilliant scientist, was totally without understanding of Middle-East politics or the personalities involved – both British and Arab. Ben Gurion, not inclined to accommodate opposition, had at times collaborated with the British, in his efforts to crush those who opposed him, on both the left and the right.

Britain, who had survived the war without the imposition of bread rationing, now imposed it, and other measures. It chose to divert scarce resources from the suffering British people in order to support a war machine whose sole purpose was to suppress Jews – those in Israel, and those who wanted to come to Israel. Britain was prepared to, and actually did, devote unlimited resources to maintaining its power in Israel, while literally taking it out of the flesh of its people back home.

iii

Mordechai briefed Jonathan and Milada. "I am in the Palmach," he explained. "There are many areas in which we take issue with

Ben Gurion. But for now we have agreed to cooperate – on immigration, for example. Even the Irgun wants that. They feel as strongly as we do. Of course many other issues divide us from them. They are in favor of free enterprise – we are very much against it. But at least we and Ben Gurion subscribe to the principle of socialism. Our main difference is that we seek a neutral Israel, while Ben Gurion has committed Israel to as close an alliance as is possible with the United States. We do not think that in the long run, the United States will prove to be such a good ally . . . The fact of the matter is, that if the United States chose, it could pressure Britain into giving up the Mandate and allow unlimited immigration into Israel."

"But it hasn't," Milada said angrily.

"And it won't. The Arab oil interests are very strong in the United States. This goes back a long time – to just after the First War, when Britain and the United States were busy competing with each other for Arab oil. But Franklin Roosevelt, who Jews made the mistake of thinking was their friend – had already made all the necessary arrangements with Ibn Saud of Saudi Arabia. This has to exclude any really meaningful help from the United States."

"We're in this alone, then," Jonathan acknowledged sadly.

"Very much so. The world will offer little by way of help. The sympathetic may shed some tears – after we're dead. This is another reason for my being here – to collect arms. If it shoots, we want it."

"I'm sure I can help there."

"I was hoping so. We have been collecting arms since the First World War – but they are small arms, and they come in all shapes and sizes – and calibers. When the war comes, we will be at a great disadvantage. The Arabs are very well equipped – by the British mainly. And they have been buying up surplus American equipment in Europe. It has not been made available to us. They want to know who wants it, and where it is going, and ask a great many questions – which disqualifies us. They do not want to sell us arms."

Jonathan was disheartened by Mordechai's revelations that the United States was not being as helpful as it might be in regard to Israel. Yet, it was obvious that if the United States chose, it could, without any effort, tell the British to get out of Israel and allow

Israel to immediately proclaim itself an Independent Jewish Land. Britain, though victorious, was beaten, beaten into the ground, in worse shape than Germany, with considerably less chance of recovery, now a pauper nation, dependent upon hand-outs from the United States. Under those circumstances, it wouldn't have been very difficult to tell Britain what it had to do.

"Mordechai," Jonathan said, "you can count on me for full cooperation."

"I thank you."

"No, it is I who thank you. We will work well together. We have the same cause. You will be staying here?"

"That is the plan. I will want to talk with the DPs."

"Start whenever you are ready. And I will begin to look into the other matter."

Mordechai Gilboa brought hope. Someone from Israel had come. Someone cared. They could go to Israel. Not today. Not tomorrow. But soon. Mordechai organized Hebrew classes. In Israel they would need to speak Hebrew. Yiddish was fine, but they didn't speak it much in Israel any more. Hebrew was the national language.

He also told them that their chances were good for winding up back here – or, worse still, in a British prison camp in Cyprus. The majority who wanted to go to Israel were prepared to take the chance.

Jonathan discussed Mordechai's work with Milada. She was delighted. He also discussed another matter. "I believe I can get you a visa for permanent residence in the United States."

She looked at him with disapproval. "No, thank you."

"That's what I thought you'd say."

"Then you were right."

"I'm due back Stateside. I'd like to see my parents. Then I'll return here. I'm up for discharge pretty soon. But I'm trying to delay it for as long as possible – there's a lot of work that needs to be done here – with Mordechai . . . I'd like you to come with me to the United States – just for a visit. I want you to meet my parents – and I want them to meet you." He put his hand on hers.

She put her hand on his. "I'd love to meet them. But not now. I might get in. But I might not get out. I never heard of anyone being issued with a visa to get back into a DP camp."

"Okay. I understand what you're saying. When I return, and

when you and I and Mordechai finish our work here – then we will all go to Israel. Together. There's going to be a war there. I have to be in it."

"So do I."

"It's settled then?"

"Settled."

Mordechai began moving the DPs out. They were headed for Genoa or Marseilles, or one of the other Mediterranean ports, depending upon which one was open. The British knew what was happening, and would apply pressure on the French and the Italians to close the ports to illegal ships trying to transport illegal immigrants. But both the Italians and French were sympathetic to the cause of Jewish immigration to Israel, and while one port was closed, others would open, in defiance of British wishes to the contrary, with the situation changing periodically.

The DPs were taken to the appropriate port by train. Milada was usually the courier. She discovered that traveling on the trains with the Jewish DPs were those Germans, Lithuanians, Poles, Croats and others who were, in fact, war criminals in the process of evading justice, traveling now, out of Europe, to take up residence abroad, where there was no danger that they would be made to pay for their crimes against the Jews.

Milada brought this to Mordechai's attention, and spoke to him and Jonathan about it. Mordechai already knew. Milada's intelligence did not come as a revelation to him.

"We know," Mordechai confessed, embarrassed.

"These people should be brought to justice."

"It isn't the policy of the Jewish Agency – and particularly Ben Gurion."

"The Jewish Agency didn't burn in a concentration camp."

"The policy is not to take revenge."

"And they decided this," Milada shouted indignantly.

"Their sole interest is to bring Jews to Israel."

"Do you agree with this policy?"

"I didn't make it, Milada. I don't agree with it."

Milada felt the rage burning in her. It had been decided that there would be no retribution. Israel had decided it. The Jewish Agency. And who had given them the right to decide this? They stole it from the dead, those who had already been incinerated, those who had no voice, those who could not demand justice.

The "illegal" ships were loaded with "illegal" passengers, packed together in the most difficult conditions. But they were going "home", and the discomfort was just for a while – a little while.

The *Warfield*, an old American river boat, renamed the *Exodus*, carried 4,500 Jews. Twenty miles off Gaza, in international waters, two British destroyers rammed her, one on either side. British soldiers, firing tear gas, armed with pistols and clubs, boarded her. Bill Bernstein, the First Mate, was hit over the head, and later died. A young boy, an orphan who thought he had reached "home", was shot in the face at point blank range, and died instantly. The British killed at least two Jews, with many requiring hospital treatment. It took five British destroyers and a cruiser to finally subdue the *Exodus*, ramming it continuously, until it was in danger of sinking, with 4,500 Jews on board.

The "illegal" Jews were transferred to three British prison ships and returned to France, where they refused to disembark, despite being denied food and water by the British, and told they would be taken back to Germany.

The *Paducah* was forty-five years old in 1947 when it attempted to run the British blockade with 1500 Jewish refugees on board, trying to reach Israel. It was 190 feet long, 36 feet wide, 900 gross tons. The Captain, Rudolph Patzert, wrote: "*It seems to me that I was discovering what it meant to be a Jew. Now I, too, was a Jew.*" He found out the hard way, in a British concentration camp in Cyprus, where he wound up, along with his 1500 charges and the rest of his crew, including able-bodied seaman Walter Greaves, who was on his way to Israel for a second time – the first had been aboard the *Ben Hecht*; the British put Greaves in Acre Prison, warned him that he'd have a prolonged stay there were he ever to return.

Jonathan paid a brief visit to Los Angeles to see his parents. He told them about Milada – about their mutual feelings toward each other, and their hopes for a future together.

His mother said, "We welcome her. She is our daughter."

And he also told them about his work.

"We are proud of you," his mother said.

He told his father that he would be returning to Europe, and then to Israel, where there would soon be a war, and asked that his father break the news to his mother.

His mother, when she confronted Jonathan, said, "Your father has told me of your plans. I know that you wanted to make it easier for me to bear. But, remember, Jonathan, we are Zionists – going back to when we were hardly more than children, living in Russia. Now, at last, after almost two thousand years of waiting, we are about to realize our dream. And my son is going to fight to make that dream, a reality – in our life-time. Did you expect me to discourage you? On the contrary, my son, fight hard. Fight well."

"Thank you, Mother."

"You are fighting for all of the Jewish people – for the people who never had a chance to fight."

"I know. I will remember that."

"We are very proud of you."

On the eve of Jonathan's return, his father gave him a small, somewhat battered case.

"What is it?" Jonathan asked.

"Money."

"What for?"

"To buy arms."

"It must be a lot of money."

"It is. A million dollars."

Jonathan looked at the case in his hands, impressed. "I didn't know we had a million dollars."

"We don't," his father replied. "We didn't. Now we haven't got anything. It is all that we have managed to save, plus whatever I have been able to beg and borrow, and almost to steal. We'll probably get some more money, but we won't get another chance to have an Israel."

Jonathan returned to Germany. They prepared the arms he had gathered, and made ready for their journey to Israel. They borrowed three trucks from Uncle Sam – 2½ tonners with six-wheel-drive. They loaded the trucks, filled now not only with munitions but with men prepared and eager to do battle, men Mordechai had deliberately held back, in order to insure that they would not end up in Cyprus.

The small convoy started out on its journey, headed over the mountains for the obscure port of Marano, south of Undine, on the Adriatic side of Italy, to the north of Venice. Jonathan drove the lead truck, the little battered case on the seat next to him, the Shmeisser on top of it. Milada sat on the other side, near the door, the Luger in her holster, belted around her waist. Jonathan was no longer connected to the United States Army officially, but wore the uniform, and the insignia of his rank for this journey, which he thought could be useful.

The middle truck was driven by a man who, with Milada, had seen off a substantial number of Germans, and had a sten gun next to him, as did the man who also occupied the front seat.

Mordechai brought up the rear, he and his passengers in the front seat armed, as were the men in the back of the truck.

Night fell. The moon came up, bright and full. It made maneuvering the mountain roads easier. They traveled along steadily. There was an atmosphere of excitement, of anticipation. Hardly anyone spoke, except to exchange a few essential words now and again.

Suddenly, as they rounded a bend, a British military truck blocked the road. Jonathan hit the brakes hard. British soldiers stood near their truck, cradling sten guns. A captain, holding a Webley service revolver, held up his hand. He came over to Jonathan, who remained behind the wheel, taking hold of the Shmeisser.

"Good evening, Colonel," the captain said, surprised to find a high-ranking officer behind the wheel. "What are you carrying?" he asked politely.

"Blankets," Jonathan replied.

"Mind if I have a look?" the captain asked, still polite, in his standard English, as if this were just routine and he harboured no suspicions at all.

Jonathan assumed that the British must have been tipped off. There were plenty around who weren't sympathetic, and in the pay of British intelligence.

Jonathan grabbed his Shmeisser, pushed open the truck door, and jumped down from the truck. "As a matter of fact, I do mind," he said.

Milada jumped out of the truck, her Luger drawn. The Jews in the other trucks emerged, their arms ready, training them on the Tommies.

The captain pointed the Webley at Jonathan.

With the barrel of his Shmeisser, Jonathan knocked the Webley from the captain's hand. It fell noisily to the road and traveled a short distance before it came to a final stop.

"Throw down your arms," Jonathan commanded.

The Tommies did not respond at once.

Jonathan fired the Shmeisser at their feet, immediately in front of them. "Now," he ordered.

The message suddenly came through, and they complied. The captain stood by, indignant, but impotent.

"Push that truck over the mountainside," Jonathan ordered the Tommies. They stood there dumbly.

In a sudden dash Milada ran over to the British truck. She thought she saw movement inside at the back. There was a radioman trying to contact base. She fired three quick shots into the radio. It disintegrated.

"Get down off that truck," she ordered the radio man, pointing the Luger at his head. He continued to sit there, either in defiance, or petrified with fear. She fired one shot above his head. "The next one will be through you," Milada informed him.

He jumped off the back of the truck, shivering with fear. Milada slashed his face with the barrel of the Luger, the front site making a deep gash.

"You're lucky I haven't killed you yet, you little bastard," she said angrily to the radioman. "What did you say on that radio?"

"I never got through. I swear it. I was only doing my duty," he quaked.

Milada hit him again with the barrel of the Luger, harder this time, tearing open an even deeper wound. "I've heard that before, too," she said.

The captain, seething, unable to contain his anger, shouted out, "You bloody Jews – you never stop causing trouble, do you. What a pity Hitler didn't get you all."

Jonathan said nothing. He handed his Shmeisser to Milada, who slung it over her left shoulder while continuing to hold the Luger in her right hand.

Jonathan went over to the captain, whose eyes were filled with fear. He hadn't meant to say that. It had just slipped out. As soon as he heard those words in his ears he knew he had made a mistake. It was as if someone else had said them, and he was hearing them from a distance.

Jonathan gathered up the captain with his left hand, and smashed him in the face with his right hand. The captain offered no resistance, no explanation, because someone else had said those words. Jonathan hit him again. The captain would have collapsed, except that Jonathan was holding him up. He punched him again, then let him drop to the ground.

So much for dealing with allies, Jonathan thought. They were no better than the Nazis.

The Jews collected the British arms.

"Push that truck over the mountainside," Jonathan ordered the Tommies.

They moved with great speed to comply. The truck went over the edge. It rolled, and bounced, and caught fire, spiraling, alight, all the way down to the bottom, the fire still burning, but appearing quite small by this time.

"Strip off your uniforms," Jonathan ordered the British soldiers.

The sergeant stepped forward and saluted Jonathan smartly. "Sir, permission to speak," he said with a Yorkshire accent.

"Granted."

"I want to come with you."

Jonathan, and the others, were startled by the sergeant's request.

"Do you know where we're going?"

"Yes, sir."

"You are not a Jew."

"Do you have to be a Jew to want to go to Israel?"

Jonathan thought about that for a moment.

"I suppose not . . . Do you know about us?"

"Yes, Sir. Before the war my mate was in Ha'shomer Hatzier. I used to go along to the meetings with him. We were going to live on a kibbutz in Israel. Unfortunately he was killed early on in the war. But I still fancy the idea of going to live on a kibbutz."

"There's going to be a war there, you know."

"Yes, sir. I would like to do my bit. I've had a good deal of experience by this time, Sir. I'd come in useful."

"Where are you from, Sergeant?"

"Leeds, Sir."

"What's your name?"

"Brown, Sir. David."

"If you come with us, David, you'd be deserting."

"Not so much deserting, Sir, as volunteering for a higher cause."

"Your government might not see it quite like that."

"Probably not, Sir. But some governments can be a bit blinkered in that respect."

"I'm sure you're right. But it could mean never going home again.

"Yes, Sir. I understand that, Sir. It is a considered decision. I am prepared, Sir."

Jonathan was silent for a full minute. Then he turned to look at Mordechai, to see what his opinion might be.

Mordechai nodded approval.

Jonathan could see no strong objection; perhaps if they were caught, he could be accused of harboring a deserter. Not that that would matter much at this point.

"Sergeant," Jonathan said, "you've just joined the cause."

David smiled broadly. "Thank you, Sir. You won't regret it."

"I'm sure we won't."

The other British soldiers stripped off their uniforms, and helped the captain out of his. David Brown gathered them up. He spoke to his men, now standing about in their underwear. "We've had a good war, lads," he said. "We fought well. We fought for the right cause. We can be proud of that. Damn proud. But now we're on the wrong side. And for that we have to be ashamed. All the things we're doing now – it can't make any of us proud."

He turned and walked away. Jonathan and the others climbed back into their trucks. David Brown rode with Jonathan, Milada between them, the battered case on the floor.

They reached Marano without further incident. There was a former American PT (Patrol Torpedo) boat waiting for them in the harbor, manned by a Palmach crew, all of whom hugged Mordechai, and shook hands formally with Jonathan and Milada. The sound of Hebrew being used as a spoken language was beautiful music for Jonathan, an expression of the reality of Israel. The PT had been decommissioned, had no torpedo capacity and the machine guns had long since been removed. But it was fast, and with the giant diesel engines, recently overhauled, it could outrun anything the British had that might want to stop them.

The trucks were unloaded, their contents stowed aboard the now seriously overcrowded PT. Haganah/Palmach personnel would deal with the trucks, taking them up into the mountains and running them over the edge – to insure that they would not be traced to this operation. The PT carried enough extra fuel to reach Israel, and then some, in the event of an emergency; and a variety of flags – American, French, British, Italian – to be expediently flown, as the situation dictated.

The mighty diesel engines roared. They were underway, the boat cutting through the sea, leaving a giant white wake. They moved south through the Adriatic, Italy on the right, Yugoslavia on the left, past Albania, then Greece, and across the Mediterranean, heading for "home".

During the night the lights of Haifa became visible, and the lights around the Bay, at Naharia and Acre. The captain cut the engines and everyone came out on deck so that those who had not seen it before could now see Israel for the first time. The DPs wept, and sobs were plainly audible. Milada stood next to Jonathan, the tears running down her cheeks. He held her hand tightly. "I never thought I would see it," she said. "It is too bad my parents never will, and my aunts, and all of those who would have come – if they could."

Jonathan too had tears in his eyes. For two thousand years they had waited. Now there it was, but in the hands of the usurper. They would take it back and make it their own, take it back from those who had stolen it from them.

Milada spoke to her fellow DPs. "There it is," she said, "before us, too late for most. Have we been spared for this mission? We stand here now, before this promised land, and think about those who will never make it here, will never see the lights of Haifa. They will live with us forever. We will take them here in our hearts. We will not fail them."

"We will not fail them," the DPs repeated quietly, and with determination.

The engines roared again. They moved closer to the lights. They were heading for a place on the beach, to the north of Naharia, above Haifa. They flashed their light, just once. An answering light came back from the beach – just once. They moved in as close as they could to the shore.

Haganah personnel waiting on the beach, posing as fishermen launched their boats, and moved in on the PT. They unloaded the cargo quickly, efficiently, silently. The DPs came ashore. They fell on the beach, and touched their lips to the sand. Milada was amongst them. Jonathan felt that he too needed to kiss this holy ground. He knelt on the beach. He gathered up sand in both of his hands. It felt cool and good, the sand that was eternal, waiting for them. He kissed the sand. It was an act of communion. They were as one.

David Brown watched the scene. Somewhat more reserved, but visibly moved, he too now dropped to his knees, and kissed the sand. This had to be his land now.

Trucks from Kibbutz Gan Galil waited in readiness to rush personnel and munitions back to the kibbutz. There was always the danger of a British patrol trying to intercept them. Around the beach, waiting, Haganah personnel remained concealed, ready to ambush any British patrol that might approach.

Already they had knocked out the British radar station at the top of Mount Carmel that had been used to track incoming vessels, a daring attack that made many amongst the British occupiers extremely eager to return home. Israelis, dressed in British Army personnel uniforms were often able to penetrate some of the most sensitive areas. Those uniforms, recently acquired in the Italian mountains, would no doubt find a similar use.

Another Haganah crew materialized. They took command of the PT, loaded it with diesel and provisions, turned it around, and headed off in the direction of Cyprus. There they would fill the boat with DPs who were being smuggled out of one of the British prison camps there, and spirited "home" to Israel. The smuggling operation was being carried out under the noses of the British military personnel who ran the camps. Those being smuggled were selected on their potential as fighters, to be trained to confront the Arabs in the war that was pending.

All were "illegal", including Milada, stateless, without passports, entering a country the British Government said was not theirs; the British Government had remained completely consistent in this position, as indifferent now with the relatively few survivors,

89

as they had been while the millions went up the incinerator chimneys as smoke, refused permission to enter their own land. Even, for that matter, Jonathan was "an illegal immigrant". He had entered this country contrary to the laws of Great Britain.

The kibbutz trucks moved swiftly through the night, accompanied at a discreet distance by the Haganah patrol who would deal with any British forces who might try to interfere.

They reached the kibbutz. Members were waiting there in anxious anticipation, relieved now that at last the "illegals" had arrived, along with the munitions. They all greeted Mordechai warmly. Mordechai introduced Jonathan and Milada to Chaim, the *Maskaroot* (the kibbutz secretary and chief administrator) – a tall, thin man with a clip board, a pencil behind his ear, who looked like he was in a state of nervous collapse. "*Shalom, Shalom,*" he said, as if he were firing a machine gun. "Welcome to Israel," he said in English, with a heavy German accent.

"And this is David Brown," Mordechai explained to the *Maskaroot.* "Who has recently left the British Army. He wants to join our kibbutz."

"Good. Good. I'll put down his name." Chaim took the pencil from behind his ear and wrote the name on the piece of paper attached to the clip board. "We'll vote on his membership application at the next meeting. We'll want to know more about him – if he's really suitable for life on a kibbutz. He can fill out some forms later – tell us all about himself. I haven't got time to deal with it now."

"Chaim," Mordechai advised, "say something to the new arrivals. A word of welcome."

"Yes, of course, welcome." He turned to the DPs. "Welcome," he spoke in German, sounding now very relieved to be speaking German. "We're glad you're in Israel. I'm sure you're glad too. Listen, if you should decide to take up life on a kibbutz, don't ever let them make you the *Maskaroot*. It's the worst job on the kibbutz. It's sheer hell, I can tell you."

The DPs looked confused.

"Listen," Chaim said to Mordechai, deeply apprehensive, "the British could come storming in here any minute."

"Don't worry, Chaim. We've got guards posted."

"Guards. Guards. They've got the whole British army. So we kill a couple of them. They come back the next day and they break up the kibbutz. It's happened twice already. They ruined the oven in the bakery – smashed it up – a donation from a rich family in America. We didn't want to accept it. We had a big fight over it. We have to make our own way – no presents please. So they voted to take it – and it gets smashed up."

Chaim looked at the DPs as if seeing them now for the first time, and spoke to Mordechai, annoyance in his voice. "And I have to find a place for them – hide them somewhere – on the different kibbutzium – a few here, a few there. They haven't got passports. The British will throw them out – put them in another concentration camp. They're here, we don't want them dragged away – back to another concentration camp. My god, it would kill them. It would kill me. I don't even remember who I sent where. You're supposed to be able to remember things like that. I've got a terrible memory. You can't write things down. If the British come and make a search – then they'll know everything. They have to look inconspicuous – not make anybody suspicious. Listen, they all look like DPs – not kibbutzniks. If they get caught, it's all my fault."

"Chaim, you do an excellent job. Everybody says so."

"I do a terrible job."

He began sorting out the new arrivals. "These three to Kibbutz Degania. These two to Kibbutz Sha'har Hamoquim, these two to Kibbutz Ein Gev. Maybe these two we can keep here." He turned to Jonathan. "And the guns and the bullets" – the disapproval in his voice suggested that he was annoyed with Jonathan for contributing further to his problems – possession of an illegal firearm in the hands of a Jew could be punished by death. "It's good to have them – it's marvelous. We need them. We're desperate. But where do you put them? Under the manure piles of course. The British aren't so enthusiastic about looking there. We got guns under practically every manure pile in the country – or parts for them. I've run out of manure piles. We need some more cows. Maybe we should ask for a donation of cows – never mind principles – it's an emergency."

Chaim sorted out men and munitions. Haganah personnel facilitated the distribution of both. Afterwards Chaim sat down and drank a glass of tea, with lemon they grew on the kibbutz. "The worst job in the world," he said to Jonathan and Milada. "I'm telling you, I don't sleep. I just lay there and worry – until I hear everybody and everything is safe. I'm responsible. Listen, I'm no good for this job. Nobody wants it. They elected me. I didn't want it, either. Everybody wants to work with their hands, be a farmer, feed the chickens, milk the cows. It's against everybody's principles to be an administrator. They think it's an expression of decadent capitalism. But they have to have it. Why me? They think I'm a *Yekkie*" (a German Jew: a term of derision sometimes; at other times, a term of affection, depending how it is used and by whom). "So I must be a good administrator. I'm not. I'm not even a real *Yekkie*. I was born in Poland. I went to Germany with my parents after the First War. I grew up there."

"So you must be a *Yekkie*," Mordechai teased Chaim.

"See," Chaim explained, "I can never convince anybody."

"Chaim," Mordechai said cautiously, "Jonathan has brought you another little problem."

"I don't need it."

Mordechai put the case on the table next to Chaim.

"What is it?" Chaim asked suspiciously.

"A million dollars," Mordechai replied.

"What am I supposed to do with it?"

"We thought you'd have some idea."

"I'm a kibbutznik. We don't handle money."

"You do."

"Not a million dollars. What is it for?"

"To buy arms."

"I've had enough excitement for one night."

"Give it to whoever deals with these things. Find out who. You got a telephone."

"Sure. 'Hello'," Chaim said into a telephone he was pretending to hold. "I got a million dollars here. Do you want it? You don't. Do you know anybody who does? Check around. Find out. We'll bring it over to them – unless they're in the neighborhood some time and they can drop by and pick it up when it's convenient." Chaim put his hand on the case. "There's really a million dollars in there?"

"I presume as much," Jonathan replied. "I haven't actually seen it."

"I've never seen a million dollars," Chaim said, impressed. "Let me take a look."

Jonathan opened the case and threw back the lid. High denomination green American dollars lay in piles, neatly bound.

"And you want me to take charge of this?" Chaim asked, increduously.

"Of course," Mordechai said.

"Supposing I do, and I say to myself, 'Chaim, take it and run. Go to America. A million dollars is a lot of money. You could live in Miami Beach – have a wonderful life. Nobody would elect you *Maskaroot*'."

"Because we don't think you will."

Chaim capitulated, shrugged. "You are probably right. I suppose it's the Jewish Agency that deals with this sort of thing."

Chaim closed the case, took it reluctantly by the handle and shuttled off tiredly, holding the case as if it were a dead animal.

In the morning they met Mordechai's wife, Hamalia, and their two children, Rachel, who was three, and Eitan, age five, who reminded Jonathan of Huck Finn, with his freckles, his blond hair and blue eyes.

Where had his father been, Eitan demanded. Working out of the country, Mordechai explained. Doing what? Helping refugees. Helping refugees, how? To prepare for a good life in Israel.

"I'm glad, *Abba* (father). They will have a good life in Israel. I will help them, too. The young children can come and play in our kindergarden. We have many things."

"They will like that, Eitan."

"Will they speak Hebrew?"

"I think you will have to help them learn."

"I will do that, *Abba*. In Israel you have to speak Hebrew."

"Of course."

Eitan turned to Jonathan and Milada. "And who are these two *chaverim*?" (good friends/companions).

"Milada is from Czechoslovakia", Mordechai explained.

"She is a very pretty lady. Does she speak Hebrew?"

"Not yet. You will have to teach her."

"I will. Do you think she will learn quickly?"

"She is very bright."

"I'm glad of that, *Abba*."

Milada beamed with pleasure. "May I hug you?" she asked Eitan.

Mordechai translated.

Eitan frowned. Eitan was not sure he wanted a strange lady to hug him, even if she was pretty, even if she was a good friend. "Well," he said with reluctance, "if she has to."

They all laughed.

Milada knelt down and hugged Eitan, then Rachel.

"My Sabra children," Mordechai said proudly. He spoke to Eitan. "And this is Jonathan, from America." He gave Jonathan's name the Hebrew pronunciation: *Yonatan.*

Eitan wasn't taking any chances this time. He offered his hand. "*Shalom*"

Jonathan took his hand. "*Shalom*, Eitan."

Eitan said to his father, "I'm glad that at least he has a Hebrew name."

Jonathan stooped down and hugged Rachel. She looked at him shyly, her big brown eyes filled with adoration, and spoke a whispered, hardly audible "*Shalom*".

"*Shalom*", Jonathan replied, kissing her lightly on her cheek.

vii

It was night. Jonathan sat behind the wheel of the hijacked British Army truck, wearing a British military uniform. David Brown sat next to him, now attired in the uniform of a British captain. In the back of the truck, British-uniformed Palmach men sat clutching their British-made Sten Mark 5 submachine guns, ostensibly guarding the Israeli prisoners in their charge, who appeared to be manacled, but who, within seconds, could find their freedom, and access to the Stens and grenades brought along for their use, and for those of the men whom they had come here to liberate.

They drove up to the gate of Acre Prison, considered impregnable. "Captain" David Brown announced, "We've got a load of Irgunists (right-wing "terrorists" whom the British particularly feared and hated) in the back for you."

"Well done, Sir."

"All of them are highly dangerous."

"We'll know how to deal with them, Captain."

"I'm sure you will, Sergeant."

"We're too soft on those buggers."

"I couldn't agree more."

"Take 'em out in the back, and get it done with. A bullet in the brain solves all your problems with these bloody Jews."

"I wish we could make Whitehall see it that way," David said.

"Somebody ought to tell those bods walking around in grey suits what we got to put up with here – your life isn't worth anything. If the Irgun don't get you, the Haganah will. They come out of the walls. They're everywhere. You never know when you're talking to one."

David laughed. "You're right, Sergeant. Stay alert."

"I do me best, Sir."

The gates were opened. They drove into the courtyard, and were directed toward the cell blocks.

Jonathan and David exchanged glances.

"You handled that very well," Jonathan said.

"I like being a captain," David reflected. "You reckon they'll let me be one in the Israeli army?"

"No doubt about it."

Jonathan cut the engine.

A British corporal and four men stood by to receive the prisoners, their arms at the ready. The Palmach "prisoners" emerged followed by their "guards".

Suddenly, as per schedule, there was an ear-shattering explosion from outside the walls, followed by another. The ground shook. A siren wailed. The lights went out, the electric cable now severed by the Palmach attackers outside.

The British troopers took up battle positions. They began firing into the night, they knew not where, nor at whom.

The Palmach within dispatched the British guards. The Palmach "prisoners" snatched up the stens and grenades, relieved the corporal of his keys, and raced into the cell block. Most were already familiar with Acre Prison, having been inmates here at one time or another during the period of British rule.

The outer gates were opened. A British armored personnel carrier started to move out. It traveled a short distance, then exploded. It burst into flame, and lit up the night. Some well-placed Molotov cocktails did the work.

From without, the Palmach fired their stens at the prison. From within they fired at the British, who were not immediately aware that they were also under attack from within.

Meanwhile, the Palmach "prisoners" made their way to the

cells. The guards were now gone, having joined in the fray at what they thought was the only point of assault.

The Palmach men shone their flashlights into the cells, recognized their *chaverim*.

"*Shalom*, Ezra."

"*Shalom*, Isaac."

"What took you so long to get here?"

"The food's been rotten."

"It's better than on my kibbutz."

They unlocked the cells and took out their men, presenting them with the arms that had been brought for their use.

Once outside in the courtyard they joined the battle, the former inmates particularly pleased to be paying a bit back to their British tormentors.

When the firing ceased, Jonathan and David, and the Palmach men scrambled into the truck. As they reached the entrance, David fired a flare, to signal their presence, so they would not be fired upon.

viii

The British, beaten, humiliated, decided it was time to leave. Though Churchill was said to be sympathetic to the idea of an independent Jewish state, the Foreign Office was not, and, consequently, it did not happen during his period in office.

The Labour Party said publicly that they favored the establishment of an independent Israel. But that was when they were out of office. Upon assuming the role of government, they soon discovered that they could not make independent decisions on foreign policy; on the contrary, the Foreign Office ruled the Labour Party. However, there was no conflict between Foreign Office and Foreign Minister. Ernest Bevin, a notorious anti-Semite, who sprang from the depths of low-class society, and sounded no different from any good Nazi: Hit the Jews where it hurts most – he said – in the pocket.

The Oxford and Cambridge-trained men from the Foreign Ministry obviously loathed Bevin, but otherwise could not have found anyone more compatible or more pliable. There was a complete and total meeting of minds between Bevin and the Foreign Office.

96

It wasn't just in the pockets where Jews were hit; the British Government hanged Jews in Israel – just like the Nazis did.

The British, to try and ameliorate some of the humiliation that had been thrust upon them by the Jews, claimed that they had been in fact "protecting" the Jews. Against whom? Themselves? The Arabs, they would have said, whom they had supported for the last thirty years, and whom they now, on the eve of their departure, supplied, equipped, presented with fortifications and strategically useful positions. The Arabs would throw the Jews into the sea – they insisted, aware that they had done everything within their power to insure that this would happen. Then, they said, in the generous way everyone knew the British had, they would return to save the remnants, if the Jews begged them to do so.

The League of Nations had presented Israel to Britain, not as a gift, but as a mandated territory to be reconstituted into a Jewish state. The British Government instantly betrayed this misplaced trust when other interests offered the opportunity of greater rewards. The Jews had not needed the League of Nations to offer them up as a mandated entity; they should have then and there proclaimed their independence.

Now the United Nations voted for an independent Jewish State; neither then nor now did Israel require their permission or their votes in order to come into being. But the votes were forthcoming, anyway. Somehow Ben Gurion felt that the UN, and the world generally, were doing Israel a favor to let them exist. He, and many of his followers, did not take Jewish existence as a right, but as a privilege – to be granted by those on the outside.

The Jewish leadership never learned that they did not have to ask permission to exist. Perhaps it was in the Jewish psyche to ask: Please, may we exist, Sir? But that's what Israel was for – not to have to ask permission to exist.

The UN said Yes, but the Arabs didn't. They knew not to ask permission to destroy Israel, though they certainly had everybody's tacit permission. The Syrians came roaring down from the Golan Heights – originally meant to be a part of Israel, but annexed by France and presented to its Arab friends in Damascus. The Lebanese sent troops, the Saudis, and there were regular Palestinian forces. The Arabs had a total of 270 tanks, 300 aircraft, 150 pieces of field artillery. All the Arabs were there – to pick the bones of the soon-to-be vanquished Israelis.

Many Palestinians fled – unfortunately not all – upon instructions from Arab sources to do so, to return later, and enjoy the fruits of Arab victory, all that the Jews had created in this land.

Israel was not so well equipped. Israel had about ten thousand rifles and small home-made automatic arms. This was the sum total of their equipment for confronting the Arab hordes. They could only lose once, and Israel would be no more.

America, Israel's "great friend", who had vied with the Soviet Union to be the first to recognize Israel – and won – promptly imposed an arms embargo on Israel. This was not a friendly act; they had voted for Israel to exist, and now they were prepared to watch her die.

Jonathan and David and some of the men from Gan Galil were assigned to the defense of Jerusalem. Milada remained at Gan Galil, to take her stand with the defenders of the kibbutz, in the direct path of Syrian tanks on their way to Haifa, and ultimately to Tel Aviv, where they could meet up with their Arab allies, coming north from Egypt and enjoy all the pleasures of Israel's first all-Jewish city.

The kibbutz had its rifles, some of them of World War I vintage, with a multiplicity of calibers; and its home-made sten guns – a part made at each kibbutz – and now assembled and ready for use. And a reasonable supply of Molotov cocktails.

The British-made Syrian tanks approached, moving confidently, aware that there was little to fear, little to impede their progress – just a few people, with some small arms. And behind the tanks were the Syrian troops, to pick off any who might have survived, except, of course, for the women, who were meant to fill a special role.

Milada stood behind the stone fortification. Not far away, Mordechai waited, and just beyond Mordechai was Chaim, the *Maskaroot*, and the rest of the kibbutz members who were defending Israel, and their kibbutz, against these impossible odds. The children had been evacuated – to Haifa – for safety. Relative safety. The lower part of Haifa, the port city, was Arab, the slopes and the Carmel, Jewish. How much chance would the Jews of Haifa have when the Arabs broke through the thin lines of defense offered by Kibbutz Gan Galil and the other kibbutzim attempting to hold the Galilee, and protect Haifa?

The Syrian tanks moved through the outer perimeter of the kibbutz, barbed wire that was never meant to contain tanks. And then they approached the stone fortifications, built hurriedly for this moment. Milada remained calm. This was the moment for which she had been kept alive, for which she had waited. This would be a chance to pay some of it back – for her mother, for her father, for her aunts, for all of those who would never have the chance to do so.

The guns from the Syrian tanks fired at the water tower. It crumbled, hung by a thread for a moment, and crashed to the ground.

What was the difference between these Arabs who filled the oncoming Syrian tanks, the Arab infantrymen who followed behind, and the Nazis? None. None! was the answer Milada gave herself. Killing them was killing Nazis. At least now she could fight back. She thought about death. But it did not worry her. She had lived next to it for as long as she could remember, lived with it. And now when it faced her again, it was with calmness, with resolution. Still, the thought of Jonathan fighting for Jerusalem filled her mind. She could see him clearly now. For him, she wanted to live. But, if she were to die, it would be in the sacred process of fighting back.

The Syrian tank was almost upon her. She flung a Molotov cocktail.

The tank burst into flame. The hatch jerked open. An Arab appeared. Milada shot him with her Luger, and he slumped over. There was another tank, just behind, firing, about to breach the stone fortifications. Milada jumped up on the tank, and emptied her Luger into the slit. It stopped firing.

Through the corner of her eye, she saw other British-made Syrian tanks burning. Mordechai was flinging Molotov cocktails. And Chaim. But other tanks had breached the stone fortifications, and were actually in the kibbutz, crushing their houses, the dining hall. The barn was on fire. She grabbed up two Molotov cocktails and rushed at the tanks, one for each. They burst into flame. There were still two more, firing their guns, shattering the kibbutz. Milada had Molotovs for each of them.

But now there were the Syrian infantrymen, firing their British-made submachine guns. Milada stood behind a stone column, her heart racing, breathing hard, exhilarated to a degree she had never known before. She felt her mother was watching her, her father, her aunts, those who could not be here. They were pleased for her. They were laughing now. She could not remember them laughing before, not in all the time they had been victims of the Germans.

She fired the Luger. The Syrians dropped. For my mother, she thought. For my father. For my aunts. The Luger was red hot. She pushed in another clip. "For all those who didn't make it here," she said aloud.

The Syrian tanks that could, turned and ran, exposing those amongst the infantry who still stood upright. They got picked off, and joined their dead comrades strewn about the kibbutz.

Milada saw blood running down her left arm. She had been grazed on the shoulder. She had never felt it, never been aware of it, too excited in the thick of battle to have paid any attention. Now there was some pain.

Hamalia, Mordechai's wife, now a medic, came, and treated the wound.

"You will have to be evacuated," Hamalia said.

"I'm all right. I'm staying here."

"But you must."

"The Syrians will be back. I have to stay."

They counted the disabled tanks. There were fourteen.

They had won this one. They were still here. Israel was still theirs. In the Arab view it was but a skirmish. They could lose any number of those, even lose the war. What had they lost – some men? They had plenty of those, and they were all expendable. Some equipment? There was plenty of that – endless amounts of it – nations lined up to supply them with it.

The barn burned. There was no water to put out the fire. The cows had all been taken to a safer place. They watched the barn burn, helpless to do anything about it.

Quickly they gathered up the arms and ammunition with which the Syrian dead had now provided them, and waited for the Syrians to return.

The Syrians regrouped, added reinforcements – more tanks, more men and came back again. Now at Gan Galil there was a quiet confidence. They were battle-tested veterans; they had faced the best the Syrians could throw at them, and they had repulsed them. They knew they could do it again.

In the meantime, Milada's Luger had a chance to cool. They had mixed some more Molotov cocktails, hurriedly rebuilt the stone fortifications, and joined in the battle for their survival once again.

"For myself!" Milada said aloud, throwing a Molotov cocktail. "For myself!" she said, as she squeezed the trigger of her Luger and watched the Syrians die. When enough of them did just that, the survivors turned and ran. But even victories have their price, and Chaim lay dead. Kibbutz Gan Galil no longer had a *Maskaroot* – even a reluctant one.

Gan Galil held. Sha'har Hamoquim held. Degania held. Sasa held. The Galilee held. The Negev, in the south, held. Beersheva was still in Jewish hands, despite the mighty Egyptian army. The New City of Jerusalem was still Jewish. The Old City had not yet been liberated.

Israel held. The price was high. Many would never see the fruits of victory for which they had paid the highest price of all – so that others might taste it. The kibbutzim, the moshavim, the settlements – they were in ruins, devastated by Arabs who could not create, but only destroy.

Then there was a truce. Israel needed a truce – to prepare for the second round. And the Arabs needed to regroup and resupply. Arms came to Israel from Czechoslovakia, communist Czechoslovakia. A man by the name of Robert Maxwell, a Czech Jew, a British war hero, now British agent – as well as a secret Israeli one – negotiated with the Czech regime. The regime in Prague was mainly Jewish, old communists now in power, and non-Jews who were sympathetic. They had the strength, and the inclination, to say yes to Israel – to insure that Israel would survive.

They sent thirty-five planes, three tanks, five field guns, small arms. Israel was now prepared. And they – the Czechs – incurred the wrath of Stalin; he was prepared to recognize Israel, not allow the Czechs to supply her with material that might ensure her survival. He later eliminated the Czech leadership – killed them off.

Robert Maxwell, as a British agent, built an empire. When it became apparent, many years later, to the British Government that Robert Maxwell was also an Israeli agent, they pressed the banks to refuse further loans, and his empire crumbled. He died, an elderly man, on his yacht, in the Mediterranean, under suspicious circumstances, and was buried in Israel – as a hero, which he so richly deserved.

Though Israel was now a free and independent nation, a member of the United Nations, Britain could see no reason for accelerating the release of the Jewish Displaced Persons it had imprisoned in its concentration camps on Cyprus. As far as Britain was concerned, the war they had fought against Israel for almost thirty years had not ended, merely took on other forms, now greatly exacerbated by the reality of Israel's existence. They did not feel that it was incumbent upon themselves to accentuate that defeat by providing Israel with reinforcements detained in their detention camps.

They, like their Arab allies, saw Israel as a temporary phenomenon, against whom they would wage a war of attrition, except when they waged an actual one. Battles could be lost, almost into infinity, without serious consequences, but the final one – the one in which they were at last victorious – would bring Israel's existence to an end forever more. In between they might suffer bouts of humiliation, as, for example, some years later, when five British-piloted Spitfires, based in Egypt, violated Israeli air space – obviously testing Israel's defenses for future military action against Israel; Israeli planes scrambled to confront the intruders – and proceeded to shoot all five of them down, without loss to themselves.

Though humiliated, Britain did gain considerable military knowledge: It was a mistake to violate Israeli air space.

ix

The truce ended. Round two began. If the Israelis had held the Arab advance before, now they went on the offensive. The New City of Jerusalem had remained under Arab siege, and virtually cut off. Anybody who has ever been to Jerusalem, traveling up from Tel Aviv, knows how high it is. Supplying Jerusalem had never been easy, even during Mandatory days, when Britain "protected" the Jews. Proof of that was the trucks that lay derelict off the road, victims of Arab attack.

For Jonathan and David Brown, and the others, there had never been a truce; their job had been to try and keep the road open. That meant killing Arabs, and trying to break the siege that had cut off the New City of Jerusalem and the Jews who were trapped inside. With dwindling supplies of food and water, their situation was becoming more desperate every day.

Amos Bar-Lev, Haganah commander, was in charge of the sector, a fifth- generation Sabra, whose family had orange groves. He spoke Arabic with the same fluency as Hebrew, and with an accent indistinguishable from that of the Arabs. He had also served six years in the British Army. The tactic he had devised was to hole up during the day, then to emerge at night, and approach Arab lines, calling out in Arabic. They were bringing reinforcements, he would explain. They had gotten lost – had been wandering about in the dark. Arabs did not like fighting at night – had a pathological fear of night. Amos Bar-Lev took advantage of that. That was when he and Jonathan and David Brown and the others attacked.

David Brown had integrated well into the Israeli military; the three men had become good comrades at arms, though this army was different from any they had known before.

"Too bad I never made it to Captain," David Brown joked.

"Too bad I lost my colonelship," Jonathan countered.

"What are you too complaining about?" Amos Bar-Lev asked. "I don't even have a rank."

There were no officers. No ranks. In this army, there was someone in charge. He was in charge because the others were prepared to follow, because he led from the front. Because he had some special knowledge, some special talents.

"Glad you came along?" Jonathan asked David.

"The best thing I ever did in my life," David Brown replied.

The order came to advance – break the siege. They could wait no longer. They moved forward foot by foot – forward and upward, because the Arabs continued to hold the high ground. The British had seen to that.

An Arab machine gun had them pinned down – regulars from the Arab Legion, British trained, British equipped. The gun commanded a wide area. Jonathan and David ran up the slope toward the machine gun, spitting fire from their own weapons. David got it, and fell to the ground, rolling back down the slope. In the same instant Jonathan was hit, rolled and came to rest next to David. Jonathan leaned over David. The blood from his wound fell onto David's hand.

"Thanks for bringing me along," David said. And then he died.

Jonathan lost consciousness. A medic got to him. They evacuated him to the medical facility further down the slope. He had been hit in the stomach.

When Jonathan regained consciousness he remembered about David, and felt a terrible sense of loss.

Amos Bar-Lev was there. Referring to David Brown he said, "He was a good soldier. We'll never forget him."

The Arab siege that blocked Jerusalem had been broken. Amos Bar-Lev helped Jonathan into a truck, and sat next to him, the first convoy to reach Jerusalem. It was Passover, and they carried matzos for the first Seder in almost two thousand years that Israel would celebrate as a free and independent nation.

The besieged Jews welcomed their liberators with tears of happiness, embraced, laughed, cried, spoke their prayers.

X

On all fronts the Israelis moved forward. Resistance had been broken in all sectors. The Arabs were on the run. General Yadin, in a surprise attack, had thoroughly defeated the Egyptian Army, and secured the Negev. There was nothing to impede the Israeli advance. They could have been on their way to Cairo and Damascus, Baghdad, Beruit, and Amman. Jordan could have been permanently eliminated as the bastard child of Britain, and reconstituted as a part of the Biblical legacy, and historical political proclamation that was the Balfour Declaration.

In Cairo and Damascus and in all of the Arab lands they could have imposed a peace agreement – the victor decides the terms – removed all weapons from Arab hands, and prevented the introduction of any further armaments into those Arab countries who had sought to destroy Israel. Then there would have been peace, because the instruments of war would have been removed from Arab hands.

But that wasn't the way it happened. Harry Truman, the then President of the United States, told Israel to stop. And Israel stopped. They didn't have to stop. They didn't have to listen to Harry Truman. They didn't owe Harry Truman anything. Had they forgotten that he had imposed an arms embargo on them – meant, except for the determination and courage of but a handful of people, that Israel would be eliminated forever? That had not been the act of a friend.

Had they forgotten that Franklin Roosevelt had concluded an agreement with King Ibn Saud of Saudi Arabia that precluded the possibility of a free and independent Israel? Had they forgotten Roosevelt's betrayal of the Jews? Had they forgotten that America had never made any effort to inhibit Britain from its terrible persecution, no different from that of the Nazis? If they hadn't forgotten, they – Ben Gurion – decided not to remember.

Ben Gurion thus insured that the Arab countries were free to wage constant and continual war against Israel. For the Arabs, losing them all was not a serious deterrent. Only the last one would count – the one that destroyed Israel.

They stopped – with the Old City of Jerusalem still in Arab hands, and left the Jordanians free to vandalize the historic Jewish cemeteries, to use the headstones in the construction of lavatories. They stopped with the scab of Gaza still running. They stopped with Syria occupying all the strategic heights. They stopped when Arab-occupied Jordan was but ten miles from Tel Aviv, cutting off Hebron as a Jewish entity, one of the four Jewish towns in Israel in which Jewish habitation has been perpetual, uninterrupted by the events of history – as well as the area of Judea and Samaria, historically, and inseparably, part of Israel.

The truce agreement was never anything but an expression of the state of war that continued to exist, and even peace agreements were but instruments of that war, an expression of expediency, and not of genuine peace, since the Arab psyche, the Arab history, the Arab culture, precluded the possibility of anything that resembled a genuine peace. Having been humiliated at frequent intervals, every Arab knows that he must exact retribution, which can only come in the form of Israel's demise, a reality that can be clearly envisioned, and not only by Arabs.

xi

Jonathan recovered. He made his way back to Gan Galil. There he found Milada. She was waiting for him. They fell into each other's arms, and held each other tightly.

9

Alan Brady has been imprisoned, pending court action. Bail was refused. Leah was indicted as an accessory, but given bail. For the moment she remains free.

Now they are in the ante-room of the prison, set aside for inmates to discuss their legal strategies. Alan is here, and Leah; Alan's father, Dr. Morton Brady, eminent molecular biologist, and university professor, a heavy-set man with thick glasses, and thinning black hair. Jacob Ben Zvi is here too, the man charged by Peres, the Prime Minister of Israel, with "helping" Alan Brady. And also a lawyer, James R. Rutherford Jr., of Peabody, Rutherford and Smithers, slight, almost gaunt, except for his nose, hair combed over a mostly barren scalp, about fifty, with round, rimmed glasses. He is uncomfortable here, in this setting, with these people. His eyes survey the room, the barred windows, the people, then back to the barred windows again. He probably feels claustrophobic, doesn't like being locked in, particularly with clients such as these.

Only Leah is aware of his attitude, of his condition, and watches him with a combination of amusement and distaste.

Ben Zvi says, trying to sound the part of the sage, concerned and conciliatory all at the same time – practically impossible for most Israelis, who are generally extremely abrasive – "Listen, listen to me – I, the State of Israel – we have only your best interests at heart," he appeals to Alan and Leah. "Believe me, when I say it: plead guilty. We'll plea-bargain. It's the only way."

"No," Leah says unequivocally. "We want a trial by jury."

"Alan," Ben Zvi says, "you'll get a year – two at the most." He turns to James R. Rutherford Jr. "Isn't that right, Mr. Rutherford?"

James R. Rutherford Jr., distracted from contemplating the iron bars, replies. "Yes. Yes. A year, maybe two. You can't always be sure."

"There you are, Alan," Ben Zvi says triumphantly. "A year or two. You won't give Israel a year or two of your life? Listen, Alan, we got you the best lawyer in Washington. Money was no object. From his mouth it comes. You just heard it."

"I don't know," Alan says, pain and doubt in his voice. "What am I guilty of?"

"Giving away government secrets," Ben Zvi informs him. "They know everything. They have all the documents you sent – with your fingerprints on them."

"Because you sent them back!" Leah says indignantly.

"We had no choice. Listen. It wasn't really the government's fault. You got in with rogue operators. All right – you weren't to know. They wanted to play like they were spies. They used you."

Ben Zvi has developed this line all by himself. It wasn't the government's fault. It was "rogue operators". He has even looked up the word "rogue" in the English dictionary he always carried with him. English had so many words. You couldn't know them all. But you want to be sure you are using the right ones. "Rogue": a dishonest, tricky, worthless person. A rascal. A mischievous person. That was the right word – a perfect description of those people who had made use of Alan J. Brady. This was a "rogue operation." He had given it out to the press, and they picked it up. It had nothing to do with the government. Peres liked that.

"Tell him, Mr. Rutherford. He's guilty."

"Yes, Mr. Brady. Guilty."

"From the mouth of the best lawyer in Washington, and the most expensive. For you we have not spared any expense. One of the oldest law firms in Washington. And one of the best. I checked, Alan. Believe me, I checked. Nothing but the best for you. Old Americans, all of them. There isn't a Jew in the firm. I on purpose went to an all-American law firm. It was to protect you. You should appreciate it."

Leah does not raise her voice, heavy now with sarcasm, which goes over the head of Ben Zvi. "You are right, Jacob. Peabody, Rutherford and Smithers is one of the oldest law firms in Washington. And they are very good – there's no doubt about it. They have always had some very good connections."

"See!" Ben Zvi says, pleased. "Even your own wife says so."

"The trouble with those connections, Jacob," Leah continues, "is that they were Nazi connections – before, during and after the war. It was all in the documents Alan copied. Too bad those 'rogue' operators didn't tell you all about it. It was common knowledge around Washington even before Alan told those 'terrible old rogues'."

James R. Rutherford Jr. reddens. "Everybody is entitled to legal representation."

"The firm was instrumental in concealing property," Leah continues, "gold, diamonds, jewelry, paintings, cash, stolen by the Nazis, and later returned to them after the war."

"That was actually during my father's time," Mr. Rutherford Jr. says, absolving himself and the firm. "And we do have a Jew in the firm. You haven't got it quite right, Mr. Ben Zvi. Just one, it's true. But he looks after our Jewish clients. And we do have those. Some of them have been with us for a very long time. And we value our Jewish clients. Many of them are fine gentlemen."

"You have done well, Jacob," Leah says sarcastically.

Jacob writhes in discomfort. "Listen. Listen. They make a good impression. That's what counts. That's what we want. That's what we want for you."

"Jacob, you listen to me," Leah says. "The United States Government had an agreement to exchange intelligence with Israel. They failed to live up to their part of the bargain. Why don't we bring a case against the United States Government. We'll find out who was responsible for the decision not to supply Israel with that intelligence, and we'll put them on trial." She turns to Mr. Rutherford Jr. "We can do that, can't we, Mr. Rutherford?"

"I – I don't know," he replies, rather disoriented by this time. "It would be highly unusual."

"If we have a jury trial," Leah presses on, "we can ask those very questions: Who failed to supply Israel with intelligence that the United States was bound by agreement to provide – and why?"

"That's not the issue," Ben Zvi says.

"It's very much the issue – one amongst many," Leah says with rising indignation. "I don't want Alan to go to prison – not for a year, not for two – not for fifteen minutes. Nor do I want to go to prison."

"You'll get off! You'll get off!" Ben Zvi reassures her. "It's practically guaranteed – if you plea-bargain. Isn't that right, Mr. Rutherford?"

"We have reason to think that that might be the case. But there is no guarantee."

"Israel betrayed us, Jacob. They used Alan, and when they didn't think he was going to be of any more use, they threw him – and me – out of the Embassy, into the waiting arms of the FBI. They told Alan we had passports at the Embassy – we were Israeli citizens."

"You don't appreciate we're giving you special treatment," Ben Zvi tries to explain.

"And we got it, too. That's why we're here – with this Nazi law firm – that you brought around – trying to push us into pleading guilty."

"Please, Mrs. Brady," Mr. Rutherford Jr. says, pain in his voice. "We are not Nazis, despite some of our previous connections."

Dr. Morton Brady says, "I told him not to join the navy. I told him they were anti-Semitic. But he wouldn't listen to me. And look what happened."

"I didn't join the navy. I was a civilian analyst. They came to me," Alan attempts to defend himself.

"Sure. He went to the best college in America. The best brains in the whole country go there. When the government want somebody special, they look there. But my son has to be a dope – and go off to join the navy." Dr. Brady points an accusing finger at this son. "I told you not to join the navy!"

Alan rolls his eyes, and speaks to no one in particular. "I got two citations for my work. I was very good at it."

"Too bad they didn't give out citations for spying for Israel." Dr. Brady turns to Ben Zvi. "Then he could have three." He speaks to his son. "I've got citations, too." He speaks to Ben Zvi. "From two different presidents of the United States – for my work." He turns back to his son. "And I didn't have to join the navy. And I didn't have to be a spy, either."

In anguish, Alan asks, "What was I supposed to do, Dad?"

"What the navy hired you to do – not spy for another country, even a friendly one."

Angrily, Leah says, "I'm proud of what Alan did."

"He disgraced the whole family – that's what he did. He ruined our lives. We can't go out in public. The press is always there, hounding us. The worst spy of the decade, they call him. My son. He made his mother ill. My colleagues watch me from the corners of their eyes – the father of the spy. I teach at a gentile university. One of the few Jews. We have to set an example. Some example – 'the father of the worst spy of the decade'. That goes down well. I know what they're thinking. I know what they're saying."

"Morton," Leah says to her father-in-law, "stand up and fight. Stop being a frightened mouse."

"I don't want to fight. I don't want to fight with anybody. I'm a

scientist. I'm making a contribution. The presidents acknowledged it. Two of them. Now I'm 'the father of the spy'. That's how
the world knows me. Never mind my contributions to science – to
making a better world. I'm the father of the spy. I *am* frightened.
Why shouldn't I be frightened!"

"Because there are some things bigger than ourselves. Israel,
for example. Your son saved Israel! Doesn't that mean anything to
you? Doesn't that make you proud?"

"I've got other children, too. I'm not proud that their lives are
ruined." He turns to Ben Zvi. "My other son is an auditor – for the
American Government."

Leah is irate. "I don't know how that sniveling coward can live
with himself – denouncing his own brother – doesn't have the
guts to come out and fight for him. What kind of a son did you
raise?"

Dr. Brady speaks to Ben Zvi. "That's the kind of daughter-in-law
I've got – she doesn't hesitate a moment to insult me. My son has
three children to support – and a wife. If he didn't come out and
say he was against what his brother did, they would have fired
him. You can't work for the American Government and have a
brother who is the worst spy of the decade."

"Unless you betray him," Leah says.

"And my daughter," Dr. Brady goes on to Ben Zvi, "she's a
musician. Who wants to hear a cello played by the sister of a spy?
She plays magnificently. She'll never work. She'll never play her
cello in public."

"And that would be a blessing," Leah says, "considering the way
she plays. I think she must be tone deaf. She's certainly deaf to
her brother's plight."

Alan says, "Leah, I don't think you're being fair."

"I don't think your family is being fair," Leah says. "They're
nothing but a bunch of sniveling cowards."

"She knows everything," Dr. Brady says to his son. "She's had
two years of college and she knows it all. She can insult us – the
whole family – and just two years of college." He turns to Ben Zvi.
"She dropped out. She's a drop-out. She works in public relations.
It's very uplifting. Public relations. She tells people: 'Eat cheese'.
Cheese isn't good for you. But she says 'Go eat cheese.' Two years
of college. We didn't want our son to marry her. She's not up to
our standards. We never said anything. We hoped he'd be sensi-

ble. But he wasn't. You can see how stupid he is. He married her. And all we get from her are insults."

"At least I'm loyal to your son – which is more than the rest of you are."

Alan says, "You have to see it from their point of view."

"I have. And they're traitors and cowards."

Dr. Brady says to Alan, "We have to be grateful to Israel for offering to help."

Leah replies. "We've already seen the kind of help they provide."

"Alan, listen to me," Dr. Brady says, "Plea-bargain. For God's sake, take what you can get. You have already caused this family enough trouble. Don't make any more. We don't want it. We don't need it. Our lives are in ruins. How will a trial help? Every day there will be headlines – about my son, the spy. How he sold out his country. Show us you care for us, Alan. Because we care for you."

Alan sighs, appears to shrink into himself. "All right, Dad. We'll plea-bargain."

"Thank God."

"Alan, no."

"I can't subject my family to this any more."

"You'll go to prison, Alan."

"Not for long."

"You don't know how long."

"As long as you won't have to go, too".

"How do you know I won't?"

"You're just an accessory – accused of being an accessory. You haven't done anything."

"Alan, it's you I'm thinking about."

"Please, Leah, let's not make it worse."

"You really want to give in?"

"It's not giving in. Not really. It's the best way. I'm sure of it."

Leah is deeply disturbed. "You don't want to fight."

"No, Leah. I don't want to fight. I want to put my faith in justice – that justice will be done."

"Maybe I only have two years of college, Alan, but I'm smart enough to know that your faith is misplaced."

"I can't take it any more, Leah. Stop fighting me. Stop fighting all these people. I want to plea-bargain".

Leah is silent for a time. Then she says at last, coldly, "All right, Alan, we'll plea-bargain."

There is a trace of a smile on Mr. Rutherford Jr.'s thin lips, "I think that's the wisest course," he says.

10

David stands in front of the mirror, slips the large gold-plated Star of David, attached to a long, heavy-linked gold-plated chain over his head, and studies himself in the mirror for a few moments. The Star reaches down toward his waist.

He then takes a package from his desk – in the store they had put a ribbon around it, but he had taken it off and thrown it away – and goes down to the study where he knows he will find his mother. She is immediately aware of the Star, but makes no comment. He hands her the package. "For you," he says.

She is mildly surprised. "A present?"

"Kind of."

"Thank you. For any special occasion?"

David shrugs. "No. Not particularly."

"How kind of you. May I open it?"

"Yes."

Slowly, deliberately, Sandy removes the wrapping. There is a white cardboard box. Sandy opens it. Inside is a large brown plastic cross, on a chain, with a white plastic Jesus nailed to the cross.

"Thank you," she says, with a gratitude she does not feel, unwilling to over-react, to feel the pain that this present is meant to cause. This is her son, after all, and she is cognizant of the pain that she causes him.

"What am I supposed to do with it, David?"

"Wear it – like I wear mine." He takes the Star of David in his hand and holds it out for her inspection. "I suppose I should cut it in half – being that I'm only half Jewish."

"David, Jews don't seek converts."

"They do when they're your mother."

Sandy looks at the cross. She takes it from the box, and puts it around her neck.

"So you think it suits me?"

"Very well".

"I used to go to church with my mother and father – your grandparents – right until the time I went away to college. It was a very pleasant and agreeable experience."

"I'm sure it was – for you."

"And for them. And still is."

David speaks with scorn in his voice. "And they believe this myth about a virgin birth – and a resurrection."

"It's very comforting."

"So are drugs."

"Isn't that what religion is?"

David is taken aback for a moment.

Sandy presses her advantage. "Your father and I have always been in complete agreement on this issue. You are the one who has become involved in religious affairs."

David, recovering, says, "They are to do with my culture, my history – who I am, and what I want to be."

"Do you want to take away their faith?"

"I wouldn't care so much if their faith had to do with sun worship. But the faith they've got – it has more to do with extermination camps."

"That's pretty harsh, isn't it, David?"

"Not them, personally. But their faith. Christianity. Hitler said he was doing the work of the church."

"That's not the church your grandparents attend. David, are you isolating yourself to the extent that you see only enemies out there?"

"We have friends. Some. A few. I know about them."

"And I am your enemy."

"Sometimes."

"That's why you gave me this cross?"

David does not reply. His silence is agreement.

Sandy is visibly shaken. She struggles to control herself, to not let David see how upset she is. "You have divided up the world – and I'm in the wrong part of it."

David nods his head slowly. "At least drug addicts don't go around putting you in concentration camps. They might hit you on the head to steal your money – but not because you're a Jew."

"You're making a good case for drug addicts," Sandy says sarcastically. "David, do you have any idea how much your grandparents love you?"

"A lot."

"That's right. A lot. And do you love them?"

"Of course. But different from Grandma Milada."

"How, different?"

"Grandma Milada is Jewish."

"And yet, on religious issues, you're on opposite sides of the fence."

"Those are personal matters – personal decisions."

"I don't think she would be all that enthusiastic about a Bar Mitzvah for you."

"If it ever came to that."

"Your father never had one. His parents were against religious expressions. But Grandma and Grandpa Fraser would be delighted if you had a Bar Mitzvah."

"How do you know?"

"Because it would make them happy if you were happy."

"They'd probably like it better if I got baptized."

"Then I wouldn't need to convert."

"That would make things easier for you, wouldn't it."

"You obviously want to hurt me, David."

"I'm the one who's been hurt – very deeply hurt – by you."

"That isn't the way I meant for it to be."

David shrugs, unconvinced.

"David," Sandy says, "you are my son. You are yourself, but you are also mine, and you always will be. All of you. I love you. I love you unequivocally."

David feels uncomfortable.

"Then, why don't you become Jewish? Or keep on wearing that cross."

"Wearing a cross doesn't exactly suit me," Sandy replies. She picks up the cross and fingers the plastic Jesus. "In church we used to sing a lot of songs about *him*. As I recall, he used to figure rather prominently in most of them. He was, of course, Jewish."

There is irony in David's voice. "And I'm only half-Jewish. Funny, Jesus is more Jewish than I am."

"He was never anything else."

114

"He never made it very big with the Jews. He's sure caused us enough trouble."

"That wasn't his intention."

"Too bad your lot didn't put that message out a long time ago."

"He complained that the Jews were back-sliding – like now, in many ways. Rome ruled Israel. You could get on with Rome, if you wanted to. You could become a Roman citizen. There were a lot of advantages to that. A lot of Jews took the plunge."

"Became Roman citizens?"

"That's right. Jesus was afraid Jews might lose their identity. Jesus agitated. The Romans weren't happy. The Romans nailed him to the cross – their way of dealing with such things. There were no doubt Jews about who didn't like Jesus stirring things up, beating the drum for the old-time religion and spoiling things for them. But Jesus wasn't the only one; there was a lot of agitation. The country was seething with rebellion against Rome. The Jewish connection ran very deep – then – as now. Jews were afraid that the Romans – with their many gods, would swamp the Jews who had but a single God. You know about Bar Kochba, don't you, David?"

"No."

Sandy shakes her head with condescending disapproval. "Your Jewish education has certainly been neglected. You'll have to speak to your father about that. And it hasn't got anything to do with religion, either. It's his history – and yours. The least you – and he – can do, is know it. You really can't expect me – a mere gentile, not a member of your tribe – to know your Jewish history."

David feels that his mother is winning the battle here, if not the actual war. "But you do."

There is the sound of victory in her voice. "As a matter of fact, yes. Bar Kochba led the Jewish revolt against Rome. He and his forces captured and held Jerusalem – and they defeated the Roman Tenth Legion. Rome may have been invincible – but not to the Jews . . . The trouble was – there were more of them than there were of you. Obviously, the quality of the Jewish forces was infinitely higher than those of the Romans. But the Romans had the advantage of superior numbers. And slowly, through attrition, the Jews were worn down. And then, at the fortress at Betar, near Jerusalem, Bar Kochba fell. 580,000 Jews were killed in battle.

That was the end of Jerusalem – and the beginning of the Expulsion. The surviving Jews had to flee and find a place in other lands."

David looks at his mother with a new, grudging respect. "How come Dad didn't tell me about Bar Kochba?"

Deeply pleased with herself, Sandy replies, "I suspect he doesn't know."

"But he should. I'm sure Aaron knows. If I'd gone to Rabbi Moreheim's Bar Mitzvah classes – then I would have found out about Bar Kochba."

"All you have to do is read your own Jewish history, David."

"Are you going to tell Dad about Bar Kochba?"

"I might. If he's interested. Then again, if his own history is important to him, he should have read it. It signaled the beginning of the Jewish exile. For almost two thousand years Jews kept Israel in their hearts. That's why Israel is so important to us now. It exists. It's real. It's very precious to us."

"Us?"

"Yes, David. 'Us'. If it's important to your father, and to you, it has to be important to me, too. If I had never met your father, Israel would still be important to me."

David, suspicion in his voice, asks, "And is Jesus important to you, too?"

"Historically, yes, but for what he was, and not for what he wasn't. Long after the events, the myth of Christianity was created. It may have been Greek in origin, and endowed Jesus with powers that he never claimed and never had, and have no basis in reality. They produced a religious tract called the New Testament, to embody those myths. It as all made-up, and make-believe, and included very considerable amounts of warmed-over Judaism."

"Didn't people see that it was all made-up and make-believe?"

"People bought the whole message – because it felt good. It answered their needs. It gave them a measure of comfort, or what they saw as comfort, in their own personal domain that was filled with fears and anxieties – and still is, and does, for that matter. But it was a dangerous tract because it promoted the idea that Jesus had created a new religion – called Christianity – and that the Jews had rejected it – and him. It was, and continues to be, the basis for anti-Semitism. Jesus was the lord. The Jews rejected the lord, and his teachings – in fact, killed the lord – and needed to be punished for their treachery. That punishment included exile from the Land of Israel. They had to wander, as a people scorned, from country to country – until they repented, and accepted Jesus Christ as their lord and savior. Then, and only then, would they be allowed to return to the Land of Israel."

"But we got back there before that happened," David says triumphantly.

"That's the part the Catholic Church doesn't like. It was the Church that perpetuated the myth of Jewish guilt, and has been promoting it ever since, with the resultant suffering thrust on the Jewish people. As far as the Church was concerned, the more the Jews suffered, the better. It was their punishment for rejecting him. And it would hasten the day when they would 'see the light', and accept Jesus."

"I'd sooner be dead than convert," David says passionately.

Suddenly he is aware of the significance of his words. So is Sandy. They look at each other for what seems a very long time before either of them speaks.

"It's different when you're Jewish," David says defensively.

"Jews have chosen death rather than conversion," Sandy says to David.

"You just told me about Bar Kochba – they must have felt pretty strongly about being Jewish. So you can understand how I feel."

"I do understand, David. Judaism is a very powerful force. If you didn't feel so strongly about it, I'd be very disappointed. Judaism has survived despite the best efforts of the Church – of the collaboration between the Nazis and the Vatican. More recently the Church has absolved the Jews for Jesus's death. But it's really only 'political correctness." They can't eliminate 1300 years or so of overt anti-Semitism, by exonerating the Jews. They still want Jews to 'repent' and accept Jesus. They are still against the existence of a free and independent Israel, inhabited by Jews who never have, and never will, accept Jesus. Even today they look upon Israel as a temporary phenomenon. And they're doing their best to support Israel's enemies."

"I wish we'd talked about all this before, Mom. You're a lot smarter than I realized."

Sandy smiles. "Thanks. And if it will impress you any further, David, the Old Testament is historically correct."

"It is? I guess I'd never really thought about it one way or the other. But, sure, why not? It would have to be, wouldn't it? Didn't God speak to Moses on Mount Sinai – and give us the Ten Commandments?"

"I suppose he did, David. Do you know about General Yadin?"

"Sure. He kicked the Egyptians out of the Negev – so it could remain a part of Israel."

"He was an archeologist before he was a General. He knew, from reading the Old Testament, that there was a road through to the Negev. He looked for it, and he found it. It wasn't much of a road. Maybe it hadn't been used in a thousand or so years. But it was there – all overgrown – like any road would be that hasn't been used for a thousand years or more. Leading his army, they followed this road, and surprised the Egyptian Army in an attack that resulted in the Egyptians being thrown out of the Negev."

"I didn't know that about General Yadin. It's a great story."

"It's absolutely true."

"I think I owe you an apology," David says contritely.

"What for?"

"For being such a rotten kid."

"You're not rotten. You're great."

He throws his arms around Sandy. "I'm sorry, Mom."

She hugs him tightly to her.

"There's nothing to be sorry about."

"There is. That cross."

"What do you want me to do with it?"

"I don't suppose you'll want to wear it."

"No, I don't suppose I will." Sandy takes the cross from around her neck. "I don't want to be seen as rejecting your presents, David –"

"That's all right."

Sandy drops the cross into the waste basket. "I don't think I'll be needing it."

"I don't think so either, Mom. But that doesn't mean I'm happy about having a gentile mother. I still want a Jewish one."

11

Mark continues writing his report: "There was a secret partnership between Allen Dulles of the United States, Jack Philby, the father of British spy Kim Philby who ultimately defected to the Soviet Union, and Ibn Saud of Saudi Arabia. Their objective was to put Hitler into power. Jointly they financed the Nazi war machine, and sabotaged the escape route to pre-independence Israel. They, and the American oil companies, are largely responsible for the Holocaust. Going back to the beginning of the 1920s, the American view of a free and independent Israel had already been determined: The creation of such a country would inhibit the flow of Arab oil, and should never be allowed to happen.

"This position was reiterated in 1943, by Franklin Roosevelt, the then President of the United States – whose own hands were dripping with Jewish blood – when he said, 'The defense of Saudi Arabia is vital to the defense of the U.S.', and merely confirmed what was an already-established policy. The implications were unmistakably clear – there would be no State of Israel as far as the U.S. and Saudi Arabia were concerned.

"If Chaim Weizmann, the brilliant scientist, and David Ben Gurion, the not-so-brilliant Head of the Jewish Agency for Israel, had been able to grasp the U.S./Saudi position, which was absolutely consistent since its inception, they might have avoided the groveling and the negotiating which they thought would be useful, but wasn't, in advocating their cause.

"The American Congress may have had some doubts about Saudi Arabia, but certainly no U.S. Administrations did, who merely circumvented the Congress, encouraged the oil companies to deal with Saudi Arabia as if they were U.S. representatives, which in reality they were. In 1947 a secret agreement was concluded in which ARAMCO expanded its Government Relations Department; U.S. diplomats and CIA agents were transferred to ARAMCO to make this arrangement work more effectively.

"Currently the climate in which to do business is extremely good. Saudi Arabia purchased military equipment worth seventeen billion dollars during the course of one year. They concluded a twenty year arrangement for the purchase of $150 billion worth of military equipment, which, fortunately, it would never use, since there are few Saudis about who possess the skills required. But since the commissions involved, to be paid to members of the Saudi Royal Family and their friends, amount to between twelve and twenty billion dollars, it does not matter to them, and apparently not to Israel, at this time.

"Well-connected individuals have been able to foster trade between the two nations – John McCone, William Colby and Richard Helms, all former CIA directors and former ambassadors to the region as well – amongst them Andrew Kilgore and Parker Hunt. Vice-President Agnew and Edward Muskie were also involved.

"The Saudis had one hundred billion dollars in oil money, exacted from a world that for the most part couldn't pay it. It happened during a time when America lost a war, and a president, and the Arabs generally, Saudi Arabia amongst them, saw this as an opportunity to raise oil prices. From the two dollars and fifty cents that the Saudis had been getting for a barrel of their oil, they now extracted as much as forty dollars a barrel.

"There were many about who objected, but nobody was going to do anything about it, which showed the extent to which the United States had placed itself in the hands of Saudi Arabia.

"Amongst other things, Saudi loaned its money to U.S. banks, who in turn had to find something to do with it, and did. They loaded it off onto Third World countries who didn't want it, didn't need it, and couldn't absorb it, but who managed to spend it anyway. The problem was, they couldn't pay it back. This did create some very serious problems, from which the world never really recovered.

"Saudi Arabia also financed every terrorist organization operating in the Middle East, and much of Africa, channeling money, generally through the Palestine Liberation Organization. An Islamic fundamentalist country, it is often at odds with other Islamic fundamentalists.

"The Saudi Royal Family is self-proclaimed, and not descended from the Prophet Mohammed as they like to claim. In order to project themselves into the descendent realm, they hired the same fixer who managed to find a connection between King Farouk of Egypt and Mohammed, who had little trouble finding one amongst the Saudis.

"On the other hand, the true descendent – King Hussein of Jordan – regards the Saudis as just so much Arab trash, but nevertheless acknowledges the financial advantages inherent in a relationship with Saudi Arabia.

"If Mohammed was not actually instrumental in bestowing the status of royalty on the 'Royal' House of Saud, Ibn Saud had the foresight to take matters into his own hands: On one occasion he killed 400,000 Shi'ites; on another he beheaded a thousand. He managed 40,000 public executions, and 350,000 amputations – for infringements of his laws. If not actually Mohammed anointed, he made himself into King of the Hill, named the country after himself, and was there when Roosevelt wanted to chat.

"They didn't always get the kind of press they would have liked. The wounding words that followed the execution of a Saudi Princess who did not conform, cost them five hundred million dollars in an effort to cover it up, which failed, and was all money wasted. To rectify the problem they bought the press, and can now put to death anyone whom they choose, virtually without any unpleasant words from the Western media.

"That large sectors of the Western Press are in the Saudi pocket will come as no surprise to anyone. The United Press International was taken over for four million dollars. The Saudi Embassy makes great effort to cultivate journalists, who are directly or indirectly in their pay.

"Although there is considerable opposition to the 'Royal Family' within Saudi Arabia, it is unlikely that they will be toppled, though rebellions at the top can never be ruled out, but these palace coups are meant to change personalities and not the status quo. If that were to happen, then the United States would intervene to restore the monarchy with which it has worked so well for so long.

"With its immense power, Saudi Arabia can, and has, demanded the elimination of Israel, a process which is under way. Israel has the capacity to reverse that process, but appears not to be inclined to take any action to do so. Perhaps history and conditioning preclude the possibility of Israel making any decisive move which would eliminate for all time the threat to her continued existence.

"In Israel's case, a major nuclear power – perhaps the third or fourth or fifth – with the most sophisticated nuclear weaponry, which includes delivery systems that can be propelled 5000 miles, the mere threat to deploy would cause the Saudi leadership and their American partners to suddenly reverse their position vis à vis Israel's continued existence."

12

Aaron Haliday stands in front of the pulpit. He wears a grey suit, and a necktie that is maroon and blue. Over his shoulders is a *tallis* – a prayer shawl – a *yarmulke* on his head.

Rabbi Moreheim, in long gown covered by his *tallis*, his head also covered with a *yarmulke*, stands next to Aaron, his hand on Aaron's shoulder. Rabbi Moreheim, in his middle forties, with full black beard, looks like a prophet straight from the Old Testament.

The choir sings the liturgical music appropriate for this day. Jim and Miriam Haliday sit in the front row, next to Sandy and Mark and David. Rabbi Moreheim's synagogue is filled to overflowing – with friends and relatives: the proud grandparents, aunts and uncles and cousins – not all of whom are Jewish.

Miriam and Jim are bursting with pride, though they try to appear calm and casual. But the tears of joy are streaming down Miriam's cheeks. And tears have welled up in Jim's eyes.

The singing ends. In the beautiful synagogue, with the stained glass windows, depicting Moses receiving the Ten Commandments on Mount Sinai, there is complete silence.

Today is Aaron Haliday's Bar Mitzvah.

Rabbi Moreheim breaks the silence. "Today is truly a day of joy," he says to the congregation in his deep, booming voice, and warm southern accent. "Aaron Haliday, following in the long tradition of our people, has come of age today. We welcome him.

"I have had the pleasure of working with him, of helping to bring him to this day. It is an honor that, as Rabbi, has been bestowed upon me. I thank Aaron for being who he is, for making the position of Rabbi such a rewarding one.

"I thank his parents for instilling in him the pride of our Jewish culture and heritage. He is a credit to our people. He always will be, cognizant of how deep our roots are. Jim and Miriam Haliday, take all the pleasure today, and always, that you so richly deserve."

Rabbi Moreheim sits down.

The choir sings again.

They finish. Aaron, completely composed, takes hold of the pulpit with his hands. He smiles down at his mother and father, who acknowledge his smile. He nods to David. David nods back.

Aaron surveys the people before him. "Thank you for coming here today, to share this with me." There is no script. Aaron's words are his own. Rabbi Moreheim wants it that way. "I have so many 'thank yous' to give, because there is so much gratitude. I'm grateful to have been born a Jew. I accept this privilege filled with humbleness, aware of the responsibility the accident of birth has placed upon me. How fortunate I am. If I had been able to choose, this is what I would have chosen.

"I have a very special thanks for Rabbi Moreheim, who has done so much to open my mind and my heart to my Jewish being. He has made me rich, by opening the doors to my faith, to let me see the magnificence of our heritage. It all belongs to me. And on this day, I can claim it as my own.

"But I am aware that to claim those riches, I must also take on the responsibilities that go with them. And that is what this day is for – to affirm that I am ready, able, and very willing to accept responsibilities as a Jew. I accept them – not just accept – but welcome them. I am eager to serve my people.

"No, today I am not a man. Not yet. I will take it each step in turn, and carry all that I can of that responsibility. I am glad for your welcome. I will always try to be worthy of it.

"I also need to say thank you to may parents. I hope that I have been the son that they want. I have tried. They are such remark-able people. I love them very much. They have given me this day. I give them my word that I will try never to disappoint them. Their Jewishness, which they gave to me, is mine forever, and it will be my strength for the whole of my life.

"For my father there is special gratitude – because he was not born Jewish. He asked to take on our heritage, and make it his own. He wanted my mother's people to be his people, and that is what they became. Now I have two Jewish parents.

"Our sacred language is his sacred language. This magnificent synagogue is his synagogue. Our Rabbi Moreheim is his Rabbi

Moreheim. I have a Jewish Dad all the way. He chose to be a Jew – chose the hardships and the tribulations, as well as the joy, of being a Jew. And for him – this day is, and will be, just one amongst many."

Aaron finishes his talk.

The choir sings again.

His listeners sit in silence, moved by Aaron's words.

Rabbi Moreheim removes the Torah from the Ark, and hands it to Aaron, who cradles it firmly in his arms. Resting it on the dias, he removes the cover, and unfurls it. He finds the place, and begins to read in Hebrew.

Afterwards, with the Torah in his arms, Aaron, accompanied by Rabbi Moreheim, moves slowly along the aisles, the congregation touching the Torah as he passes – a gesture of love, of respect, of holiness, of a oneness of the people whose scroll it is.

Aaron stops now near his father who touches the Torah. Then his mother touches it. He waits for David to touch it. David hesitates, almost afraid – as if the scroll is not really his, too.

"Touch it," Aaron says.

Their eyes meet.

"Touch it, David."

Slowly David complies. He feels as if he would like to hold it, take possession of it – never relinquish it.

The two boys nod to each other.

Now Aaron moves off.

Later, when the ceremony is completed, David and Aaron embrace.

"You were great," David says.

"Thanks. You're next."

"I don't think so. I don't think I'm going to make it."

"Sure you will. Just have some faith."

13

S andy is having lunch with Miriam, in town, near their respective offices, in sight of the Capitol building. Miriam is an economist, employed by the Department of Commerce.

Sandy says, "Aaron did a beautiful job. You can be very proud."

"We are."

"Sometimes I think it would be easier to just give in – and convert. It's what David and Mark both want. At least then David could have his Bar Mitzvah."

"Easier, Sandy? I'm not sure. You can make a case both ways."

"I know. I've argued both sides".

"That's the point – you shouldn't need to argue. If the debate is raging, then you don't want to convert."

"That's a very convincing argument."

"Jews don't look for converts."

"I tried to explain that to David. He wasn't convinced – at least, in his mother's case. Is it wrong to do what your husband and your son want?"

"If you're compromised in the process."

"I am Jewish, Miriam," Sandy says with some force.

"Except for a formal commitment."

"You can't be Jewish without it?"

"I'd love to see you make that commitment, Sandy."

"And, if I did, how would I look to you then?"

"Like you had joined us."

"Otherwise, I'll always be on the outside – looking in?"

"It comes to that."

"There is a price to pay then, for joining."

"That's why I don't think you're ready, Sandy. And that you mustn't do it until you are. You shouldn't have to feel that you are paying a price – that it's costing you something to become Jewish."

"I wasn't born Jewish. I can't change that."

"Jim wasn't born Jewish."

"He had no doubts – no questions?"

"None."

"Would you have married him otherwise?"

"It was never a factor. It was never an issue."

"What if it was?"

Miriam thinks about it for a moment before she replies, then speaks unequivocally. "I wouldn't have married him."

"Your commitment is very strong."

"That's why it was never an issue. But it was what Jim wanted. I had never suggested it."

"Growing up, I didn't know a lot of Jewish people. I must have known Jews, but they didn't look any different from anybody else. They didn't have horns or anything – although I think my father thought they did."

"It's ironic that he should wind up with a Jewish son-in-law."

"It's not been a problem. He adores Mark. He couldn't love him more if he were his own son. They go hunting and fishing together all the time down home. He sees Mark as the best thing that ever happened to him. And then getting David for a grand-son – he thinks the ground David walks on is holy."

"And if you converted?"

"It wouldn't worry him – or my mother. My father would be there two hours early for David's Bar Mitzvah."

"Mark has altered some of your father's prejudices."

"He has – yes."

"Then could they be some of your own – buried deep – learned at your father's knee?"

Sandy thinks about that. "I don't know. When I met Mark, I committed myself then."

"A full commitment, Sandy."

"I didn't think that it could be any more full."

"'Full' means conversion, Sandy."

"I suppose 'full' means different things to each of us. Miriam, are we splitting hairs?"

"Do you think that that's what we're doing? Are you creating a definition that's convenient?"

"You mean I should be probing for the hidden anti-Semite in me?"

"Is there one?"

Sandy is visibly distressed. "I don't know."

"I'm not suggesting there is, Sandy. Look, you're very close to me. We couldn't talk this way if you weren't. And you must feel that I'm close to you. If you didn't, you wouldn't have asked for this talk. I don't know if I'm helping you much. Maybe I've done you more harm than good."

"No. I need to look at myself. You've helped me to do that. Maybe down deep there is something. The gentile world has had almost two thousand years to condition us. Have I been immune? I'd like to think so. Mark is my life. He is the air I breathe. And my son is what we have done together. He is my Jewish son. How important is that condition in my psyche? Has it been of sufficient importance to prevent my son from having his Bar Mitzvah? Am I trying to keep him from making that official step – his Bar Mitzvah – into Judaism? Is that how I see it – unconsciously? If he had his Bar Mitzvah he would then be – officially – a Jew. Am I keeping that from happening – without realizing it? It could all be true, Miriam. I think I had better face up to it. Have I said to my husband, 'I am committed', and inside, I could only go so far? And that I wasn't really committed after all – not fully committed? I'd hate to think that these two men in my life – who have given me everything – I have not been able to give them all of me – that I have been holding back a part that I didn't really want to give."

"You've brought up some serious issues, Sandy."

"I know."

"I think it would be useful if you talked to Rabbi Moreheim."

"I don't know him. We're not members of the synagogue. It would be an imposition."

"You do know him. You saw him at Aaron's Bar Mitzvah. That is the man. And besides, David is involved. I'm sure he'd be delighted to talk with you."

"Will you phone him first – and ask him if he's prepared to see me?"

"Of course."

"Thanks."

"He must know the situation very well. David went to some of his Bar Mitzvah classes with Aaron."

"Am I in need of psychological help, Miriam?"

"How do you feel?"

"Shaken up."

"I can understand that."

"I've always thought of myself as a pretty straight-forward person – without complications. Maybe there's more to my 'conversion' problems than I had ever realized. And that there are some complications."

14

S andy sits with Rabbi Moreheim in his study.
"Thank you for seeing me, Rabbi."

"Thank you for coming, Mrs. Spaulding. It's an honor and a pleasure to have you. I know your son David fairly well by this time. He's a remarkable boy."

"Thank you for saying so."

"He and boys like Aaron Haliday make my work deeply rewarding. They are obviously very high flyers, and very serious."

"Too serious?"

"Not more so than suits them."

"Rabbi, forgive me for going off the subject for a minute, but when I heard you at Aaron's Bar Mitzvah – and talking with you now, I detected a very familiar accent, much like my own. Could it be that you're also from Georgia?"

"I am, Mrs. Spaulding, from Atlanta."

"Connected to the Moreheim family who have the department stores, and the cotton mills?"

Rabbi Moreheim smiles. "The same, Mrs. Spaulding."

"I didn't make the connection at first. Moreheim is a very familiar name in Georgia. Are you any kind of relation to Major Moreheim?"

"Joshua Moreheim – I'm a direct descendent. The Moreheims are a German Jewish family. They came to Georgia in the 1840s."

"Then our family has a very direct connection to yours. Two of my ancestors fought in the First Georgia Cavalry – commanded by Major Moreheim. I have been hearing about him my whole life. 'Some more like him and we would've won', is the way my Daddy tells it. It really is a great pleasure to meet you. I never thought I was also going to be meeting 'Johnny Reb'."

Rabbi Moreheim laughs. "'Johnny Reb'. I like that. At college they'd call me that. It suited me."

"It suits us all."

"They never understood us – the Northerners."

"We had our pride."

"And they've spent a hundred years accentuating the differences."

They are both silent for a time, pleased by this encounter.

Sandy is relieved, and at ease. She speaks first. "I'm glad I came, Rabbi. I think we're going to get on just fine. I'm sure you won't have any problem understanding what I'm thinking and what I'm feeling."

"I hope not, Mrs. Spaulding."

"I'd feel a lot better if you'd call me 'Sandy'."

"Sandy it is. And I'm Michael."

She tells him the problem.

He listens carefully. Then he replies. "You can't be Jewish for someone else's sake. Only for your own."

"But it's hurting my marriage. And I'm hurting my son."

"You're feeling under considerable pressure."

"A great deal of pressure."

"You don't like being pushed, Sandy. We're all old rebels, after all. I understand this very well. Our southern women are very strong and determined. They want to make up their own minds – in their own time – when they're ready."

Sandy nods, pleased.

"I know," Rabbi Moreheim continues. "My wife is from South Carolina – also from a German Jewish family – with a distinguished record . . . Do you have in-laws? What do they feel?"

"My father-in-law is dead. I never met him. He died prematurely – as a result of wounds he suffered during Israel's War of Independence. My mother-in-law is very much alive. She's a professor of Modern History at UCLA. She was in a concentration camp. And later she too fought in the War of Independence. She's one of Israel's heroines."

"How do you feel about her?"

"She's Mark's mother. I love her."

"And if she weren't?"

Sandy thinks a moment. "I'd love her anyway."

"And how does she feel about you?"

"I'm sure she loves me. We have a good relationship. But I feel she's holding back – that if I were Jewish – she could go the whole way. But I suppose she's relieved that her son didn't marry a *shiksa* who drags him off to revival meetings in a Baptist church."

"They'll have to be patient, Sandy."

"They've been patient. Their patience has worn thin. Maybe I'll never be ready. Maybe it isn't what I want."

"Don't you?"

"I don't know. Maybe deep down I am rejecting the idea of becoming Jewish. I spoke about this with Miriam Haliday. It raised some very interesting – and disturbing – questions. I am gentile, after all. I am a product of my conditioning. I had many years of not being Jewish – of being gentile. You know what this means. You know the implications. We have a long history of antagonism – and worse – directed toward the Jews. Is it all down there, inside of me, festering away?"

"Do you feel compelled to look?"

"I don't know. It frightens me. I don't want to look. I don't want to see. What if it's there? What if it's true? Then I'm a liar, and a hypocrite. I've lied to my husband. I've lied to my son. And I've lied to myself. But what else can I do, except look?"

"Do you think this is a gentile condition – or just yours?"

"I think it's both. When you stop to look at what the church has taught, and what has emanated from those teachings – strong anti-Jewish feelings must be the result. And am I a product of that? Have I been immune? When I look, when I examine myself critically – I'm not sure that I have been immune – that I am immune."

"Logically, you are."

"But emotionally –"

"Are you taking on the guilt for what others have done?"

"That, too. And maybe compounded by the suspicion that I am like the rest. Is there a gentile guilt complex? I don't think so. There should be. Our guilt is enormous. We could never face up to it. How do I fit in? How does it affect me? I've opened this box. I never knew it was there – and now suddenly, out comes issues with the profoundest implications. Do I now go ahead and convert – as a means of overcoming what might be the hidden anti-Semite in me?"

"No, Sandy. I don't think it will resolve anything. I would like you to convert. I would welcome you. I would like to know that your son David could stand before the Western Wall in Jerusalem, and have his Bar Mitzvah. But conversion isn't a medicine. You can't take it for your husband's sake, or your son's. You can't take it for your own sake. You will need to work that one out. I am here. I'll help you. You can come and talk with me at any time."

"I'd like that. I'd appreciate it very much. I need to examine myself critically. I'm not sure I'm going to like the person I might see."

"You might also be over-reacting."

"There is a lot of tension. I've let down the people I love most. There must be a reason. I hate what I think I see."

"We'll talk about it, Sandy."

"I want to face it – no matter what the pain."

Sandy lapses into silence. She is deeply distressed. There are no tears, no danger of any. She will confront her feelings. She will talk further with the Rabbi. A couple of solid Georgians can work things out – particularly when both of their ancestors fought together in the First Georgia Cavalry.

"There is another thing," Sandy says at last. "It's not directly concerned with my personal problems – the Brady Affair."

"It's deeply disturbing, Sandy."

"Mark – my husband – used to think that he would get off with a short sentence – spying on allies is a common practice."

"But now he's not so sure?"

"New documents have come to light. It's in the interest of both Israel and the United States to put him away for a long time."

"How long is a long time?"

"Forever."

Rabbi Moreheim is visibly shaken. "And do you share this view?"

"From the very beginning – I knew there was a problem – more than people saw at first glance. There was a great deal they weren't telling."

"That was my feeling – more of a gut reaction. If there is to be an extended sentence – we'll need to take some kind of action. But I suppose, for the moment, we'll have to wait and see."

"I think it's a foregone conclusion. The problem for Brady is – he knows too much. Neither party – the Israelis nor the Americans – want him going around, telling what he knows. He had access to everywhere – to all of America's best-kept secrets."

"We'll fight for him, Sandy. I'm prepared."

"So am I."

15

Alan Brady plea-bargained.

Leah Brady, accused of being an accessory, plea-bargained. It was assumed she would be given a suspended sentence.

The United States Government double-crossed the Bradys.

What could the Bradys do about it? They had given themselves over to the "mercy" of the U.S. Government, who was not about to give any.

Alan Brady was sentenced to life imprisonment.

Leah Brady was given five years.

Had the Bradys opted for a trial by jury, the government would probably have dropped the case, because, as the constitutional lawyer, Alan Dershowitz, observed in his book *Chutzpa*, "The government would have had to declassify much of its secret evidence, and the defendant would have been free to put the government on trial for its duplicity in denying Israel intelligence information to which it was entitled under an executive agreement."

Leah was right.

The others were wrong.

16

Sandy and Mark feel outrage and indignation as a result of the sentences imposed on the Bradys.

Sandy phones the First Secretary at the Israeli Embassy, Shlomo Ha'gill, whom she and Mark know quite well.

"I want to come and see you, Shlomo," Sandy tells him.

"It will be a pleasure. Anything in particular you want to talk about?"

"I'll tell you when I see you."

"I'll look forward to it, Sandy. It's always good to talk to someone from the Spaulding family – everybody is so involved with Israel. We know how much you care. We really appreciate it."

"I'm glad you do, Shlomo."

They make a date.

Later, Sandy appears at the Israeli Embassy, from where, some time earlier, Alan and Leah Brady had been ejected. After clearing security, Sandy is allowed to enter. She is greeted at the door by Shlomo Ha'gill, an athletic-looking man in his early thirties, here by virtue of the fact that his father is in the Cabinet rather than because of his experience or skill.

He takes Sandy's arm and leads her into his office, and holds a chair for her on the other side of his big desk. First Secretary Ha'gill takes his seat behind the desk. There is a pack of cigarettes on his desk – Marlboros. He takes one and lights it with a lighter.

Intuitively Sandy draws back, trying to avoid being engulfed by the smoke.

First Secretary Ha'gill smiles, speaks of the cigarette in his hand. "Very anti-social. I know. But we Israelis are like that."

Sandy knows. She tries to avoid frowning, and nods her head.

First Secretary Ha'gill exhales a cloud of smoke. "You have to take us the way you find us," he says, shrugging, obviously aware of the reputation that Israelis have created.

"Now tell me, Sandy, you're here because you want to launch another campaign on behalf of Israel – if it's a forest, we'll go and see someone from the Jewish National Fund. If it's helping new immigrants, we can bring in my colleague from the Aliyah section. Just tell me, Sandy. I am at your disposal."

"I want to talk about the Brady affair."

First Secretary Ha'gill looks pained, as if he has been struck.

"Sandy. Sandy. We don't need such a conversation."

"We need it desperately. It is absolutely imperative that you understand our feelings in this matter, Shlomo. We completely and totally reject Israel's cowardly and unacceptable behavior in this matter. I want you to convey our feelings to your government."

"We had to do what we had to do. You have to understand this. We didn't want a confrontation with the United States."

"Israel has acted in a cowardly fashion throughout. Israel is groveling."

"We don't think it was cowardly, and we don't think it is groveling. It is not very nice of you to say that. We are a country surrounded by enemies. We don't have to go around looking for more."

133

"We want Israel to demand the immediate release of Alan and Leah Brady."

"Just like that. Let them out of prison. They broke American laws – and Israel has to get them out of prison. Even if we had the influence – we wouldn't interfere. What right have we got to interfere in the internal goings-on of another country?"

"Shlomo, you're talking to me, not the press. They are in prison because Israel betrayed them. Israel got them into prison. Now it's up to Israel to get them out."

"Why don't you bring your fight to the American Government direct – through the American people."

""Because only Israel can bring sufficient pressure to bear."

"We are not such a strong power. We don't exert much influence on the United States. We don't exert any influence. It's the other way around. You know this as well as I do."

"Israel has only to make it unmistakably clear that there will be no further negotiations with any Arab country – until the Bradys are released."

"You're against peace? We want peace with our neighbors. We don't think it's such a bad thing. You want us to jeopardize this? For one man – and his wife? We can't do it. We won't do it. You shouldn't ask. We got enough problems. Why are you trying to make them worse? You want to talk about planting trees in Israel we can talk about that. Not about the Bradys. There are all sorts of unfortunate events connected with that situation. We'll work behind the scenes. We can do things quietly. Through diplomatic channels. There are things I can't reveal to you."

"Shlomo, I happen to know you're talking a lot of rubbish. No one in the Israeli Government is, or has any intention of, working behind any scenes, or doing any work at all on behalf of the Bradys."

"This you know? You have special information?"

"As a matter of fact, I do."

"What – what kind?" There is panic in the First Secretary's voice.

"It's apparent that Israel wants Alan Brady to stay right where he is – preferably forever. He knows too much – about Israel – Israeli politicians – all the events that have occurred between the United States and Israel – that Israel – and the United States – would not like to reveal."

"Such as! Such as!" First Secretary Ha'gill demands.

"Such as," she mocks him, "The Brady Papers."

"How do you know about this?" he demands, trembling. "How? How?"

The First Secretary crushes out his cigarette, and immediately lights up another one.

"Shlomo, in due course we will have a great deal to reveal. It would also appear that Mossad is rather put out about Brady – that they weren't running him – and some other Israeli intelligence body was. They seem especially eager for Brady to stay in prison. It's more than sheer vindictiveness. Do you think Mossad is angry because he knows too much about them – and that it hurt their relations with American intelligence? Shlomo, this suggests to me that the Mossad is seeking, or already has, influence far beyond its brief as an intelligence-gathering organization – but has aspirations of running the Israeli Government, at least from behind the scenes."

First Secretary Ha'gill crushes his cigarette in the ash tray. His hand is shaking. "Nonsense! Nonsense!" he says.

The cigarette butt has not been entirely extinguished. A part of it burns, its foul smell making Sandy move her chair further back.

The First Secretary lights up another cigarette.

Sandy says, "I want you to convey our demands to the Government of Israel."

"It's pointless. Pointless. Quite pointless. Out of the question."

"We'll demonstrate in front of the Embassy to press our demands."

"I thought you were supposed to be a friend of Israel. This is not friendship."

"And we'll ask people to withhold their contributions."

"Are you trying to strangle us? That is not friendship. Tell me something – why are you so involved in this Brady matter?"

"For the sake of justice."

"There must be other causes – also where you could fight for justice. This is a Jewish problem. This isn't your problem. You are just playing with it."

Sandy is at first startled. She has not expected this.

"This isn't your fight – so why bother? You are not Jewish. Don't meddle in Jewish problems. We don't need gentiles telling us what we have to do."

"Fighting for justice isn't a Jewish right. I am as involved as any Jewish person. And I certainly have the right to be."

17

Sandy is meeting with Harry Cantor, Head of AIPIC – American Israel Public Information Committee – in his Washington D.C. office. AIPIC is the Israel Lobby. It brings members of Congress to Israel for a look around. It tells them of its virtues, and is supposed to wield enormous power – but doesn't.

Harry Cantor is American born, in his fifties, wears a smart blue suit, has most of his hair. Sandy knows him fairly well. They often meet at Washington functions.

Sandy tells him, "We want Brady and his wife out of prison."

"We all want Brady and his wife out of prison."

"I'm glad to hear you say that, Harry."

"I'll even go so far as to say he should never have gone to prison in the first place. But then, that's my opinion. That's the opinion of most of the people around here. Unfortunately, the Government of Israel doesn't employ us to give them our opinion. They have a totally different one."

"Presumably you've made your feelings known."

"They got the message."

"Hopefully it has, or will have, some effect."

"None whatsoever."

"You'll no doubt report my feelings in the matter."

"No, that isn't what we're here for. The Government of Israel pays out huge amounts of money so that they can try and influence other people – not so anybody can try and influence them. You want the Prime Minister to know what you're thinking – write him a letter."

"Would that do any good?"

"Of course not. They get thousands. They have a guy around who reads the mail. Sometimes they send back a standard reply: *"The Prime Minister of Israel thanks you for writing, has taken your words into serious consideration, and will take appropriate action."* It serves for almost everything. Israel has other problems. They want to forget about this one."

"I'm sorry, Harry, I can't."

"Making a nuisance of yourself is going to help?"

"I think so."

"This isn't an Israeli priority. If they leave it alone, they're convinced it will just go away. I'm not sure it's doing anyone a favor to stir things up."

"I've hardly begun, Harry."

"It doesn't make Israel look very good."

"Israel hasn't behaved very good."

Harry throws up his hands in capitulation. "I know. But what am I supposed to do, encourage you? One part of me says, 'Yeah, fight 'em.' The other part says, 'Don't waste your time. Israel doesn't need it.' You want to help Israel, don't lean on her. She's a frail structure. I get paid for giving out positive information. This isn't positive. You're a friend of Israel – lean on the U.S. Government. Tell 'em they got it all wrong. This guy and his wife should be out."

"You know very well that it's Israel that has to exert its influence."

"Of course I do. It won't. Even if it had any. Look, they messed up – it's like 'Friendly Fire'. You shoot your own people. It happens all the time. Brady is a victim of 'Friendly Fire'. You want to allocate blame – what would it alter?"

"I don't care about blame. Most of them are implicated. I want the Bradys out of prison."

"I admire your motives – and your vehemence. But tell me something, Sandy, how does a nice gentile girl like you get involved in these Jewish problems? And why?"

"Justice."

"The world is filled with 'just causes.' Why pick on this one? It's remote and removed from you."

"My husband is Jewish. My son is Jewish. I consider myself Jewish. I feel it's my responsibility to be involved in this one."

"This one could pull us apart, Sandy."

"The Jews have to fight, Harry. I'm just joining in with them."

18

Mark details the events of 1973 into the computer: "It was made apparent to the Israeli leadership that the Arabs would attack, with full information provided as to when, where and with how much. Every detail was known, and supplied, to the Israeli leadership – and ignored. The responsibility must fall squarely on the shoulders of Moshe Dayan, the Minister of Defense.

"He, and those who served under him – Yes-men with eyes as blinkered as his own – refused to see what the newest recruit stationed on the bank of the Suez Canal saw and knew: Egypt was preparing for war, preparing to re-cross the Canal, over-run the thin, hardly-defended Bar Lev line, reclaim the Sinai, and as much of the rest of Israel as they could, in conjunction with their Arab allies. Syria, in the north, could reclaim her part of Israel, at least as far south as Haifa.

"The Prime Minister, Golda Meir, essentially a 'party hack', devoted to the Ben Gurion concepts of kibbutz socialism and social democracy, with strong ties to the United States, had, as her main regret, the rejection of Israel by the Socialist International. Despite beating the drum with such vehemence for the socialist ideal and ideology to which she had devoted herself completely, Israel was nevertheless barred from entering this otherwise easily accessible conglomerate – the Socialist International – most of whose members bore highly dubious credentials.

"She placed her faith in her Minister of Defense, and was surprised to learn about the Arab attack, which came as no surprise to anybody else.

"Israel suffered terrible losses, and was about to lose the war. This was the one Israel couldn't afford to lose, because it would be the last, and Israel would be no more. Dayan had gotten this one completely wrong. In 1967 – the Six Day War – it had been tanks and air power that demonstrated Israel's might. An Egyptian pilot had only to see an Israeli plane, and he would proceed to eject, attempting to save his skin, while his Soviet Russian-made aircraft crashed to the ground. Israeli tanks had mashed the Soviet tanks and left the Sinai desert strewn with the results. In many cases Soviet aircraft had been manned by Soviet air personnel; and while they did not eject with the same alacrity as their

Arab friends and allies, they were no match for the Israeli pilots, who killed them and their planes with satisfying regularity. This was also true of the tank crews, Russians, who were seen by their masters as gaining battle experience while having the opportunity to kill Jews, but who died in large numbers. Hundreds, and probably thousands, of Russians died – in their tanks, in their aircraft, as ground crews, and as advisors – in their efforts to eliminate Israel, in conjunction with their Arab allies.

"Not only had the Arabs lost their war against Israel, but so too had the Russians. Both had been deeply humiliated. In Czecho-slovakia, people marched through the streets of Prague, in spontaneous demonstrations, carrying the Star of David – the flag of Israel – to celebrate the Israeli victory over Russia. These were not Jewish people, but Czechs demonstrating how they felt in this otherwise uneven struggle. Even in Poland they exalted the victory of 'their Jews' over their Soviet oppressors.

"Israel held five Soviet airmen as prisoners of war, whose five aircraft the Israelis had shot down, and who, only by good fortune, were still alive. Israel should have made the most of the situation, paraded their captives before the television cameras, flaunting their victory, not merely over the Arabs, but the Soviet Union as well. This, such a television appearance would have said, is what happens to those who attack Israel. But they didn't do it. They sent the Russians home, through the good offices of the Rumanians, who hadn't broken off relations with Israel, as the other Soviet satellites had. (Rumania still had a lot of Jews, who were a valuable commodity, in the sense that they could be sold for hard currency and allowed to emigrate, generally to Israel).

"The Russians sought a way to overcome Israeli air and tank power, came up with a simple, cheap and effective answer, one so simple that even an Egyptian could make effective use of it. And did. Wire-guided missiles could be fired, by one man, from a mile away, and eliminate an Israeli tank. Heat-seeking guided missiles could also be extremely effective against Israeli aircraft, and were. It was not necessary to confront Israel with expensive aircraft that wound up as scrap iron, and killed off Arab pilots, even if they were highly expendable.

"The United States had informed Israel of the new Soviet/Arab weaponry and tactic, which Israel completely ignored. The Arabs had five years in which to prepare for the next war, made good use of every day, learned to overcome their fear of the night, learned to use the weaponry the Soviet Union was providing in order to avenge the defeat that they both suffered. At any time Israel could have crushed the Arabs, and their hopes for revenge, but didn't. Because they didn't think any threat existed, despite the constant warnings provided by the intelligence services.

"Then it happened. And it was almost too late. Israel asked the United States for immediate help, for immediate re-supply, because they were out of everything with which to defend themselves. They assumed that the 'great' Jewish Secretary of State was prepared to help them. But they were wrong about this, too. Henry J. Kissinger had been recruited by U.S. Intelligence many years before, during the time he served in the U.S. Military during World War II. Now he was quite prepared to see Israel overrun, serving America's purpose, and not Israel's, which were in direct opposition to each other. Kissinger refused to answer the phone – when the calls came from Israel, begging for help. But, then at last, in desperation, Israel left the message: They were going to 'drop it'. Kissinger got the message. Israel was to be re-supplied.

"An Israel response with the ultimate weapon would have had the most profound effect on her Arab neighbors, and would serve as a major deterrent to further aggression.

"In the end Israel won a great military victory. General Sharon, in defiance of orders, crossed the Suez Canal. He did so at a point he had staked out much earlier, in consideration of a future need. And now he trapped the Egyptians whom he could easily have annihilated. In the end the Arabs surrendered again. The Israelis had won this one, too. And the Arabs had lost – again – massively. It was no more of a defeat than they had suffered on all the other occasions. But how many victories such as this could Israel afford?"

Claire comes into Mark's office. She closes the door behind her. She sits down in the chair on the other side of his desk. There is a determination about her, bordering on truculence. It isn't the Claire he knows. He doesn't think he's going to like this. Intuitively he braces himself for whatever is to come, his elbows on the arms of his chair.

He waits for her to speak. It is a while before she does.

Then she says, "I've been working with you for quite a while now."

Mark nods. This is the prelude to something else.

"And the whole time," Claire goes on, "I've been in love with you. From the first day, Mark."

Mark closes his eyes, as if doing so would obliterate Claire, and also prevent him from hearing her words.

"It's a funny thing about love," Claire says, "you can't always help who you're in love with. You can't just turn it on, and off. Not that I ever tried to turn it off with you, Mark. And of course you knew. You had to know. I was never very subtle."

Mark opens his eyes. He takes her in. She is still there. She is still speaking. He looks down on his desk. He sees the desk set. David and Sandy had given it to him for his birthday. It's nice. He likes using it.

"Even if it were possible to turn off love," Claire continues, "I wouldn't have – not my love for you. I've enjoyed every minute of it. I'm enjoying it now, Mark."

"Claire, I don't need this."

"I do. Mark, do you believe in love at first sight? I didn't used to. But it happened. And what else could I do, except believe? I like being in love with you, Mark. . . . I'm sorry about all those nice young men that you and Sandy were always bringing around. They were nice – almost all of them – very carefully selected. Thanks. Thanks for trying. But it wasn't going to work, Mark. Because I was in love with you. As I say, I couldn't help myself."

Mark hopes this will end. He does not know what point she is making, beyond the obvious. What is she expecting to come of this confession?

"What did I expect? I'm not sure. I never really thought you were going to take me in your arms and say that you loved me, too. That wouldn't have been you, Mark. For you there was just Sandy. I admire your loyalty. No, I don't really. I want something from you, Mark. It's very simple. I want your baby."

Mark closes his eyes again. This is worse than anything he could have imagined.

"It's not too much to ask, Mark. I've thought about it for a long time. I want your baby. What's wrong with that? If I had your baby – I'd have you forever."

"Claire, we've worked together all these years. Don't spoil it. Don't hurt me this way."

"Why?"

"Is that what you want to do? Hurt me?"

"I suppose. I love you, but that doesn't mean I don't want to hurt you. I want to hurt you very much – because you have hurt me – because of your indifference."

"Claire, talk sense."

"This is sense. My sense. Loving you makes no sense – it leads to nothing – to nowhere. But I can't help it. You stand next to me – like you have been doing – all these years. And I feel you close, and I know how much I love you. I feel the physical sensation of love. I feel it now. I want your baby, Mark. It isn't too much to ask."

"This is very painful for me, Claire."

"You don't know what pain is. I could tell you. Listen, Mark, don't worry, I won't go parading around Washington saying, 'Look at this lovely baby. He's Mark's. Do you think he looks like Mark? There is a resemblance. It's very strong.' I'll disappear. I'll go back home – to Des Moines. I have parents. They'll welcome me and my baby. They'll be happy to have a grandchild. They're very comfortable. The child won't be in want of anything – except a father. But it won't matter. I'll love him enough for both of us."

"Claire," Mark speaks firmly, "it's out of the question."

"Why? Are your genes so precious that you only dole them out sparingly?"

"What you're suggesting is irresponsible."

"Possibly. Probably. At least in your eyes. As a mother, I'll be completely responsible. It won't affect you, ever. I won't contact you. I'll have what I want – a part of you – and the rest won't be necessary. Life will go on for you as before – but for me it will be different. I'll have what I want for a change."

"Claire, why don't you take a few days off. You have been working too hard."

"I don't want a few days off. I like working hard. I like working close to you. I'm not making any demands, Mark. Just your baby. I'll tell you when it's the right time – nothing prolonged. And then when I'm pregnant – I'll disappear. I'll disappear from your life forever. I'll have what I want. Who is it going to hurt?"

"Everybody. Your suggestion undermines the basic structure and stability of the family unit."

"Your righteousness is the height of pomposity. So Sandy loans out her husband for some social work – to help the deprived.

142

Could she object to that? She wouldn't object if you passed out the Thanksgiving turkeys to the needy, served it up to them on trays. She'd say how marvelous you were, how caring, how socially involved. My need is even more acute. There is nobody else who can help – who I want to help. I'm sure she wouldn't mind lending you to me to help someone suffering from the most acute social deprivation."

"Claire, I'm sorry. This is no good. This kind of talk is deeply disturbing and upsetting. It's completely destructive for both of us. There is absolutely no possibility of my doing what you suggest. It's pointless, I see, to try and explain why – because all my arguments are logical –"

"And mine are emotional. Of course they are. Why else would I be in love with you? Having your baby – that's logical."

"No, it isn't."

"You might not think so – from your point of view. From mine it's perfectly logical. They say emotion is stronger than logic – that the heart has it over the head. I agree. But here I'm combining both."

"Claire, you need help."

"Of course I do. And I want you to provide it."

"Medical help."

"Psychiatric help, you mean. Now you're trying to take refuge behind the medical profession. That's very faint-hearted, Mark. That isn't like you. If you can't deal with it with your gun, you don't know how to deal with it. I don't need a shrink. There's nothing wrong with me."

"I'll take you home – to our house, Claire. Come and stay with us for a couple of days."

"Your house!" Claire cries out, sarcasm in her voice. "What a great place. Uncle Mark and Aunt Sandy can look after me, tuck me in bed, and give me a good night kiss. Maybe your son David could read me a good night story."

"Then let me take you back to your apartment."

"I could check with David and ask if he wouldn't like a little half brother. No, I don't need you to take me home. I don't need you to look after me."

Mark stands up.

"I'm taking you home, Claire."

"I'm not crazy, and I'm not emotionally disturbed. I don't need

143

you to escort me around this city. I've managed all these years without your help, thank you very much."

"Let's go, Claire."

Claire stands up, too. "I'm going. But I don't want you or need you to take me. Do you understand, I don't want you!"

"I'll get Bill to take you home."

"I don't want Bill, either. I don't want anybody. I'm a big girl. A foolish one. But then I can't help that. I'll take off a few days. I need to rest. I need to think."

Mark opens the door of his office, steps into Bill Cooper's office. "I'm taking Claire home," he tells Bill. "She isn't feeling well."

Bill steps out of his office, into the corridor. Claire is there.

"I'm feeling just fine. And nobody is taking me home."

She steps into her office, grabs her coat and handbag. "Nobody is taking me home!" she screams, and storms out of the office.

"What's this all about?" Bill asks, confused.

Mark runs after her. He sees the elevator close behind her. He runs down the stairs. She is gone.

Mark is shaken by the encounter. He is concerned for Claire. He ponders her irrational request, finds it very upsetting. He tries to work and can't. He gives it enough time for her to reach her Georgetown apartment — if that is where she is going — and phones her. There is no answer. He tries again. He tries several times. Ultimately Claire picks up the phone.

"I'm worried about you, Claire."

"Don't. Stop bothering me. Stop phoning me. I want to think. Leave me alone. I won't be coming to work. Maybe never. Just leave me alone."

Claire hangs up.

Tiredly Mark puts down the phone. He doesn't know how to deal with this. He'll tell Sandy about it, discuss it with her.

144

19

Sandy speaks with Ralph Lowenberg, Executive Director of B'nai Israel, founded long before the Civil War, devoting itself to philanthropic and communal activities, to helping Jewish youth – on and off campus – and providing adult education.

They have met on various occasions, but do not have an intimate relationship.

Sandy says, "It is absolutely imperative that the Jews in this country stand behind the Bradys."

Lowenberg, in his early sixties, heavy set, almost regal, in a tailor-made grey suit, has the ear of presidents and virtually everyone in Congress.

"Mrs. Spaulding, what you fail to understand," Lowenberg says slowly, articulating carefully, as if speaking to a foreigner with only a limited comprehension of English, "is that the people in this country are not behind the Bradys. They do not support what the Bradys have done. On the contrary, the Jews in this country want to distance themselves from the Bradys. If you were Jewish, Mrs. Spaulding, you would understand that."

"I think that's irrelevant. Jews can't run away from this issue by ignoring it."

"We are deeply embarrassed by it. It doesn't affect you in the same way. You may be sympathetic, and we appreciate your sympathy, but I assure you it is completely misplaced. We neither want it nor need it."

"But yours is an organization that supports Israel. How can you repudiate this man who did so much for Israel – who saved Israel?"

"We can, Mrs. Spaulding, and we have. We accept that he is guilty, and that he got what he deserves. His actions are a source of deep embarrassment for us. We are extremely vulnerable – and his actions, however commendable the motive – have made us even more vulnerable. This is what you fail to understand. If you were Jewish, you would."

"I don't believe the bulk of the Jewish people are prepared to push their brother into the gas oven."

"We don't need that kind of criticism, Mrs. Spaulding."

Sandy's eyes fall on the plaque on the wall, behind Ralph

Lowenberg. It says in Hebrew: *KOL YISRAEL AREIVIM ZEH LAZEH.* Just below, in English, it says: EVERY JEW IS RESPONSIBLE FOR ALL THE OTHERS.

"Do you believe what that plaque says?"

Lowenberg turns to look at it, as if he needs to be reminded of its presence. He reads it now.

"Indeed I do," he says. "And for that reason it is absolutely essential that we repudiate the actions of the man. We are responsible for each other, but not when individuals violate the law. That is their problem. They should know better. In the eyes of the non-Jewish world, we are guilty, too."

"Which is saying you're more interested in how you appear, than in achieving justice."

"Justice has been done. It has our approval. We are not questioning it, or have any intention of questioning it. Our efforts now are devoted to damage control."

"And you think that if you distance yourselves from Alan Brady, the gentile world will not see you as equally guilty."

"They will understand our position."

"I seriously doubt that, Mr. Lowenberg. Where they want to see dual loyalty, they will see dual loyalty. And no matter how loud you protest, and how long, you will not change the mind, or the attitude, of one single gentile. You need to fight. You need to protest this immoral and illegal conviction of a fellow-Jew. This is how you will be judged. Alan Brady is in a concentration camp, Mr. Lowenberg – an American concentration camp."

"You are seriously over-dramatizing this situation."

"They put one Jew in that concentration camp – in order to frighten all the rest."

"And we are frightened. I won't try to deny that. We are terribly vulnerable. Do you think what your husband did in Dario's restaurant was a good thing? It wasn't. I deplore it. For a moment of his satisfaction – he did irreparable damage. Irreparable. I tell you, Mrs. Spaulding. Here we try to educate. We do not look for confrontations. As a non-Jew, how can you know what we have endured, what we continue to endure? Alan J. Brady has destroyed in one minute what we have spent a hundred years trying to build. We build bridges. He destroys them. You come here, applauding his action – and you want me to applaud with you. I will not. I cannot."

"I don't believe that you speak for the majority of Jews in this country."

"If I don't, then I must work harder than I have. They look to us for leadership. I am not afraid to lead. I tell my people, stand up when we are right. Don't try to defend the indefensible. We want the non-Jewish world to look at us and see that we are loyal Americans – fully, completely devoted to the American cause and ideology. We don't question America's ways. Our loyalty is here, in America. Is that too much to ask for a Jew – for an American Jew? Look how Jews are treated in the Soviet Union. It's better here for us. Why do we have to go around stirring up trouble? Of course we're devoted to Israel – we have historical connections. But our first loyalty is to America. And our second. And our third. All our loyalty. There is no other. That is what we fight to make non-Jews understand!"

"And do they, Mr. Lowenberg?"

He thinks about this for a moment. "No. No, they don't. Not all. Some. Not all."

"Those who want to."

"Yes. Those who want to."

"And the rest – they're not getting the message because they don't want it. No matter how long and how loud you profess your loyalty, Mr. Lowenberg, it has absolutely no meaning for those who feel the need to attack you. Because you feel vulnerable in this area, this is where you are to be attacked. Anti-Semitism has very deep roots, and is purely an emotional response. If you think that you can fight it by setting the record straight, then you are completely wrong. If you prove your loyalty today by showing the non-Jewish world that you repudiate one of your finest, bravest, most concerned individuals – and they believe you – then the gentile world will find something else. They will attack you, wherever and however it suits them: You control the money – the media – Hollywood –"

"None of this is true. This is what we try to explain."

"That is my point, Mr. Lowenberg. The truth is lost on those who do not want to hear it. Israel is being crushed out of existence by the United States. This is what Alan Brady told you. You should be fighting for him, and fighting for Israel's continued existence, against the American wishes to the contrary."

"I assure you, Mrs. Spaulding, we do not need non-Jews coming

147

here to tell us how we should conduct ourselves. Where were these gentile saviors when we needed them most?"

"Where are the Jewish ones when we need them now?"

"Sufficiently sensible to go on protecting our people."

"If that's what you call protection, then the Jews are in serious trouble. How far do you think you are from that concentration camp? If they can do it to Alan Brady, they can do it to you – to anyone whom they choose. They can bend you to their will, make you conform to their requirements, which are the opposite from your own. They don't want an Israel; you will have to stand by and see it destroyed. The two thousand year old dream that people like my mother-in-law and my father-in-law made come true, will be ended forever more. In a minute it will all be gone . . . Mr. Lowenberg, my son has a book. In it, it says, in Hebrew, '*Lo Ta'amod Al Dam Reyeicma*.' It means, 'Don't Stand in Your Brother's Blood'."

Later, Sandy meets Mark for lunch at Dario's. She tells him of her encounter with the Executive Director of B'nai Israel.

Mark says, "I'm not surprised."

"I expected more."

"Did you think you could convince him?"

"I needed to try," Sandy says. "I suppose I thought I could move them a bit."

"They have already made their position pretty clear."

"Are they representative of the majority of Jews in this country?"

"I doubt it. The problem is, there's no leadership. You would think that Brady's father could do something. He's an eminent scientist – maybe get the scientific community involved."

"Mark, for the Jewish people, this is amongst the most important issues since the end of the War."

20

The prison guard unlocks Alan Brady's cell. Two men enter. They are well-dressed, in suits, and ties, obviously employed by the United States Federal Government, probably the Department of Justice. Alan Brady occupies a lot of their time and thoughts, as he does that of the State Department, and the Department of Defense. The FBI is of course involved, and the National Security Agency. Brady knows most of America's secrets, and this is not good for all of those who wanted to keep those secrets secret. And Israel has those secrets now.

Brady is useful to America. For the government he will fill the roll of the Jewish traitor supplying America's secrets to Israel. Life imprisonment? It is but a short time for his heinous crimes. And he will serve to obscure America's crimes against the Jews, against humanity, her support for the Nazi cause, her efforts to eliminate Israel.

The two men shake hands with Alan Brady. They are not unfriendly. They want his cooperation. His help. They do not want to antagonize him.

"Good morning, Mr. Brady," the One says.

The Other just nods.

"'Morning," Alan Brady says, not really convinced that it is such a good morning. What do they want? He has spoken to a lot of people. They all want something.

"Are they treating you all right?" the One asks.

Treating me all right? It's a prison. With bars, and locks. That's a funny question. They'd be treating me all right if they said Go Home. But they're not likely to do that.

"Yeah, great," Alan says, sarcasm in his voice.

If the two men hear the sarcasm, they ignore it. They are not here to discuss prison reform.

The One takes a thick white envelope from his inside jacket pocket and hands it to Alan.

"What's this?" Alan asks.

"Open it," the One says.

Alan complies. There are eight or ten sheets inside, folded into thirds. He unfolds them, and looks at the top sheet. It is covered with names.

"What is this?" Alan asks, perplexed.

"A list," the One replies.

"Of what?" Alan asks, still perplexed.

"We don't think you were working alone," the Other says. We're convinced you had accomplices. Look over that list, and tell us which ones they are."

Alan is surprised. "But you know I didn't work with anybody else. I told you. You polygraphed me for hours and hours."

"Just give us the names," the Other says impatiently.

Alan looks at the list. At the top of it is Ralph Lowenberg, Executive Director of B'nai Israel. He's heard the name. It's no one he knows. He glances down the list. There are other names – heads of Jewish organizations and Jewish causes, people with Jewish-sounding names he's never heard of. And there's a name – a familiar name: Brady, Dr. Morton.

"That's my father," Alan says in surprise.

"He could've been working with you," the Other says.

"That's crazy. You know he wasn't."

"We don't know anything," the Other counters.

Alan turns over the pages, glances at more names: Spaulding, Mark; Spaulding, Sandy. Never heard of them.

"Just check them off," the Other instructs Alan.

"But how can I check them off?" Alan asks angrily.

"Things will go better for you if you do," the One says, trying to inject concern in his voice.

"But you want me to implicate people who aren't implicated."

The Other shakes his head dubiously. "We don't know they're not implicated. We think they are. And we think you should tell us."

"I haven't got anything to tell you, because you already know everything."

What are they trying to prove – that he's a traitor, that Jews are traitors? How reminiscent of Nazi Germany. He has had a great deal of time to ponder this issue. That is why he is here – the similarities between the two: The concomitant need to destroy the Jewish people, more recently, to destroy Israel.

Alan hands back the list.

"No, you keep it," the One says.

"And study it," the Other says. "There must be lots and lots of people you've been working with. And we want you to tell us who they are. We want you to tell us everything. You know, Mr. Brady, you have a wife. And she's in prison, too. Things could go very bad for her."

Alan deliberately drops the list on the floor.

"I don't think you want to do that," the Other says. "If you're smart, you'll.pick it up, and go through it carefully. And you'll tell us about everybody. There isn't any point in trying to cover up for anybody. The truth has to come out – and it will be better for everybody if you tell it."

The two men are ready to leave.

The guard comes for them.

"Study it," the Other advises Alan. "Just check off the names, and get in touch with us. Tell one of the guards. They'll know where to find us."

The two men leave.

Alan sits on his bunk. He looks at the list on the floor. Slowly he reaches down to pick it up. He holds it in his hand for a moment. Then he tears it up into little pieces, and lets the pieces drop to the floor, like snow flakes.

He pulls his legs up onto his bunk. He leans forward, wrapping his arms around his legs. He looks up at the bars over the window, and the bars of the cell. This was not supposed to happen. He wonders if somebody will come along soon and say "It was all a mistake. You can leave now." Somehow he doesn't think so. They said, "Life. Life imprisonment." That's a long time to spend here, in a place like this, with bars on the window, and bars for a door, and bars that make a cage.

21

It is in Senator Ron Williamson's large and pleasant office. Senator Williamson is Alan J. Brady's elected representative in Washington. He has never met Alan Brady, though he is familiar with the situation. He knows Dr. Morton Brady quite well; he was present when the presidents presented their awards to Dr. Brady.

Sandy is in his office. They are discussing Brady. He is completely sympathetic.

Williamson is a man in his late fifties, with silver hair. He has been in the Senate a long time. He looks like a senator. Sandy and Mark have known Senator Williamson for many years, having visited each other's home from time to time.

"There is no significant pressure from anybody in the state – groups or individuals – for Brady's release," Senator Williamson says. "I would have thought there would be a great outcry. We have a significant number of Jewish people."

"Perhaps the people are afraid. The charge of 'dual loyalty' is very effective, " Sandy says.

"I realize this. But no other group of people would allow themselves to be bullied by such utterly ridiculous charges. Can you imagine it happening to the Italians – or the Irish – who give their allegiance to a Pope – to a man in Rome whom they allow into their bedrooms, to be told what to do there? Certainly not. They'd laugh at such charges. They'd certainly ignore them. And they'd be right to do so."

"The Jews are victims of history."

"Could it be that they let themselves be victims?"

"There could be something in what you say, Ron. They expect to be victims – therefore they are. Not all Jews, of course. There are different responses to different situations. In regard to Brady, I'm not sure. There isn't any leadership. That's why I was hoping you could help."

"I need a mandate. I need to be able to say, this is what my constituents want. You know how things work in Washington. I've been in touch with the President in this matter. I did it off my own bat – because I felt Brady was being railroaded. The President isn't at all sympathetic. After all, it's the Administration that did it to him in the first place. The President wrote and told me that Brady had had a fair hearing, and that the court has imposed a just sentence. End of case. End of chapter."

"And end of Brady," Sandy says thoughtfully. "I can't let it happen, Ron. I have to fight. I have to ask you to fight. I have never seen such injustice."

"I'll always do what I can, Sandy. The Senate is a pretty sympathetic place. We have a good record when it comes to Israel."

"Israel is under a lot of pressure."

"From the oil lobby. They run things, Sandy. They are the government. I'm here to fight them – and I do. I'm aware of the extent to which Israel is under pressure. They needed to bring their case there. Congress would listen – with considerable sympathy. I'm not absolutely certain that everybody in Congress would be sympathetic when it came to taking unshakeable and definitive opinions and views. The Administration has already made us take sides: Who rules, they asked, Washington, or Jerusalem? So Saudi

Arabia was provided with the most up-to-date and sophisticated electronic surveillance equipment known to mankind – all the better for eliminating Israel."

"Dual loyalty, Ron."

Senator Williamson laughs bitterly. "You're right. I voted for Saudi Arabia to have that electronic stuff. They came to me and said, 'Choose, Ron. What's it going to be – Washington or Jerusalem?' I didn't have the courage to tell them to go and get stuffed. I was scared, Sandy. I really was. I knew very well that back home the Administration would be saying to my constituents, 'Ron Williamson is a disloyal American. He takes his orders from Jerusalem, and sells out Washington. Which country does Ron Williamson live in, anyway?' So I took the easier way. Admittedly, it's been a bit hard on my conscience. I want to see Israel survive, Sandy. I really do."

"So now you know how the Jews feel about being charged with 'dual loyalty'."

"We're all vulnerable somewhere."

"Where do we go from here, Ron?"

"We need a campaign. Maybe it would work if somebody came around and said to those of us in Congress: We want Brady out."

"I'm saying it, Ron."

"It's a pretty lonely voice. Too bad they put Leah Brady in prison, too. I'm sure she could have made a good case. It's always a lot more effective to have your wife campaigning on your behalf."

"Like Avital Sharansky."

"She's first class. I had her in here. I did everything she asked. You couldn't say No to her."

"Brady is our Sharansky."

"It would also be easier if Brady was Russian – and was imprisoned in Russia."

"It looks like the Russians are more compassionate than we are," Sandy observes. "At least they didn't put Avital in prison, too."

"But we're smarter. We put the wife away, and we don't have the same problem. How would it look – Leah Brady in the Kremlin, asking for help?"

"I somehow don't think she'd get the same sympathy there."

"Probably not. I understand Israel has caught a number of spies in the employ of the American Government."

"One of them was an American citizen," Sandy informs the Senator. "The CIA recruited him. He was a fairly high officer in the Israeli Army."

"What happened to him?"

"The Israelis sent him back quietly."

"I suppose if the Israelis had shot him the CIA wouldn't have worried unduly about it."

"Of course not. He would have been just another Jew – who served their purpose, and not his own."

"Sandy, it's my firm belief that Israel owes this man Brady something – considering what he did for them. They've got the clout, if they want to use it. They could get him out."

"They don't want him out. He knows too much."

"And I don't suppose they want any further confrontation." The Senator shakes his head and sighs deeply. "It looks to me like there are more people who want him in than want him out."

22

Leah and Alan embrace warmly. They cling to each other – as if this could be the last time it will ever happen.

They are in the visitors' room. The two men who came to see Alan before are here now. They have brought Leah with them. It is not a visit that they have arranged out of compassion.

The One says to Leah, "Mrs. Brady, we gave your husband a list of names, and asked him to tell us which ones he had worked with. He isn't being very cooperative. We brought you here because we thought you could help persuade him."

"Which names are these?" Leah asks.

The Other gives Leah the list. She glances over it quickly. She says to Alan, "Did you work with Ralph Lowenberg, the Executive Director of B'nai Israel?"

"Of course not,"Alan replies.

"Or Dr. Morton Brady? – I believe he's your father."

"Not him, either."

"Come on, Mr. Brady," the Other says, "That's a big list. There must be someone on it you worked with."

"I didn't work with anybody. And you know it," Alan says, exasperated.

"Alan, they're trying to present the Jews as traitors."

"I know."

"In the best Nazi tradition," Leah says.

"That's being harsh, Mrs. Brady," the One says. "It would really be much better if you could get your husband to be more cooperative."

"They want you to betray your people, Alan. They are Nazis. They're no different."

"Mr. Brady," the Other says, "in an effort to keep your wife in good health, I strongly advise you to cooperate with us."

Leah turns defiant. She looks at One, than at the Other, and speaks to Alan. "No matter what they do to me," she says, "you must never bear false witness against your people."

"Do you have any idea what we can do to your wife, Mr. Brady?" the Other says menacingly.

"Alan, we won't let them intimidate us."

"Don't be a fool, Brady," the Other says. "She's in our power. We can do what we like. Are you going to let that happen?"

"Leah -"

"Never mind about me. They're Nazis. We have to fight them."

"She sounds brave now, Brady. Try to imagine your wife writhing in pain."

"Don't betray our people, Alan!"

"Why can't you ask me to do something else?" Alan demands.

"Because this is what we want."

"Then take it out on me."

"Name names, Brady."

"Alan! Alan! Don't! Don't ever! Promise me. I want to hear you say it. Say it, Alan, 'I promise'."

They look at each other in silence.

Leah says again, "Promise me, Alan. I want to hear it – in your own words . . ."

"Leah, I promise."

"I heard you say it, Alan. No matter what they do to me – remember. I have your promise. In this Nazi milieu, we have nothing left but our integrity. We can't throw that away – no matter what. Otherwise they will have won. That must never be allowed to happen."

155

The two men from the Department of Justice realize that they have lost this round, and they remove Leah. There is no final embrace. There is no touching, not even of hands.

Alan stands there, despondent, bereft.

Leah is returned to her prison. She suffers from an intestinal condition. It goes untreated. They chain her to her bed. They do not do this surreptitiously. They want to make it apparent that all the power is theirs.

23

The car jumps the curb and smashes Bill Cooper into the wall of a building. It is broad daylight. The car backs off and drives away. It is meant to look like an accident – just an ordinary hit-and-run. The driver is drunk. The driver is asleep.

But anybody who sees it knows that it's no accident.

Bill Cooper is dead on arrival.

They got the license plate number. It is an untraceable number. It means that a governmental department is involved, a governmental department that doesn't want to be traced. The police in Washington D.C. know this. They don't pursue it any further.

They would have preferred to get Mark Spaulding first – but it was Bill Cooper whom they saw. Spaulding would just have to wait. But they'd get him, too.

24

"*Yishkadal Yishkadash Shmea'rabou*. . . ." Rabbi Moreheim chants in Hebrew.

Bill Cooper is lowered into the freshly dug grave.

Helen Cooper, the widow, stands close to the grave, crying silently. Her son and her daughter, in their early twenties, are on either side of her, giving support.

Sandy clings to Marks's arm. Mark has his hand over David's

shoulder. David holds his arm around his father's waist.

Jim and Miriam Haliday are here with Aaron. So are relatives and friends and many from the congregation of Rabbi Moreheim's synagogue, here to pay their last respects.

Rabbi Moreheim says, "This man, loving husband and father, was brought down by the forces of evil which he had been fighting, the evil that was there, lurking. Bill Cooper has paid the price of that evil, as if he were a soldier killed in battle.

"Bill was my friend; our friend; a loyal son of his people, a truly great American, who fought for his country in the most important and meaningful way. His murder is a terrible loss to us personally, and to an entire nation who is poorer because he is no longer with us. It remains for us to carry on fighting on his behalf, for his principles . . .and to find and punish the perpetrators of this crime . . ."

25

Mark sits in front of his computer. The office is empty, except for himself. Bill isn't coming back – ever. Mark half expects him to come through the door, papers in his hand, eager to discuss some aspect of their report. But Bill, even if he were to come back, couldn't get through the door. It's locked. The venetian blind is drawn, so that no one can see in from an adjoining office or roof, or from a scaffold.

On Mark's desk is the Jericho. The holster is in the drawer. Mark feels a need to be ready, fully alert. He knows they could get the car; it's in the underground parking lot. For anyone determined to get in, it wouldn't be any great problem. He'll need to check out the car before getting into it.

He'd told the researchers, secretaries, and the support staff not to come in. The United States Center for World Study would stay closed for the entire week, out of respect for Bill, in his memory. Bill probably wouldn't have wanted them to do that – he'd say, Take a day, if you have to. There's work to do, let's get on with it. You don't need a whole week in my memory.

He is going to miss Bill very much. The office won't be the same without Bill. Nothing was going to be the same without Bill. How much of Bill's death was his responsibility? They were playing a dangerous game. Bill was a casualty. He, Mark, could be the next one. The United States Government needed to open its archives; the guilty had to be exposed. Uncle Sam had more than his share of dirty secrets – dirty, rotten, filthy secrets that made it apparent that America wasn't just the land of the free and the home of the brave; it was the home of a strong, subversive entity into whose grip America had fallen victim. And it had cost: the price was 57,692 American dead. If anyone wanted to see the cost, they could count the names of the dead on the Vietnam Memorial, right here in Washington, not a long walk from this very spot.

All the Jews were vulnerable. They were on the list. Alan Brady headed the list. And Israel was on the list. The American Government made that obvious. Israel was highly expendable. Israel, in the eyes of most of the world, was an artificial entity, the creation of some Jews' over-active imagination. It impeded better relations with the Arab world. Who wanted Israel? Who needed Israel? Almost nobody.

Mark knows he has to press on. The work is more urgent than ever. He hadn't meant to come in today. They are sitting *shiva* at Bill's house. He and Sandy and David were there earlier. What do you say to people whose husband, whose father, has been mur-dered? Not so long ago they were at Bill's son's Bar Mitzvah; and his daughter's Bat Mitzvah. Now there was no father; no husband.

At home, earlier, he had paced the floor, and wondered if there was any way this could have been prevented, if they could have taken some precaution that might have kept this from happening. Bill was aware of those destructive forces, but in the abstract, not in the real terms that rose up to kill him. He remained the college professor, the academic, who knew about evil, who knew of the malignancy that was a part of the American structure, but learned about it in real terms, the hard way, from experience.

He had tried to phone Claire. Claire worried him. If she was in her apartment, she wasn't answering her phone. She needed some time off. Did she know about Bill? Maybe she had gone back to Des Moines. He had no number there. No address. Her life there was far removed, remote, as she had chosen for it to be, from her life in D.C. He had driven over to her apartment building. There was no response to the bell.

Is it just a question of a couple of days off work? Will she come back? Could things ever be the same? Maybe they could have a more mature relationship – the personal aspects out of the way. He would certainly be prepared to try. Claire was a good worker. They worked well together. He would have preferred not to lose her.

Sandy had been restless, too. She sat in the den, her eyes filled with tears. In the end she said she was going in to the office. Mark decided he might as well go, too.

Mark begins to write on the computer, contributing further to his report:

"Israel is a nuclear power, ranking well ahead of Great Britain, with perhaps fewer nuclear weapons than China, but with a sophistication that leaves China far behind. France, Number Three in terms of actual nuclear weapons in its arsenal, nevertheless lags well behind Israel in many aspects of its military nuclear program, as does even the United States. Israel has a strike capability of fearsome proportions.

"Israeli attack aircraft can deliver nuclear weaponry where and when required; there are short and long range missiles fitted with nuclear warheads, as well as two submarines that can fire nuclear warheads while submerged. Israel also has nuclear landmines, for use on the Golan, against the Syrians. There is nuclear artillery.

"Further, it is believed, Israel has thermonuclear weapons – H-bombs – and neutron bombs. These, in practical application, would inactivate the Arabs on whom they were unleashed, but leaving the structure intact. (Israel also has biological and chemical weaponry facilities.)

"Their Jericho missiles can hit Baghdad and Teheran, as well as Baku and Odessa. Israel has targeted as many as eighty sites as possible recipients of nuclear devastation – amongst them: Cairo, Tripoli, Damascus, Ain Oussera in Algeria (their nuclear establishment), Kahuta in Pakistan (their nuclear facility), and others. As early as 1973 Israel was said to have a miniaturized nuclear bomb that would fit into a suitcase.

"With a 1650 pound nuclear warhead, Israel's rockets have a range of 3600 miles. With a reduced warhead of 650 pounds, their rockets can travel 5500 miles.

"With such massive strength, it is obvious that Israel can, (or, as it certainly should have done) confront any or all of the major

159

nuclear powers and state her requirements, to which they would have no choice but to comply. By virtue of her strength, Israel can dictate the terms for her own survival. She can take her seat amongst the major nuclear powers of the world, who would have no choice but to accept whatever terms Israel might choose to impose, concerned with her own continued existence.

"The Arabs' loftiest aspiration continues to be the elimination of Israel. In this, the Administration of the United States of America fully concurs, as Alan J. Brady has made apparent. In fact, the American Government views the disappearance of Israel as an important objective, and pursues this goal with alacrity. As a counter-measure, the Government of Israel decided to reveal its nuclear strength, without actually admitting to it.

"This took a very considerable amount of maneuvering; they set up a disgruntled nuclear technician, by the name of Mordechai Vanunu, whom they obviously invited in to the nuclear establishment at Dimona and told him what to photograph. On his own Vanunu would never have known what to photograph; it is clear that someone guided him in his efforts, since his technical expertise was too limited to be able to discern the functioning of the devices he was told to photograph.

"He ultimately made his way to Europe, where his photographs appeared in the London Times, who revealed that Israel was the Number Six nuclear power in the world.

"So the world knew, and Israel could deny it, but no doubt the Arabs got the message. And that was what Israel wanted.

"Israel carried on the fiction that Vanunu had sneaked into Dimona and took 'Forbidden' photographs. They then went to the trouble of sending a Mossad agent to London to facilitate his return to Israel, and actually kidnapped him in order to bring this about. Back in Israel he was sentenced to eighteen years in prison.

"Israel's conduct in dealing with Mordechai Vanunu spawned a very considerable amount of condemnation and hostility generated by the London Times, who felt that it had an exceptionally good excuse for beating Israel, with Vanunu as the very effective stick."

The phone rings. Mark picks it up. "Spaulding."

"Mark, it's Claire," a voice says weakly.

Concerned, Mark asks, "Are you all right, Claire."

160

"Not really. Listen to me, Mark. Don't talk. Don't ask questions."

Her voice tapers off. There is silence.

Mark is aware that his hand that holds the phone is shaking. "Claire?"

"I'm here, Mark. Can you hear me?"

"Not too well."

"I'm sorry about that, Mark. I'm sorry about a lot of things. Listen to me. It's my fault. It's all my fault. Everything is my fault. To spite you, Mark, to hurt you – I told everything -"

"Told what, Clarie? To whom?"

"George Warton. The Defense Department. That we have the Brady Papers. That's why they got Bill. You're next. I killed him. I can't live with that. I can't live with what I have done to you. They'll kill you, too, Mark."

"Claire -"

"I don't want to live, Mark. I can't. I've taken sleeping pills. The whole bottle. It will be over soon. All over. I'll be glad. Then I'll have some peace."

"Claire!" Mark shouts. "Don't do anything!"

"I've done it, Mark. It's too late. The whole bottle."

There is silence.

"Claire! Claire! Can you hear me?"

No sound comes through.

"Claire!"

Mark listens intently. He hears nothing.

He puts down the phone and dials the police.

"An attempted suicide . . . Georgetown." He gives the address.

He rushes out into the street and hails a cab.

"Georgetown," he says to the driver. "In a hurry."

They move out into traffic. The driver says to Mark, "You can say 'hurry'. And I can try to hurry. But there ain't no hurrying, Mister. Anybody can see that. Not in this here city. Not going to Georgetown. I'm sorry about that, man. I'd sure like to oblige. But 'hurry' – that's one thing you just can't do nohow."

26

Mark reaches Claire's apartment building. He pushes the button. He pushes it frantically. There is no response. The police should be here. Maybe they're not answering the bell.

He pushes the Superintendent's bell. And he pushes Claire's bell again, holding it down. Then it's the Superintendent's bell again. Silence. Silence.

A man appears, presumably the Superintendent, looking from behind the glass outer door with a combination of annoyance and suspicion, uncertain as to whether he should bother opening the door.

Mark pounds frantically on the glass door. Now the Super is mostly annoyed. But the urgency of Mark's pounding creates an element of curiosity. He moves slowly toward the door, opens it a crack.

"I've come about Miss Alderson in 708. She may be ill."

"I don't know nothin' about that. I ain't seen her around for a while. You a doctor?"

"No. A friend. She phoned me a little while ago."

"Then you shoulda' asked her, Mister."

"She told me she was ill. She could be dead by now."

"Dead!" the Super repeats in surprise.

"Are the police here?" Mark asks.

"Police? I ain't seen no police."

"I phoned them."

"They ain't come, Man. I would'ah seen 'em if they did. No one can't come in here without me seein' 'em."

"We'd better get up to Miss Alderson's apartment."

"Won't do no good. I ain't got the key."

"We'll have to break down the door."

"I ain't breakin' down no doors."

"I'll do it."

"You can't do that neither. That sort of thing ain't permitted."

"The lady could be dead. Dead! Do you understand me? Dead!"

"You sure?"

"No. But she took a bottle of sleeping pills."

The Super thinks about that, inquires dubiously, "A whole bottle?"

"It would appear so."

"Then maybe we should get up there. But you got to take the responsibility for that there door."

"I'll take it."

They take the elevator up to the seventh floor. They go to Claire's apartment. Mark rings the bell. He pounds on the door.

"Claire! Claire!"

No response.

It's a very solid door.

"You sure you gonna be responsible for that there door."

"Absolutely sure."

"Them there police sure ain't in no big rush gettin' anywhere these days – what with all them murders they got to deal with."

Washington D.C. is Murder City. Crime City. Drug City. The nation's capital. It all happens here. You have to wait your turn to be carted off, hauled away. Mugging, rape, robbery, assault, stick-up, store break-ins. Attempted suicide? Wait your turn. At least you know who did that one. Only one suspect. And you did it by choice. You didn't have to do it. If we get there quick, we might be able to save you. Yeah, maybe. So what? You might try it again. If you want to go, why should we stop you? It's nice and neat – pretty neat. You should see some we have to deal with – face shot away. And plenty of blood. And then you got to try and find the guy who did it. All in the nation's capital.

Mark throws himself against the door. The wood splatters. Part of the door clings to the lock. Mark throws himself against the door again. The door falls away.

The Super is impressed. "You sure is one powerful man."

Claire is in bed, looking very pale. The telephone receiver is off the cradle, laying on the floor, hanging from the cord. The empty pill bottle is near by.

The Super nods. "You was right, Man. She sure do look dead to me."

Mark shakes her. She is unresponsive flesh.

Mark picks the phone receiver off the floor. He rings the police again.

163

27

It is at home. Sandy says to David, "Are you interested in doing something useful for your people?"

"Which people are those, Mom?" David inquires, a note of suspicion in his voice.

"The Jewish people."

"Oh, those people. I thought they were your people, too."

"You don't seem to think so – nor does anybody else."

"What do you want me to do?"

"It isn't so much that I want you to do anything. It's – if you want to. I'm demonstrating in front of the Israeli Embassy – on behalf of the Brady's. Would you like to come with me?"

"Do you think it will do any good?"

"I know it won't do any good if we don't make the effort."

"I'm not sure."

Sandy shrugs. "Up to you. Here's something real to do. But you don't have to. Don't feel obligated, David."

"Who else is going to be there?"

"Rabbi Moreheim."

David is surprised. "Rabbi Moreheim."

"That's right. He organized it."

"Was it his idea?"

"Mine, actually. I suggested it to him. He thought it was a very good idea."

"I'll come."

"Good."

They go to the Israeli Embassy. There are about fifty people there.

Rabbi Moreheim shakes hands with David. "Glad you could come," Rabbi Moreheim says to David.

"So am I."

They carry placards that say: ISRAEL BETRAYED THE BRADYS. IS-RAEL, DEMAND THE IMMEDIATE RELEASE OF THE BRADYS. ALAN BRADY IS IN AN AMERICAN CONCENTRATION CAMP.

The press is there. They do a lot of interviews. They take a lot of photographs.

Shlomo Ha'gill, the First Secretary at the Israeli Embassy, comes out to talk with Sandy and Rabbi Moreheim. He tries to restrain his anger.

"How does this help Israel?" he demands.

"We want to be proud of Israel," Rabbi Moreheim explains. "What Israel did to the Bradys does not make us proud."

"You have to understand our position," Ha'gill says.

"We do. And you have to understand why we are taking ours."

Shlomo Ha'gill does not even try to conceal his anger now. He storms back into the Embassy.

Returning home afterwards, Sandy asks David, "Glad you came?"

"Yeah. I feel like I did something."

"Me, too."

28

The telephone rings in Sandy's office. She picks it up.

"This is Jacob Ben Zvi," the voice at the other end of the line says. "I am from the Brady Campaign."

Sandy didn't know there was one. The man has an Israeli accent.

"In fact," Ben Zvi continues, "I am the world-wide head of the 'Campaign for Alan Brady.' In Israel I represent the 'All-Party Knesset Committee for Alan Brady'."

Sandy is deeply suspicious.

"I hope your efforts extend also to Leah Brady," Sandy says coolly.

"Of course. Of course. She is in our heart. Always in our heart. I have heard about the wonderful work you are doing for Alan Brady."

He has obviously seen the pictures in the papers of the demonstration in front of the Israeli Embassy. That wouldn't have pleased him much. It had had very good coverage. No doubt this man and Shlomo Ha'gill, the First Secretary at the Israeli Embassy, had conferred on the subject. One of the pictures in the paper was that of Ha'gill looking very distraught as he spoke to Rabbi Moreheim and herself, with David looking on. David had been delighted with the picture. He'd cut it out and hung it

165

up on his bedroom wall, and shown it to his friend Aaron with such evident pride. "I really am glad I went with you," he'd said at home later. "I felt like I was doing something. Something really important." Sandy had replied, "You were. Something really important."

Ben Zvi says, "I would like to meet with you, Mrs. Spaulding, and talk with you – and hear all about your work for Alan Brady."

"And Leah Brady."

"Naturally. It goes without saying. I want to tell you what we are doing. And I want to discuss how we can work together."

Sandy feels herself bristling. The man is no doubt an Israeli Government representative – the same government that had betrayed Alan Brady in the first place. This is the enemy, she thinks – dressed up to look like a friend, but not sufficiently well-dressed to be very convincing. But she would meet with him, hear what he has to say, let him provide a further insight into the insidious behavior that has characterized Israeli actions from the beginning. And he will hear what she has to say.

"Yes," Sandy says, "I'm sure we will have a great deal to talk about."

They make a date. A little while later Ben Zvi comes to her office.

She does not find him an impressive figure, not disarming, not someone she would trust, or believe.

"Please call me Jacob," he tells her.

She does not want to call him Jacob. She does not want the intimacy of a first name relationship. She does not tell him to call her Sandy. She does not like the man, or the man's mission.

"Mrs. Spaulding, I am glad – we are glad for your involvement in this cause. It makes me feel good – that you care so much. We appreciate it deeply."

"I'm really glad to hear that, Mr. Ben Zvi."

Jacob Ben Zvi winces slightly, aware that he has not put himself over as the friend and confidante he would have preferred, insisting as she does upon calling him Mister.

"But I am not sure how much it helps the cause," Ben Zvi goes on, "demonstrating in front of the Israeli Embassy."

"I am. Otherwise I wouldn't do it."

"Your heart is in the right place, Mrs. Spaulding. But do you know, the truth of the matter is, it doesn't help Alan Brady. In fact, it hurts him. It hurts him very much. It gives the wrong impression."

"To whom?"

"To the friends of Israel."

"Tell me, Mr. Ben Zvi, what are you and your committee doing?"

"We are working behind the scenes."

Sandy smiles to herself: working behind the scenes – it rolls off so smoothly, and is obviously well-rehearsed, has no doubt been repeated many times.

"Working how, 'behind the scenes', Mr. Ben Zvi? What are you doing there behind the scenes?"

Ben Zvi pauses for drama. Sandy thinks that this must be rehearsed, too.

"It is very delicate," Ben Zvi says reluctantly.

"I'm sure that it is," Sandy says, her voice heavy with sarcasm, lost, or ignored here. "Why don't you give me a clue."

"It has to remain secret – at least for now."

"I don't want to pry, Mr.Ben Zvi, but quite frankly, I don't think you're doing anything – at least nothing constructive – nothing that includes making the effort to get these two people out of prison."

Ben Zvi appears wounded. "Mrs. Spaulding, we want to avoid a confrontation with the United States. This is perfectly reasonable. It would be bad for the Jews. The Jews in this country will be the ones to suffer."

"I don't think the government of Israel cares a damn for the Jews in this country – except as a source of money."

"That's a very unkind thing to say, Mrs. Spaulding. We feel very deeply about the Diaspora. We have things under control. We ask you, please, don't upset the boat. Do you want us all to drown?"

"The fact of the matter is, you are in control of nothing."

"Perhaps it is only damage control – but we know this is what has to be done. We ask for your help and your cooperation. That is not too much to ask, Mrs. Spaulding."

"You are asking the Jews to surrender."

"If you were Jewish you would understand what I am trying to say, Mrs. Spaulding. This is not really your problem. You have decided to make it into one. To play with it. To involve yourself. All very nice – but it is us it hurts. Israel. Jews. All of us."

"On the contrary, Mr. Ben Zvi, mine is a Jewish family, and my birth as a non-Jew has nothing to do with it. Judaism is my chosen way of life. But further, as a lawyer, I want to see justice done."

"My very point, Mrs. Spaulding. You want justice. So do we. We have been fighting for it for almost two thousand years – and we have seen very little of it. Now at last we have our own country. In it we can see some justice. We need to protect it."

"The Jews of America need to stand up for this man, and this woman. We can't hide from this one. You, and Israel, are doing us a grave disservice – and at the same time you are inflicting the most serious damage on Israel itself."

"I feel that you are being insensitive to the problems Jews face. Jews are in an extremely exposed position. Israel is in an exposed position. You would be doing us both a service to leave things to me – to my committees – here and in Israel. For us this isn't a hobby. This isn't a play-thing. This is life or death."

"You are right Mr. Ben Zvi. For us it is life or death. And how we go about it will decide whether Israel survives, whether we survive as Jews. We need to take the strongest possible action – as opposed to your policy of inaction. You are leading Israel to the slaughter. We don't want that to happen. And neither do we want to disappear. This is what you are trying to make us do. You want us to be invisible – pretend that you did not betray this man."

"We know that we are in danger. That's why it's more sensible for us to repudiate this man."

"It's not safer to push our brother into the gas oven. You have merely bought some time. But the rest of us will invariably follow."

"You talk very casually about gas ovens."

"We know them from first-hand experience. They are a part of our life. We know when the threat is there. We live and relive the torment and torture of the concentration camp every day of our lives. This happened to us. If you recall that picture in the paper, Mr. Ben Zvi, someone in that demonstration carried a placard that said, 'Alan Brady is in an American concentration camp'. That's right. As long as he is there, we are there, too. Jews are vulnerable – and the only way we will ever become less so, is to fight – to demand what belongs to us, our rightful safe and secure place. That has been in very short supply for us throughout our history. Israel's existence was supposed to provide it – for all of us. But it hasn't. In fact it has created insecurity – a new insecurity –

betrayed itself, and all of us. When they imprison Alan Brady, and we let them do it, they know they can do it to the rest of us, too."

Ben Zvi does not reply. He just looks at Sandy, overwhelmed, in awe, with a begrudging admiration that he does not want to feel. Perhaps he has not convinced this woman of the correctness of his arguments, the reasonableness of his cause, but others will listen – have to listen. The Government of Israel knows what it is doing. It knows what it has to do. He will lead, and the Jewish people will follow. The Government has a program. It all makes sense.

Sandy clutches the arms of her chair. Her heart is beating rapidly. The words had flowed out of her, spontaneously, expressing all that was deep inside her – perhaps until now – the feeling that went with them, repressed. Now they are out. She feels overwhelmed. But she also feels very good. Absolutely marvelous.

29

Sandy continues to sit in her chair, long after Ben Zvi has departed. She had said "we" and "us". We and us – not "they". "We" the Jews, "Us" the Jews. Not "they" the Jews. What had suddenly brought about this change, almost in mid-sentence? "Us" the Jews. She likes this. "We" the Jews. It is comfortable. It is right. It is her.

"We Jews," she says out loud. "We Jews!" she shouts out.

I am one, she thinks.

She smiles. Then she laughs – out loud. "I am a Jew!" she shouts.

How do I know?

Because I feel like I am.

Not until now? Why now?

Because I have been in the Jewish wars. This one. It's a nasty war. Brother against brother. Like the War Between the States. I am for Alan Brady. I fight for him. I fight for him because he is a Jew, who fought for a Jewish cause – who fought to save Israel. What else could I do except fight for Alan Brady?

I am in the Jewish war – deep into it. I deserve to be a Jew. I have earned the right to be a Jew.

169

Why now? Why has it taken so long?

Why? Why?

Because I needed the blood of battle. The encounters on behalf of Alan Brady. I needed to know what it felt like to be a Jew. Needed to know what it felt like to be told this was not my fight because I was not a Jew. Needed a Ben Zvi to come here and say my efforts were those of someone pursuing a hobby – not someone who had suffered two thousand years of persecution, and dreamed, generation after generation, of the redemption of Israel.

No, not my culture. Not my background.

But it is now. I have the blood of battle on my hands. That blood will never come off – the battle of Ralph Lowenberg, and Jacob Ben Zvi – and the war that killed Bill Cooper.

But why now? What has taken so long? Your husband asked. Your son asked.

They want you to be one of them.

And you said no. Did you not feel like one of them?

Yes. Yes and no. Not all the way.

Why? Why?

I was afraid.

That down deep you were the anti-Semite you talked about to Miriam and Rabbi Moreheim?

No! No! But could my culture and history and background have conditioned me, left a residue of the Christian values that reek of anti-Semitism? They could.

But did they?

I don't believe it.

Are you sure?

Absolutely.

Then why?

I was afraid.

Afraid? Afraid of what?

The suffering. The pain.

What suffering?

Of the Jewish people.

Now we are getting somewhere. Afraid that you had to take it on – their pain – their suffering?

I did not want to ache for them. I did not want to endure their two thousand years of suffering. I didn't want the concentration

170

camps to be mine. I didn't want the gas ovens to be mine. Do you know how much this hurts? Do you know the pain that I have to endure? I did not want it.

Inside me, perhaps unconsciously, I refused to take on this pain, this burden. I said no to my husband. No to my son. I understand this now. Alan Brady taught me. Leah Brady has taught me. I am with them, and I hurt.

I'm not afraid any more. Because it has already happened. And now I belong to them. I belong to my husband and his people, to my son and all of his people who will follow.

The pain is there. But I'm not afraid of it any more. I will endure it, as if I were born with it, as if it has always been with me. Alan Brady has taught me not to try and run from it, to hide from it – but to accept it – to accept it with pride.

Sandy picks up the phone. She dials.

At the other end a voice says, "Moreheim."

"It's Sandy. Listen, Michael. I'm converting."

There is a moment of silence. Then, from the other end of the line, "Yahoo!" the victory cry of Johnny Reb.

"That is, if you want to do it."

"Yes, Sandy, I do. This is a very happy day."

"For me, too. Are you very busy? Can I come over and see you now, Michael?"

"I'm not busy at all. It's as if I have been waiting for you – and this was the day."

"I'm at the office, but I know I'm not going to do a stitch of work. No use trying. It isn't every day a woman decides to convert. I haven't told anybody else – not Mark, not David – not anybody. I just decided now. This moment. I wanted you to be the first to know."

"I'm very flattered, Sandy. What made you decide?"

"Because I'm not afraid any more."

"That sounds very deep, Sandy. You'll have to tell me about it when we meet."

"I'm coming right now, Michael."

Sandy rings Rabbi Moreheim's bell. Sarah, Rabbi Moreheim's wife, opens the door.

She throws her arms around Sandy. "I'm so happy," she says.

Rabbi Moreheim appears. He and Sandy hug.

"Yahoo!" They both shout in unison. And they all laugh.

"Sandy," Rabbi Moreheim says, "amongst the things that have given me the greatest happiness, are my marriage, and the birth of my children, and now, today, still another, is your decision to become Jewish. I know you had some reservations."

"I did. Because I was afraid. When you take on the responsibility of being a Jew, you take on the history, and the pain that goes with it."

"You're quite right, Sandy. You have a remarkable insight."

"And that is what I didn't want. It wasn't mine. I didn't want to have to take it on. But now I'm not afraid of it any more. Because I've acknowledged it. I can accept it. And I can hurt. I can hurt for all that our people have suffered. I can hurt for Alan Brady – and Leah. I can demonstrate with you, and I am one of you. I am a 'We'. An 'Us'. Your pain is my pain, and always will be."

"And our joy is your joy -" Rabbi Moreheim says.

"And always will be," Sandy replies.

30

Mark is driving home from work. It is night. For some time the same set of headlights have been reflecting in his rear view mirror. They were there almost from the time he had left the office. He is suspicious. But then, when isn't he?

He touches his jacket for reassurance. It's there – the Jericho. He slows down. The lights behind slow down. He speeds up. The lights behind speed up. They have been with him for some time now – on the Beltway, then off on the open road, and now on this quiet road not all that far from home.

Should he try to outrun them? They might catch up. Lose them? Why? And are they really following him? Or is it just imagination.

He turns off into a side road, a quiet country road, and drives slower than before. The lights make the turn. They are right behind him now. No question, is there? No doubt. Mark feels a sense of relief. He had been expecting something. And now, here it is. He does not want to run. He wants the confrontation. He almost welcomes it.

And they, obviously, are not making any serious effort to conceal their presence. They want him to know about them – to fill him with fear and panic. It gives them the psychological advantage, they assume. They are closing in for the kill.

Suddenly Mark swerves off the road, and onto the hard shoulder. He jumps out of his car, makes it over the log fence, and is in the woods. The car that has been following pulls up behind his. Three men jump out. Two of them are carrying cut-down pump-action shotguns. The third has a Beretta autoloader – Italian – now the official U.S. side-arm, since displacing Colt. The one with the Beretta is George Warton.

Mark watches from behind a tree, his Jericho firmly in his hand. It's dark, but not dark enough to prevent him from seeing what is happening.

"Let's get that Jew-bastard," Warton says.

The two with the shotguns look off into the woods, but make no effort to move into them.

"Come on, let's go," Warton orders the men. "We may never get another chance like this. The bastard's a sitting-duck."

"What if he's armed?" one of the gunners asks.

"He probably isn't. And besides, you guys got pumps. You won't have any trouble dealing with him."

Reluctantly they move toward the fence, Warton bringing up the rear.

The first one climbs over the fence. Then the second. Then Warton.

The three of them are standing there, looking about.

Mark steps from behind the tree, fires at the first.

He drops.

He squeezes the trigger again. The second one drops.

Warton fires at him.

He gets Mark in the shoulder.

Mark squeezes off a shot, but misses.

Warton ducks behind a tree. "You bastard," Warton shrieks. "You rotten Jew bastard. I told you I'd get you."

Mark can feel the blood trickling down his arm. With his right hand, clutching the Jericho, he rubs it over his shoulder. It comes away covered in blood.

"Get me now, you son of a bitch," Mark calls back. "Get me now!"

Warton fires the Beretta in the direction of the tree where Mark had been standing. But Mark isn't standing there now. He is trying to outflank Warton. The blood is dripping down, but he feels no pain. He feels exhilarated. Two down. One to go.

"Get me now, Warton, you stupid son of a bitch."

Warton is confused. He does not know where Mark is.

"I'll get you if it's the last thing I ever do, Jew-bastard!"

Warton steps out from behind his tree, shoots in the direction of Mark's voice.

Mark squeezes the trigger three times in rapid succession.

"It *is* the last thing you'll ever do," Mark says to Warton, as Warton drops to the ground, dead before he touches the cold floor of the woods.

31

There is a hearing. The Defense Department claims that it was the work of embittered individuals – that Warton, with the help of some friends, was out to redress the humiliation he – Warton – had suffered at the hands of Mark Spaulding.

It has nothing to do with the Defense Department, they insist. Nothing at all. The fact that it was a Defense Department vehicle that Warton employed – the same one, incidentally, that had killed Bill Cooper, has no relevance; it was merely that Warton had access to it.

The Defense Department insists that Warton acted on his own, and that they – The Department of Defense – deplore Warton's unilateral action. They don't actually say, in so many words, that they understand Warton's desire for revenge, but make it unmistakably clear that that is precisely what they feel.

Mark is completely exonerated, seen to have acted in self-defense. The newspaper columnists not in government pockets revel in Mark's confrontation. They have no question who was behind this attack, and the earlier one on Bill Cooper. There is immense gratification that Mark has acted so effectively and so heroically.

Mark recovers quickly from his wound. When his hand moves

to his shoulder, he remembers with satisfaction how he dealt with Warton and his friends. He is also aware that the other two he had dispatched bore descriptions very similar to those of the men in the car that had killed Bill Cooper. Mark feels that in a small way justice has been done – that he had been the administrator.

His picture fills the newspapers. People recognize him as he goes about his daily life. There is general agreement that he did a very good job.

Sandy, thinking about that night, trembles. How easily he could have been killed. How close he was to death.

David never felt fear for his father. He always knew his father could handle any situation.

32

"*Baruch, ataw adonai elohaynu* . . ." Blessed be thou, oh Lord our God . . ." Sandy recites in Hebrew, then in English, as she lights the Sabbath candles, reciting the traditional blessing.

She wears a white lace scarf over her head. There is a radiance, a holiness, about her as she touches the flame to each of the candles.

Mark stands near her. David stands next to his father, his arm around his father's waist, his father's arm over his shoulder.

Milada stands nearby, slightly to the side. Her hair is silver-gray. She is a handsome woman, obviously still in control. She wears a midnight blue suit. Her arms are pressed against her sides. She imbibes the solemnity of the situation. She does not want the tears of joy to flow down her cheeks, but she is reluctant to wipe them away for fear of making them too obvious.

Sandy concludes the ritual. She turns to her mother-in-law, and they embrace. The tears are running down Sandy's cheeks, too.

"I'm yours now," Sandy says to her mother-in-law. "I belong to you."

"You have always belonged to us," Milada replies.

Sandy and Mark embrace.

"Do I get a hug and a kiss from my son?" Sandy asks David. "A hug and a kiss for your Jewish mother?"

"For my Jewish mother, any time."

Mother and son embrace.

Sandy is pleased with herself. This is the first time she has lit the Sabbath candles. The first time as a Jewish woman, a Jewish wife, a Jewish mother.

They all sit down to the Sabbath meal.

The candles burn happily, merrily.

"Well, David," Sandy asks, "how does it feel to have a Jewish mother?"

"Like you've come home."

"I'm not sure that's a compliment."

"It is, Mom. That's how I mean it."

"In that case, I'm glad. I am home. Truly home. I want you to know that I did it because I was ready, because I wanted to – not because anybody pushed me into it. I have a great sense of relief. And you are right, David, it is like coming home."

Milada, who retains a touch of her Czech accent, says, "Sandy, I loved you as you were."

"With no reservations?"

"You were my son's choice. But I loved you for yourself. That you now light the Sabbath candles is a source of very deep pleasure and satisfaction for me. You always were, as far as I was concerned, a Jewish daughter. Now you have made an even more profound commitment, and I am very pleased, and very happy."

"Thank you, Milada. This is a very happy moment for me. I'll never forget it." She looks from her husband to her son. "Of course there is a down side," she says, a twinkle in her blue eyes. "Being Jewish isn't just *knaydl* soup and Israel Independence Day."

"What do you mean, Mom?" David asks suspiciously.

"Well, all of you take your Judaism for granted. It's just there. It's a part of you. You don't have to question it. But then I'm a convert. And, as you know, Jews don't seek converts – except when they're your wife and your mother – so that we converts have to work extra hard at it. We stick to the letter. We can argue Judaism with anybody. We know the rules. How would it be if we kept kosher?"

Mark looks at Sandy, surprised. "Kosher? Nobody has kept kosher in this family for a hundred years."

"That's my point. Maybe we should start. I've accepted the

tenets of Conservative Judaism. They are of the opinion that we should maintain the old traditions – at least in the home."

Mark says to his mother, "There's nothing worse than a convert."

"And that's not all," Sandy says, "You two should spend the day in the synagogue, *davening.*"

"That's Orthodox," David complains. "You had a Conservative conversion. They have regular services. We can all go together – with Aaron, and his parents."

"How did I get included in this synagogue attendance?" Mark demands humorously.

"It's what you wanted," Sandy says. "Now that I'm a Jewish wife – a converted Jewish wife, and you know the zeal of the convert – I don't want to see any backsliding around here. It's the woman who maintains and upholds the Jewish traditions in the family."

Mark says to Milada, "I'm not sure this conversion thing was such a good idea after all."

"I think it's great," David says.

"See," Mark says to his mother, "now there's conflict between my son and myself."

They laugh.

"And now," Sandy says, "we are all going to sing *Hatikva*"- the Israeli national anthem.

They look blank.

"You don't know it? Well, shame on you."

Sandy proceeds to sing it, first in Hebrew: *Kol od ba-leva penima . . .*" And then in English: "As long as in the heart, The Jewish spirit yearns, With eyes turned eastward, Looking towards Zion, Then our hope, The hope of two thousand years, Is not lost: To be a free nation in our land, The land of Zion and Jerusalem."

David goes over to his mother and kisses her on the cheek. "That was beautiful, Mom."

"Yes, I thought so," Sandy says loftily. "See that you learn it by next week. So that we can all sing it together."

"Okay, Mom. It's a promise."

Mark stands up and kisses Sandy on the top of her head. "That was beautiful."

"Thank you, Mark. That goes for you, too. A committed Zionist at least ought to know *Hatikva.*"

Milada leans over and kisses Sandy on the cheek. "I'm very happy tonight. And I too promise to learn *Hatikva.*"

"Good," Sandy says. "And there are some other Hebrew songs you'll need to know. I'll teach them to you."

33

Sandy enters the prison cell. It is dark and dank and smells vilely. It is the women's "correctional" institution in Connecticut where Leah has been incarcerated. It is the smell of human beings confined, and chemicals to cover up the smells. And chemicals meant to impede the multiplication of bacteria, which contributes further to the vileness. This is Leah's concentration camp. She is chained to her bed.

She is asleep now. It is the sleep of the tortured, of the tormented, in this "correctional" institution. This place, this chain, on this woman, is meant as coercion: Name names, tell us of the other Jewish traitors – there is a long list; just pick them out. And if you won't, we'll torture you until you do.

Sandy sits on the chair near Leah's bunk bed. She watches Leah. Despite all of this, Sandy notes, Leah remains a remarkably handsome and lovely woman. She looks filled with defiance and determination, but deathly pale, bearing the inevitable marks of torture. Sandy figures the *mezuzah* that she now wears around her neck. This is what it means to be Jewish – to sit in a prison cell with someone who is there for being a Jew. This is the pain that frightened her, that she knew she would have to endure. And now she is enduring it, face to face, looking with undiminished horror at the chain that is attached to a Jewish woman.

Leah stirs. Perhaps she senses Sandy's presence. Her eyes open. They fall on Sandy. She studies Sandy for a while, not speaking. Then at last she says, "Hello."

Sandy tries to smile. "Hello."

"You're not from the prison."

Sandy shakes her head.

"I didn't think so."

Sandy is trying to hold back her tears. She fights to do so. She knows the tears have welled up in her eyes. She does not want to break down in front of Leah. Her tears won't help.

"I'm a friend," Sandy says.

"Thank you for coming."

"You're a hard lady to get to see."

"Maybe that's why I don't have a lot of visitors."

"Are you always chained up this way?"

"Almost always. It's a part of the program – 'rehabilitation' – they call it," Leah says, smiles ironically.

The tears are streaming down Sandy's cheeks. "But why?"

Leah speaks softly, with effort. "They think it will help to convince Alan to name names – Jewish leaders he was supposed to have worked with – but didn't." She tells Sandy what has gone before. "It's to make Jews look like traitors."

Sandy sobs. She cannot control herself. The sobs come from deep inside her. Then, after a time, she manages to stop. "I'm sorry about that."

Leah smiles at her. She lifts her gaunt hand from underneath the blanket and holds it out to Sandy, who takes it in both of hers.

"Don't you have a lawyer?" Sandy asks.

"Not that I know of. If I do, he hasn't been around."

"What about Alan's parents? I read in the paper that Alan's father comes to see you all the time."

Leah shakes her head. "He's never been here."

"Then it's an unmitigated lie?"

Leah nods. "He appears better in the press than in real life."

Sandy continues to hold Leah's hand. "I've become involved in this terrible travesty of justice." She tells Leah about her efforts and herself. "Has Jacob Ben Zvi been here to see you – or any Israeli representative?"

"No."

"He told me they were looking after you. Another lie."

"They're good at that."

Sandy tells Leah of her encounter with Ralph Lowenberg, Executive Director of B'nai Israel.

"The Jewish leadership is frightened," Leah observes. "But I'm sure the people are prepared to fight for us – not just Jewish people – but all decent people."

"I have no doubt about it."

"Funny about Ralph Lowenberg," Leah says. "He was on the list

they gave Alan. With all his professed loyalty to the government –
he's still on their list of traitors."

Sandy volunteers to be Leah's lawyer, serving without pay. She
takes a notebook from her handbag. "For what periods of time
are you chained up?"

"Twelve hours. Sometimes more."

Sandy looks at Leah, shocked. "It's inhuman."

"It's part of the process."

"Nobody has seen you chained to your bed?"

"Everybody has seen me. They make no secret of it. The prison
social worker. The prison doctor."

"They say nothing?"

"They work for the system."

"What kind of medical attention are you receiving?"

"I have an intestinal problem. It started in prison. It developed
here."

"You're being treated for it?"

"No. They say I'm making it up."

"You're in physical pain?"

"Yes."

"And they ignore it?"

"They ignore the problem. They come to examine me – in
front of the guards – male guards."

"In order to humiliate you. For how long can you endure this?"

"For as long as I have to."

"Leah, in a hundred years they'll still be talking about you. You
are an inspiration to women – and to all of humanity. They won't
beat you. You're too strong. I have no doubt about it."

Leah nods. "Neither have I."

34

It is in the Old City of Jerusalem. They stand just back from the
Western Wall, in the area seen as appropriate for men and
women to fraternize, if they wish. David is here with his parents
and his grandparents. Rabbi Moreheim and his wife Sarah are
here; Jim and Miriam Haliday, and their son Aaron, David's

friend. Amos Bar Lev, Haganah Commander, Member of the Knesset, Cabinet Minister, has come with his wife. They are here from Kibbutz Gan Galil; Mordechai Gilboa, who worked with Jonathan and Milada in the DP camp in Germany, and who returned with them to Israel on the PT boat prior to the War of Independence; Mordechai's wife Hamalia; their daughter Rachel, who was three when Jonathan and Milada first met her at the kibbutz. Missing is Rachel's brother, Eitan, who was then five, the blond-haired, blue-eyed Israeli Huck Finn who had paid the price in full so that they could all gather here today. Rachel is here with her husband, Yossi Reshef, whose grandparents were amongst the founders of Kibbutz Degania. They have a daughter, Shashona, also present, almost fourteen, whose dark and won-drous eyes take in the scene. She allows herself the occasional glance at David, whom she engulfs with her eyes. When he catches her eye, and smiles at her, she turns away quickly, feeling herself blush.

Jonathan is also missing. And so is David Brown. But their presence is felt. At this place, at this time, how could they not be here?

There is a Bar Mitzvah taking place. It will soon conclude. Then it will be David's turn. It is a Bar Mitzvah of a boy from one of the Arab lands. His mother and sisters and aunts watch from the unsanctified zone and throw sweets and make the haunting Arab cry that expresses the joy of this time. They share the sweets with David and his family.

The boy, whose Bar Mitzvah it is, carries the Torah, his shoul-ders covered with a *tallis*, his head covered with a *yarmulkah*. His father is here, also carrying the Torah, his uncles, his brothers, their friends. They walk slowly toward the Wall, and they say the things that people say when they face this Wall – this Wall, that is the foundation, the life of the entire Jewish people.

This boy is a man. It is confirmed here and now. He is accepted as a responsible Jewish person, in the shadow of the Wall, that only now belongs wholly to the Jewish people, which the Arabs still claim. To thwart their ambitions, a soldier of the Israel Defense Force stands prepared, at this very moment in time, just feet away from those taking part in this holy ceremony, his Galil assault rifle ready.

Now it is David's time. He looks at the Wall – the Wailing Wall –

the Western Wall – and smiles with deepest pleasure and satisfaction. He turns to look at his family and friends gathered close to him, and feels overwhelmed by happiness, by the sudden reality that he is here, now, before this Wall, and it is the day, the moment, of his Bar Mitzvah. For how long had he waited for this, and wanted it, and thought it would never happen. But it is happening now.

The men in David's retinue move toward the entrance-way, as the women look on. The *shomer* – watchman, "Watchman of the Faith" – wants the Jewish men to put on the *tefillin* – the phylacteries – a ritualistic thong of leather that goes up the arm, required of religious Jews when reciting the first prayers of the day.

Rabbi Moreheim puts on the *tefillin*. He is not allowed to officiate here, at David's Bar Mitzvah, since his Jewish faith – Conservative – is not recognized by the ultra-Orthodox who control this domain. He is here only in the capacity of friend of the family.

Amos Bar Lev declines the opportunity to utter the ritualistic prayers. Aaron Haliday puts on the *tefillin*, followed by his father. Mordechai Gilboa declines. His son-in-law Yossi declines. Judge Fraser stops in front of the *shomer*, and offers his arm. David and Mark and the other men look on, startled.

"You are Jew?" the *shomer* asks Judge Fraser, scrutinizing him skeptically.

Judge Fraser now wears a *yarmulkah* on his head, having replaced the maroon and black I'M FOR JUDGE FRASER baseball cap he had been wearing earlier. "Of course," he replies.

The *shomer* shrugs. He may harbor some doubts, but if the man insists he is a Jew, who is he – the *shomer* – to argue?

He winds the phylacteries around the Judge's arm, recites the prayer in Hebrew, line by line, and Judge Fraser repeats the *shomer*'s words. Judge Fraser is delighted with himself. He is beaming.

David puts his arms around his grandfather and kisses him. "That was very good, Grandpa."

"I thought so myself. I might take to doing that every morning. What were them words again?"

"I'll write them out for you, Grandpa."

"I'd sure appreciate it."

The *shomer* wants Mark to put on the phylacteries. Mark has no

182

wish to do so, and resists the *shomer*'s efforts. He has never done it before; it is not his Judaism.

David says to his father, "Please, Dad."

Mark succumbs. He knows he would never refuse his son's request – this, or any other. He allows the man, who regards this conquest, and all of the others, as a *mitzvah* – a blessing, counted in his favor by God.

The *shomer* winds on the *tefellin*. Mark repeats the prayers offered first by the *shomer*.

Then it is done. "Thanks, Dad," David says.

Mark feels slightly compromised. "Any time." But he realizes he is glad that he did it, before the Wall. It is not a religious expression, but a historical one, as far as he is concerned. His father would have done it. He wishes his father were here now. His father, who had helped to make this country, would have been pleased and proud.

The boy whose Bar Mitzvah has just now been, hands the Torah – the Scroll of the Law – to David, who takes it in both of his arms.

"*Besader?*" the boy asks – All right?

David nods. "*Besader*," he replies solemnly. All right.

The boy hugs David and says, "*Shalom*."

"*Shalom*," David responds.

The boy's father hands his Torah to Mark.

"From where do you come?" the boy's father asks.

"The United States."

"We are from Iraq. Now we are all here together – in Israel – and our sons are having their Bar Mitzvah on this day, before this Wall. God is good to us."

Mark nods.

The boy's father hugs Mark. "God bless you," he says.

"Thank you. May your son bring you much pleasure."

"He does. And he will. I know that yours does, and always will. I can see that."

One of the boy's uncles gives his Torah to Judge Fraser who takes it and holds it with pride, delighted to have it in his arms, as if he has been given a gift, straight from the hand of God.

The other men take up the Torah in their arms.

David reads from the Torah.

And David has his Bar Mitzvah. He looks up from the scroll – to confirm that he is here, in this place, and that it is happening to him. There is his father, and his grandfather, Rabbi Moreheim, Jim and Aaron Haliday, Amos Bar Lev, Mordechai Gilboa, and his son-in-law Yossi Reshef, and each holds the Torah, and there is the Wall. And behind him, further back, is his mother, and his grandmother Milada, and his grandmother Ella May, Mrs. Moreheim, Mrs. Bar Lev, Miriam Haliday, Hamalia Gilboa, Rachel, and Shashona – even prettier than he remembered. They are here. And he is here, and it is real, and it is all happening to him.

His eyes turn back to the Hebrew words, and he feels comfort as he recites.

Today, David Spaulding is confirmed in his Judaism.

He goes to his mother, whom he hugs and to his two grandmothers. And his father, and his grandfather. The men shake his hand warmly. The women kiss him. He stands before Shashona. She would like to kiss him, too. But she remains immobile. He stoops down and kisses her gently on the cheek. She goes crimson.

"Thank you," he says to them all. "Thank you for coming here. Thank you for making it possible for me to be here. Today I am the happiest, and I am sure, the luckiest boy – man – in this whole world. I'll do my best, to make you proud, always."

They are silent, savoring this moment.

David says, "I'd like to have a little talk with the Wall, say thanks – to Grandpa Jonathan."

This is a Wall to which you can chat, pray, cry, make personal requests. Thousands of pieces of paper flutter in the breeze, between the ancient stones, written in many languages, requesting divine intervention, because, in this place, God is more inclined to be listening.

David goes to the Wall. So does Judge Fraser, as if in a great hurry, in order to say all that is bursting forth. Mark goes, too, but he moves slowly. Aaron goes, too, and takes a place next to David. The other men drift slowly, but purposefully, to the Wall.

Sandy goes, and Milada and Ella May, and the other women, to the section fenced off from that of the men, whom they might "otherwise distract".

David lays his hand on the Wall. He glances at the man standing not far away from him, a soldier, wearing a red beret – the Goloni Division? David wonders – one of Israel's finest. He is not very much older than David. Leaning against the Wall, near the soldier, is a Galil Assault Rifle, made in Israel. The soldier touches the Wall gently with both of his hands, and speaks to it in Hebrew.

David says softly, in the direction of the soldier, "Thank you for keeping this Wall ours. Thank you for letting me come here today." He turns to the Wall and speaks: "I have a lot of 'thank-yous'. So many . . . I wish you could've been here today, Grandpa Jonathan, standing close to me, holding the Torah. I never met you. But I know all about you. I'm sure you are here. I know you wouldn't want to miss my Bar Mitzvah. And I wish David was here – David Brown, who fought with you, so we could have Jerusalem . . . I'm named after him . . . It's what you wanted. You told Dad. I wish I had known him . . . I can see him in my mind's eye, standing near you, holding the Torah, too. He must be here. I know he will live here forever. Thank you, Grandpa Jonathan. And thank you, David Brown. I'm proud to have your name.

"Thank you, Grandma Milada, and Amos Bar Lev. Thank you, Mordechai Gilboa, and Eitan Gilboa – who gave his life so I could stand here now.

"Thank you, Mom. Thank you for becoming Jewish. Thank you for letting me be Jewish . . . Thank you, Dad, for being who you are. And thank you, Rabbi Moreheim. As I stand next to this Wall – our Wall – I pledge to be a credit to my people. On this day of my Bar Mitzvah, when I am accepted into the Jewish Community, I will do all that I can to serve my people."

David, still facing the Wall, reaches out his right arm to Aaron, who, also facing the Wall, locks hands with David.

"And thank you, Aaron," David says to the Wall, "for being my friend. And for being so certain that this day would happen for me. I needed your faith. It was always there."

Aaron, still clasping David's hand in his, speaks to the Wall. "I knew that this day would happen – because it had to happen – just as this Wall had to be restored to us – to our people. I am glad of who I am. I am glad of who you are, David. Thank you for being my friend. We will be friends forever. We will fight for Israel. And for this Wall, and for all of our people. Today, David, it is official for you. Let's go together, hand in hand."

They turn from the Wall, and they embrace each other.

Not far away, Judge Fraser talks to the Wall. "Lord," he says, "you sure been good to me – to us. Better than anybody has the right to ask or expect. I'm here, Lord, as You can see, talkin' to You direct, 'bout as direct as you can get. At first I had the feeling I was speaking to my son-in-law's Jewish God, which don't make no matter to me. But then, standing here, holding the Torah, it was plain to see that we Christians had been borrowing the Jewish God – that we had You on loan, and decided to make you our own personal property. But it ain't like that, is it, Lord? There is only one God, and we are sharing Him with the Jews.

"And anyway, I got us special connections. I got me a Jewish son-in-law – naw, not a son-in-law – a son. You couldn't want no better son, neither. And Sandy got him for me. I tell you, Lord, we been havin' one great old time together all these years. And then you give me a grandson. He's a grandson to be proud of. Today is his Bar Mitzvah. Today he's a man – a Jewish man. I'm really happy to be here, carrying that there Torah, and being a part of this here whole thing.

"Ella May was right. If Sandy loved Mark, then Ella May did, too, and there weren't no question 'bout that as far as she was concerned. It took me a bit longer to come 'round. But I tell You, Lord, I couldn't love that boy no more than I already do. Sandy done the right thing to convert. We didn't lose her because she did; it made 'em into a whole Jewish family. And that has to be a good thing, Lord. If she didn't, my grandson couldn't have no Bar Mitzvah here today – and I wouldn't be here, and I wouldn't be carrying no Torah."

Mark speaks to the Wall: "It's worked out well, Dad. I'm sorry you're not here. I'm sure it would please you – it was you and a few others who made it all possible. I know things have not gone as you would have wished. But you gave us this day, so that my son, your grandson, could have this moment before this Wall.

"We've got problems here, Dad. I'm not sure how they're going to get sorted out. I'm very concerned for this land – very apprehensive . . . Dad . . . I've never stopped missing you."

Over in the women's section, Ella May speaks to the Wall: "It's been a good day, Lord. And a good life. Thank You. You know how happy I am to be here, to be at the Wall, where our grandson can take part in this beautiful and historic ceremony. We're pleased that our daughter has decided that she wants to be Jewish. It's a very great commitment. It's a grave responsibility. But she's up to it. I know it's not easy for the Jewish people. It's not easy for this country. The Lord is supposed to be here, but sometimes I wonder. He doesn't always seem to hear his people."

Milada touches the Wall gently, rubbing her hand against the stone. "Ours," she says. "Forevermore? I don't know. It doesn't come with guarantees. Each generation has to fight anew . . . we need you . . . our Wall . . . Without you, we will become nothing. It is here, where my grandson wished to come. He understands its significance, its importance. He knows that here is the center of the universe – his, and ours, and that of all the Jewish people. Take it away, and we will be no more. It has stood up to time, to two thousand years in exile. And we never forgot it. I am so happy that Sandy has made the decision to make this Wall a part of her life. I loved her before. I do not love her more now for what she has done. But I am glad. She has said, What you are, I want to be, too. . . . Jonathan, she is our daughter. You would love her as I do . . . I miss you, my beloved. I miss you very much."

Sandy's arms are stretched out. Her palms are hard against the Wall. Her lips touch the Wall, which is smooth, and cool. "I am yours," she says. "And you are mine. I am committed to you. I have chosen it that way. I am your Jewish daughter – now – and for always. I have claimed the privilege . . . and I accept the responsibility. I am not your passive Jewish daughter. I am your eager one – your ardent one. I am your active Jewish daughter. I will speak my mind – even when you don't want to hear . . . because that is part of the commitment . . . I have. . . . a wonderful sense of being . . . a sense of being a part of this, that it is mine as much as it is to those who have been born to it. My son said it felt like I had come home. It's true . . . I have come home."

Milada and Ella May conclude their talk with the Wall. They turn to each other and embrace.

Sandy observes them from a short distance away, gratified by their closeness.

"It's a good day, Milada," Ella May says.

Milada nods.

"I can understand why David wanted his Bar Mitzvah here – at the Wall. You feel very close to God here."

"If that's a concept one wants."

"It's very comforting."

"For some."

"For us."

Milada pulls up her sleeve, to reveal the concentration camp number tattooed on her flesh, confronts Ella May with it. "If there were a god, there wouldn't have been one of these."

"And yet," Ella May says, "and I have read it often in the literature of the concentration camps – it was God that sustained those people."

"I wasn't one of them, Ella May. If I ever had believed, I would have stopped the day we were put in a concentration camp."

"We all need faith, Milada."

"Faith in our strength – military strength. Without it there would be no Wall, no Jerusalem and no Israel. Here you are standing amongst the people who created this land, and who sustain it day by day – through their strength – strength of arms. You see Mordechai Gilboa over there – his son paid for this Wall – with his blood."

"I feel very humble in their presence. I know how this land was won – and how it continues to sustain itself, surrounded as it is by enemies. We have become involved, Milada – through you, through our daughter, Mark, and, of course, David. This land is very precious to us."

"I know. And I'm very happy to hear you say it."

"Wait until you see the present we're giving David. It's a surprise. And we have decided to learn Hebrew."

"That's very courageous."

"We want to be able to read the Bible in the original. And we want to be able to pray in Hebrew. We're going to an *Ulpan.*"

"In Israel?" Milada asks.

"Yes. It's a six month course. Very intensive. We've already signed up. We'll be going home for a bit – we're expecting you and Mark and Sandy and David over Thanksgiving again this year. We're really looking forward to it."

"So am I, Ella May. I always do."

"The men will be out hunting – we've sure got a lot of quail this year. And there's plenty of deer about – with some mighty good racks. Then we're coming back here, and in six months we'll be speaking like natives."

Sandy joins them, puts her arms around the waists of her mother and mother-in-law as they go to join the others.

Now they are all together, a little distance from the Wall. Judge Fraser says to David, "Me and your grandma got a couple of presents for you. One of 'em is back home at Ashmere. And we're going to give you that when you're down. It's one of them over-and-unders – made in Italy – the sweetest 20-gauge shotgun you have ever laid your eyes on."

"Thanks, Grandpa – and Grandma. I'm really looking forward to using it."

"And that ain't all. That there other present – well – it's here. And it's a surprise. It was my idea. I talked it over with your grandma, and she thought it was a pretty good idea, too."

"You've really got me wondering, Grandpa."

"Well, you just keep on wondering, son, because I don't think you'll ever guess. But I'm pretty sure you're going to like it. You're just going to have to be patient for a while."

"I'll do my best, Grandpa."

"Now we got to get us something to eat. Nothing like a Bar Mitzvah to make you hungry – especially when you're carrying one of them Torahs around."

They all get into the minibus Mark had hired for the occasion and go part way down the slope from Jerusalem to a wooded park with a magnificent view, not all that far from where David Brown had fallen, and where Jonathan had been wounded. Wherever you go in this land, somebody had paid the price for it, in blood.

They park the minibus and they get out the hampers and they have their picnic lunch.

David says to Judge Fraser, "Grandpa, maybe you and Grandma ought to convert, too."

"Well, I'll tell you, son," Judge Fraser replies, "You really want me and your grandma like we are. And I'll tell you why: because you want allies in the enemy camp . . . Now don't that make sense to you?"

David nods. "I guess it does. I hadn't looked at it that way before."

The large Bar Mitzvah party, jovial, happy, finish their lunch and climb back into the minibus, prepared for the long ride ahead.

They move down from the slopes of Jerusalem, north toward Tel Aviv, past the orange groves, and along the coast road toward Haifa.

Then they move up into the Galilee, past the entrance to Kibbutz Gan Galil, with its nine memorials close to the gate; past the Isaiah and Zahava Spaulding Forest; past the Noah and Deborah

Spaulding Forest; past the David Brown Forest; past the Jonathan Spaulding Forest, to where the hillside is barren, and where the minibus comes to a halt.

Already a group of people are gathered nearby. The Spauldings and the Frasers and all the others get out of the minibus. Judge Fraser points part way up the barren hillside to the sign that says: THE DAVID SPAULDING FOREST. IN HONOR OF HIS BAR MITZVAH. FROM HIS LOVING GRANDPARENTS, JUDGE AND ELLA MAY FRASER.

"That's the surprise," Judge Fraser says. "Do you like it?"

David hugs his grandparents. "I like it a lot," he says, biting his lip and trying not to cry.

"And it's up to you," Judge Fraser says, "to plant the first tree. And then all of us are going to plant trees. We thought it would be kinda nice to put down something permanent in this land."

All of Gan Galil is here. It is a happy time. Sandy hugs her parents. "It's such a beautiful gesture."

Mark hugs them, too. "You couldn't have done anything nicer."

"That's the way we figured it," the Judge replies.

David is presented with the first sapling. He holds it in his hand. The tears are streaming down his cheeks. He is oblivious to the tears. They are tears of joy, tears that express the overwhelming emotion that he is feeling.

He hopes his tree will grow and be strong like those in the other forests to which this one will be attached. Gently he places the sapling into the ground. With the shovel he covers the roots with earth, and then pats the earth firmly with his hands. Taking a sprinkler he waters his tree, the first one in the David Spaulding Forest.

Then all present plant a tree in David's forest.

David speaks to all those who are assembled.

"Thank you, Grandpa and Grandma. You're right. I never would have guessed. It is such a beautiful present. It is one that the whole nation can share. I can't imagine getting anything nicer, anything more important and more useful. It expresses your love for this land, and it allows me to speak of my love. I'm so proud of you, and I know my mother is, too."

Sandy kisses David, and then her parents.

Everybody applauds.

Amos Bar Lev speaks to the assembled guests.

"I am pleased to be a part of this memorable celebration," he says. "It is an honor and a pleasure. It is indeed a happy day. We all know what has taken place here, on Galilee's Sacred Hill. We know the cost. We know the price. We have paid it. Just remember those nine memorials – and those scattered throughout this land.

"The fight goes on. Perhaps it will never end. There is one fight, however, for which we have paid over the year, and continue to pay, and may have to pay into eternity. That is the fight on behalf of the Bradys, whom we betrayed. We have to live with that. It is a bone stuck in our throats.

"I must apologize for bringing in this sad note, on such a glorious day. But I want us to remember. I know what a magnificent battle Sandy Spaulding has been waging. She is a fighter for Israel – as much so as any of us. That fight must go on. I will be a part of it for as long as I can, for as long as I am able. We must have justice for the Bradys."

All of those assembled know. They do not speak. They feel the shame with which their government has covered them.

Afterwards, there is a dinner at the kibbutz, followed by Israeli folk dancing. They do the Hora and they sing *Tzena, Tzena*.

Shashona says to David, "I'm very happy for you. Congratulations. I like the things you said today."

"Thanks, Shashona. It's nice of you to say so."

35

It is early in the twentieth century. In the domain of the Czar things were not going well, in which case it was expedient – and usual – to blame the Jews. They were, it needs to be repeated often, the ones who had killed Christ. This was a good diversionary tactic, and always worked; the great mass of people who would otherwise have turned on the government – on the Czar – could now direct their efforts elsewhere: toward the Jews.

In 1902 there were pogroms in Bialystok, Minsk, Lodz, Dusyata, Simferopol, Melitopol and Zhitomir. In 1903 they again had pogroms in Lodz, Minsk, Bialystok, Simferopol, and now added Sedlits, Melitopol, Odessa, Kishinev, and other towns of Jewish habitation. They were government-inspired, but required no great effort to stir up the local populace against the Jews, who felt they were on a holy mission, doing God's work.

Isaiah Spalczik was a great bear of a man, the local blacksmith, with arms like tree trunks, with a chest like a barrel, and who towered seemingly into the sky. His legendary strength made him famous in all of the villages around – and in many that were some distance away. In his presence the anti-Semites remained silent; they heard what happened to a few who had been indiscreet.

Isaiah Spalczik did not have to go looking for anti-Semites. They were there, all around him, a natural part of the Russian empire. Much of the time during the past eight hundred years the Jews and their Slavic neighbors had managed to co-exist. Isaiah Spalczik managed. He was liked, he was respected – by his Christian neighbors as well as by most of his Jewish ones. He did important work. Most were dependent upon his efforts one way or another.

No *yarmulkah* covered Isaiah Spalczik's head. He was not a believer. He had stopped believing even before his Bar Mitzvah – the last one to take place in the family until David had his before the Wall. Isaiah Spalczik was a Zionist. The Jewish people, he felt, needed a home of their own; living in other people's countries had its negative aspects.

The religious element too believed in a return to Israel. They had believed in it for almost two thousand years. The disagreement with the secular Zionists was over the method. Religious Jews were waiting for the Messiah to redeem Israel. They prayed hard and loud for him to appear. There were those who contended that there had been insufficient fervor, and that it was necessary to pray even harder and ever more loudly – in order to make God hear.

But either God was deaf, or indifferent, or, as the new and incipient secularism had it, non-existent. In the Czar's domain, the Zionists were stirring, those not prepared to wait for the Messiah's redemption of Israel; they knew that they were going to have to do it all on their own – they would be their own Messiah. Two thousand years of having Arabs wander about in it had not done the land of Israel much good, and there were those who doubted that it could ever be restored. Even if the Messiah were to come, he would throw up his hands in utter despair and admit defeat; remaking Israel into the land of milk and honey was considered too big a job even for the Messiah.

But already Jerusalem had a Jewish majority. Many were old people who had gone there to die, to live out their remaining years in the Jerusalem that actually existed, touching distance from the Western Well.

Those who would be their own Messiah were already making their momentous beginning, restoring this land that suffered from two thousand years of erosion, malarial swamps and Arabs with trachoma. They were in immediate conflict with those who insisted that this should all be the work of the Messiah, which others must not undertake. The Czar was no doubt filled with delight upon learning that there existed a Jewish group who had no aspirations for his over-throw, and that better still, their profoundest desire was to emigrate.

Of more concern were the Jews who insisted upon staying around, like the Bund, like the Social Democrats, like the Communists, to make the revolution and get rid of the Czar. Already, in 1905, there was the first great uprising of modern times, put down, but only for the moment; the big one was yet to come, not that far off.

The religious element had more in common with their Catholic/Eastern Orthodox counterparts than they did with their Jewish brethren who were Communists, Socialists and/or Zionists. If the Catholics and Eastern Orthodox were aware of this, it made little difference to them: a Jew was a Jew, and the same fate needed to be administered to all of them – though the Socialists and Communists were seen as being considerably more troublesome. There were also ideological conflicts between the Socialists and Communists, who rejected the Zionists entirely: they, the Zionists, were in pursuit of a crazy dream that could never become a reality. The Zionists, generally also socialists, wanted to practice their socialism in Israel, and saw their dream as both practical and realistic.

Isaiah's son, Noah, who was fifteen, belonged to a Zionist youth group. Noah's girlfriend, Deborah Moiseyivich, who was fourteen, was a member, too. Her parents did not approve of her political affiliation; they were Bundists – Jewish workers who wanted to depose the Czar and create a Jewish socialist entity with a Yiddish culture. But otherwise the two families were good friends. Isaiah and Deborah's father – who was a cabinet maker – argued endlessly over the merits of their respective cause, quick to point out the flaws in the ideology of the other. This was not mere rhetoric; these were the roads to salvation – to an end of oppression of the Jewish people. The argument was over which was the correct one. The one concept on which they did agree was that one day their respective children – Noah and Deborah – would marry.

The pogrom had been brewing for some time, though when it happened it appeared to be a spontaneous event, actuated by the drinkers who had until then spent more time talking about killing Jews rather than actually doing it. Isaiah Spalczik knew that something was in the air, though he did not know exactly what; there seemed to be fewer horses amongst his gentile clientele in need of being shod, and there were considerably less friendly hellos.

They burst into the forge – a dozen of them – with clubs and knives. It was immediately apparent to Isaiah that they had not come for horse shoes. He knew most of them – there was Stoshik and Stanislaus – he had shod their horses many times over the years. Stoshik still owed him money. Stoshik wasn't very good about paying – though there was no shortage of money for vodka. But now was not a good time to remind Stoshik about his overdue account.

Instead, with the heavy tongs, Isaiah grabbed the red hot strip of iron that had been heating in the forge, and swung it around like a mighty sword, into the faces of his attackers who screamed in anguish as they fell. He swung again, and those who could, fled.

Another group arrived, also neighbors, clients and friends – now former friends – having burned down the house next door and killed the people who lived in it. At that moment Noah appeared, the large Russian revolver in his hand, firing as rapidly as he could, until all the chambers were emptied.

"Well done, " Isaiah said to Noah.

"Do you think they'll be back?"

"It's entirely possible. Better get the shotgun. And reload that revolver. Get all the shells we've got. Go to the Moiseyivich's. See if they're all right."

Noah got the shotgun, a double-barrel hammer gun, and all the shells they had. He raced down the dirt street, toward the Moiseyivich's, the smell of burning houses filling his nostrils.

The pogromists were running about, destroying what they could, whom they could. A Russian officer on horseback, his sword drawn, was shouting encouragement. Noah shot him.

Some of the rioters fled. Noah shot several who didn't. He made his way to the Moiseyivich's house. There wasn't much of it left. The Moiseyivichs were dead. He found Deborah hiding in the cellar, in a state of shock. He brought her back to their house.

Isaiah announced. "We are leaving."

"Where will we go?" his wife Zahava asked.

"To America. We will leave now. Our neighbors – the ones we have left alive – will no doubt want to take revenge."

They loaded up the wagon, took what valuables they had, and they left – Isaiah, his wife Zahava, their son Noah, Noah's younger sister, and Deborah, and headed for the German border, where they could get a ship bound for the United States.

Ultimately they arrived at Ellis Island. The Immigration Officer who confronted them was Irish. "Name?" he asked.

Isaiah looked at him blankly. None of them understood a word of English.

"*Nomen*", the Inspector said, employing the only word of Yiddish he had learned.

"Spalczik," Isaiah replied.

"Spalczik!" the Immigration Officer asked in his thick County Sligo brogue. "What kind of name is that? You're in America now. You'll be wanting an American name – a good American name. How about 'Spaulding'? That's one for you. That'll be suiting you just fine."

The Spaulding family, and Deborah, arrived in New York. Isaiah looked about him, at the tenements on the Lower East Side, and felt physically ill. He could hardly believe this was America. As soon as they could, they moved across the river to New Jersey, where Isaiah set up a forge, but instead of horse shoes, he started making tools.

Almost from the beginning they prospered. Noah sold the tools his father made. At night he went to school, and ultimately got his degree in metallurgy. Noah and Deborah married, and a son – Jonathan – was born to them. They went from hand tools into machine tools, in time built a large factory and employed many hundreds of people.

Some years later, Noah and Deborah, with their young son Jonathan, visited Israel – then still under British occupation –

where at Kibbutz Gan Galil, they dedicated a forest in honor of Isaiah and Zahava Spaulding. Noah planted the first tree. Mordechai Gilboa, slightly older than Jonathan, watched with deep pleasure, watched the saplings grow into a whole forest.

An era or two passed. European Jewry had all but been eliminated. Israel emerged from the ashes. For Jonathan and Milada, having fought to make this dream a reality, now it was time to return to the United States. Jonathan went into the family business, which he expanded considerably.

They had a son, whom they named Mark, after Milada's father. Mark was still quite young when he made his first visit to Israel, with his parents and grandparents, where they dedicated another forest. This one was in honor of David Brown.

Mordechai Gilboa was there for the dedication, with his wife Hamalia, their son Eitan, and their daughter Rachel. So was Amos Bar Lev, the Haganah section commander under whom Jonathan and David had fought, and who was now in the government and a member of the Cabinet. He said: "This forest is a fitting tribute for this man, David Brown, who came to us, and gave us all that he had. He would like this forest, a permanent part of the land he wanted to make his own. He will be with us forever."

Mark remembered the ceremony, remembered Amos Bar Lev, Mordechai, Hamalia, their son Eitan, their daughter Rachel. His father and his mother had fought to make this country – regarded here as hero and heroine. Mordechai showed Mark around the kibbutz where his mother had fought, told him how the Syrian tanks had breached the kibbutz defenses, and how his mother had stopped those tanks forever. Mark could feel himself bursting with pride.

Then once again Israel had to reassert its right to exist – made its point – in six days. Israel did not have longer than that; America, Israel's "good friend", insisted upon a termination of hostilities. The Arabs suffered some humiliation, knew that wasn't a war lost, merely a battle, and that there would be another day. But Israel had the Old City of Jerusalem back. The Wall had now been restored to its rightful owners. Jerusalem was now one city, both halves forming the whole. Unfortunately there was a price: Eitan Gilboa, son of Mordechai and Hamalia, brother of Rachel, was killed in the process of retaking Jerusalem. So were a lot of other Israeli young men who had hardly begun to live.

196

Jonathan and Milada and Mark returned to Israel, to Kibbutz Gan Galil, where there was now another memorial: EITAN GILBOA.

Milada and Jonathan stood before the Memorial, remembering when they had first met Eitan, shortly after their arrival at Gan Galil, a little boy who had welcomed them to Israel.

"This is the price we pay for Israel," Jonathan said, running his hand over Eitan's name, etched into the black metal, the whole of which looked like a wing.

"A high price," Milada said.

Mordechai remained dry-eyed now. The tears had already flowed, enough between Hamalia and himself to make the Sea of Galilee spill over its banks. "I used to believe that we could live with the Arabs," Mordechai said. "Our whole movement was predicated on the concept that we could live together. But we can't. We never will. Not with the Arabs that surround us. Not with the Arabs who live in this country. It is not a view popular on the kibbutz – or in our movement. But this view is not mine alone today. A growing number of people are facing up to the reality – however difficult and painful it is for them. The Arabs do not want us here. And they will fight until they get rid of us. Unless we get rid of them first. That is the answer to our survival. The only answer. We need to deal them such a blow that they will never recover. We need to insure that they do not have guns – that they will never be able to hurt us. And we can do it, too. We could have done it from the start. We could have done it when those Syrian tanks were over-running our kibbutz, and we stopped them. We could have made sure that they would never come again, and we could do it now. We have everything that we'll ever need – except the will to use it."

"I strongly suspect that Israel will be pushed into it one day," Jonathan said.

"By then it might be too late," Mordechai said.

"We can't go on forever losing our best," Milada said.

"This isn't the last one," Mordechai said. "There is another one coming. Everyone knows it – except the government. I'm tired of fighting. I'm tired of war. I have been fighting the same one all my life. Now we have paid with our son. I have no more sons to give. We had only the one."

"I remember Eitan very well," Milada said. "It seems like yesterday that we arrived here, and there was Eitan. I had to hug him.

He wasn't very enthusiastic about it – but I was a guest, and he let me."

"He always reminded me of Huck Finn," Jonathan said.

"Now he's gone. Just a memory – and a memorial. We can't bring him back . . . All we can do is insure that it won't happen again. And the only way we can do that is to get rid of these people who spend their whole life trying to kill us."

There was also a memorial for David Brown, much like that of Eitan Gilboa. It said: DAVID BROWN. IF HE HAD NOT DIED FOR US, HE WOULD HAVE LIVED WITH US. He had been made a member of the kibbutz, in absentia, and would remain here forever, a kibbutz member into perpetuity, his deeds recounted to each new generation of kibbutz children – as long as Israel existed.

They then paid their respects to Chaim Goldbaum, the *Maskaroot* Jonathan and Milada had encountered the night of their arrival in Israel. Milada remembered when he had fallen. This land of tears, she thought, that never stops giving away the lives of its people. What an expensive land it is. Would there ever be peace? She doubted it. She could see no evidence of it, no hope for it.

The next forest was planted as a memorial for Jonathan. Amos Bar Lev was there to dedicate it.

"He died before his time," Amos Bar Lev said, "because he came to us and fought the war that he knew was his war as much as ours. It was a Jewish war, and he had to be in it – because he was a proud and dedicated Jew, from a family dedicated to the creation and survival of this land. We will not forget him. I will not forget him. We fought together to make this land. He has a permanent place as one of its creators."

By now the three memorials at Kibbutz Gan Galil had grown to nine. The six new additions were as a result of the Yom Kippur War.

Mark liked what Amos Bar Lev had said about his father. He was the creator of this land – as was his mother. All his life he had been surrounded by those who had done so much, given so much. These nine memorials were expressions of those who had given their all.

He felt awe, and respect, and deepest sorrow that his contribution had until now been completely nonexistent. He wondered what it would have been like to fight his way up the hills toward Jerusalem, as his father had, in the company of David Brown, and Amos Bar Lev, who was now the Minister of Agriculture.

It was a privilege, Mark thought, to be called upon to serve – to call upon one's self to serve. No one had called upon his father: he had volunteered to serve in the Army of the United States. And he had certainly volunteered to fight in Israel; in fact, those Americans who had, lost their citizenship, which was ultimately restored. And his mother had chosen. She was part of the history of this country, a legend in her time, about whom children read in their history books, at the dawn of their awakening.

You choose, Mark thought. You decide. You make the decisions. Decisions for what? he wondered. Currently the opportunities appeared to be limited. Right at the moment there was something of a war in Vietnam – not his war, not a war in which he would want to participate, in which he would want to contribute. It would never touch him – never affect him.

Had the time passed to participate in history? Perhaps each had to do it in his or her own way. But what was his way? All those around him had reached for the heights, and realized them. He hoped there would be heights which he could scale. Sinai's lofty mountain was not so far away. But what did you do when you got there?

It was a place that inspired this land, and this people. It was his, handed down to him by Moses, who had been there – on Sinai's lofty mountain. It was the heritage of all the Jewish people. The mountain would never go away, nor would the knowledge of what had happened there. It was a part of him, and each day he would scale the heights.

His father had been his beacon, the light by which he had been guided, and by which he would also be guided. His father had paid the price for the creation of this land, a gift to all of the Jewish people, into perpetuity.

Mark wished his father could be here. He missed him desperately. They had been friends, companions. Together they had hunted and fished – explored near and far domains with rod and gun. Every moment had been precious – precious then, the memory of it precious now.

36

Mark writes the concluding section of his report on the American condition, briefly presenting its history in order to make the present understandable. "The American Revolution was hardly a popular movement, with only about half the population in support. Many fled to Canada for asylum. England saw its colonial empire as a domain to be milked, to be used for its own economic gain, at the expense of the colonial population. England, like the rest of Europe, needed money to fight its wars, used its power to exact revenue from an unwilling and helpless population. Bear in mind that in England there was even a tax on windows (people bricked them up to avoid paying the tax). There was a tax on clocks. And the exorbitant taxes on sheep farmers forced many out of business.

"Long before the American Revolution, a Portuguese slaver, on its way to the West Indies, apparently blown off course, and finding itself near the southern American coast, offered the cargo to the Colonials. Otherwise, the captain explained, he would dump the cargo of captive Africans overboard. The Americans took the Africans, now their slaves, and found them work on their plantations, picking cotton.

"The North, unable to make productive use of slave labor, took a position of righteous indignation, making morality an issue that might not have been one otherwise. George Washington and Thomas Jefferson were slave owners and did not feel compromised as a result, and very likely, had they been alive at the time, would have fought as Southerners during the Civil War.

"Ultimately they fought a war that should never have been fought, that severely divided the nation for more than a hundred years, that left scars that would never heal."

Mark stops writing for a minute. He thinks about his friend Roy – Roy Maclaine, whom he'd first met Stateside during basic training – who had warned him that hostile forces were out to get him. And then they had met again in Vietnam, when Roy was a Medic, and attended to Mark's leg wound. Roy had probably saved his life – twice.

They stayed in touch. Roy wanted to be a doctor; it was a crazy, impossible dream. Milada, because Mark asked, got him into UCLA. It took some doing. Roy just didn't have the background, had never learned the discipline of study; you didn't get born a doctor, and one day emerge with a stethoscope around your neck, a diploma on your wall, and a doctor's bag in your hand. There was an interval in between where you had to qualify and that took a lot of work.

At times Roy found it pretty hard going. He'd phone Mark and say he was going to drop out.

"No, you're not," Mark would tell him. "If you could stick Nam, you can stick this. There isn't anybody there shooting at you."

"There is. It's everybody. And I can't shoot back."

"It's a different kind of war, Roy."

"I never got the training for it."

"At least you won't wind up in a body bag."

"Sometimes I think that would have been easier."

"I've got faith in you, Roy."

"That's more than I've got in myself."

"Are you going to let me down, Roy? You didn't before."

"It's so hard, Mark," Roy pleaded. "I don't think I got all that stuff you need between your ears."

"You've got it, Roy. You just keep right on trying."

And Roy did.

Mark and Milada also helped him financially.

Roy did make it. He became a doctor. He married, and he had two children.

Whenever he was in Washington – for a medical convention, or political conference – he and Mark always got together.

"The American 'melting pot' never melted, but merely boiled and simmered, and frequently boiled over. The immigrants who came in droves in the late 19th and early 20th centuries, were generally Europe's surplus, those with not much to lose, and, in many cases, not much to give either. Those who had any stake in the land of their origin, usually remained there. Those who came, brought their own prejudices with them.

"The Jews of Eastern Europe were all surplus, but from all sectors and all levels of the community, representing the best, with the best potential, as well as those with less. They entered timidly, and

201

discovered that the old enmities had not disappeared during the ocean crossing, that their neighbors were the same ones that they had hoped to leave behind.

"A culmination of that historic enmity manifested itself some years later when it was shown again how vulnerable the Jews were. The American Government murdered Julius and Ethel Rosenberg. They employed the full power, force and legitimacy of the law, including that of the Supreme Court – with only Justice William O. Douglas dissenting – to make their point. Julius and Ethel Rosenberg were found guilty of having passed nuclear information to the Russians, which they did not have, and could not have provided, but were nevertheless sent to burn in the electric chair, though they were totally innocent. This was the American Government, serving notice on its Jewish population, on whom it had already attached a left-wing label, not to oppose its own aspirations, which were decidedly Nazi and Pro-Nazi, as we have long suspected, but now are able to prove; the leading figures in American Government had created and sustained the Nazi entity.

"By giving Jews a left-wing label, they were immediately marginalized. With the inauguration of the Cold War in 1946 a 'Left' label was attached to any and all opposition, any area in which the fascist right wished to prevail. Jews were on the 'left', as defined by the far right, who were, and are, the real threat to America's democracy.

"American Jews knew that the finger was being pointed at them, and they were frightened, leaned over hard to express their patriotism, and repudiated their fellow Jews who knew how necessary it was to stand up to the large fascist entity that did, and continues to, impose a most serious threat.

"Only at the beginning of the 1960s, with the advent of a new generation, who were being called upon to serve in a war for which they had no sympathy, did any real opposition come into being. That opposition altered the course which John Foster Dulles had charted. But the American military defeat, was so unequivocal, and so traumatic that America, and Americans never fully recovered. Their confidence was shattered as they questioned the validity of this highly dubious cause, for which they could find no justification.

"Inter-racial strife would appear to offer little by way of solution. The fundamentalist Right has its own demands, different from a secularist society that demands adherence to a Constitution that requires separation between Church and State. These basically hostile – to each other – concepts contribute further to a divisive society, unprepared to accommodate views different from its own.

"Benefiting from conflict, both internal and external, carrying on its work virtually unnoticed and unmolested, are the oil interests that function in tune with Saudi Arabia, on a government-to-government basis, which Franklin Roosevelt instigated. Succeeding American administrations saw it as a good place to do business – they were absolutely right – the United States Government handed over its relations with Saudi Arabia to the oil companies. This followed a number of secret agreements, which circumvented Congress, going back to 1947, in which the Government prevailed upon ARAMCO to expand its Government Relations Department, and actually transferred diplomats and CIA agents to staff it.

"Such a cosy relationship placed America in the hands of the oil companies doing business with Saudi Arabia, and the oil companies in the hands of Saudi Arabia. Saudi Arabia has emerged as the dominant entity, buying what it wants, paying for what it gets, able to rule the United States, and push its program for the elimination of Israel."

The Report appears, authored by Mark Spaulding and Bill Cooper, a victim of the forces of fascism, with the able assistance of Claire Alderson, another victim. It is meant for the eyes of Congress, of those in government, the military, the diplomatic corps, as well as foreign governments. Not initially viewed as a document meant for mass distribution, it nevertheless arouses enormous public interest, and appears as a book that becomes a virtual bestseller, producing shock waves throughout the country.

It is a fitting tribute, and a memorial, to Bill Cooper.

37

Leah Brady serves three and a half years in prison. Her intestinal condition, untreated, grows steadily worse. Those who administer political prisoners are concerned that she might die, and that they would be held responsible for her death. They wonder if it might not be expedient to release her on parole: they would look good – humane – and she would not die while in their custody.

On the other hand, she is a trouble-maker – they know this from first-hand experience. They are deeply disturbed that they have not broken her spirit. But then, if they kill her, the repercussions might be unpleasant. They would have to contend with that lawyer – Sandy Fraser Spaulding, and her law firm in Washington: Draycott Webber Warner and Fraser. Why do these respectable law firms have to get involved with political criminals? There ought to be enough else to do in Washington to keep them busy. That Spaulding woman had already caused enough trouble – made them stop chaining Brady to her bed, made them look very bad in the eyes of the public. Now she is pushing for parole.

Well, the thinking goes, Leah Brady hasn't tried to escape, hasn't assaulted any guards. Get rid of her. If she's going to die, let her do it somewhere else.

Leah is out on parole. She is compelled to live in a half-way house – with other women who have been released: drug addicts, prostitutes, murderers – meant to facilitate her/their return to society. The half-way house is in New York City, on the Lower East Side, an appropriate setting for dealing with the degraded, where drunks and drug addicts lay in the street, and over whom passers-by need to step, or, alternatively, walk around.

It is a dangerous area. The drug addicts are not all lying prone in the street; there are those who remain upright for the moment, requiring enough money for another fix – your money extracted from you at the point of a gun, or knife, or iron bar. Leah Brady does not feel fear. She has lived in the depths, experienced all the degradation which man has consciously created – in the process of making such an institution. Here it is a hell of a different nature – by default rather than by design.

The terms of her parole require Leah to remain within a hundred miles of New York City. This means she cannot see Alan, who is in Marion Prison in southern Illinois, where his fellow prisoners are seen as beyond redemption – some for having killed other prisoners, or a prison guard in other, less well-supervised institutions. Now, here, there is no possibility of release – ever. This is what Alan J. Brady's incarceration in this place is meant to convey.

Sandy comes to see Leah at the half-way house. The two women throw their arms around each other. Leah's pain is her pain.

"I'm trying to get the Parole Board to let you go to Marion to see Alan," she tells Leah.

"What are the chances?"

"We'll fight. We could win."

"And even if we do – I haven't got the money to go there."

"It won't be a problem, Leah. Mark and I will give it to you."

"I don't want to take money from you. You've already done so much for me. I'll never be able to pay you back."

"There is nothing to pay. Leah, in Hebrew, there is the word *tzedaka*."

"It means charity. I don't want charity."

"It means 'Duty'. There is no word in Hebrew for 'charity'. This is duty, Leah – responsibility. We assume it without question – and with deep humility."

Both women's eyes fill with tears.

Sandy takes Leah's hands in both of hers. They sit silently for a few moments.

Then Leah says, "I need to get Alan out, Sandy."

"We'll do all that we can. I promise you."

"And I'll need to find a job."

"When the time comes, Leah."

But Leah, even if the Parole Board allowed it, even with the money to do so, is not well enough to make the arduous journey to the remote part of southern Illinois where Alan is incarcerated, surrounded by row upon row of razor wire. Even if she could find a job, even if someone were prepared to hire her, she cannot work: she is too ill. Therefore she has no medical insurance, and only the facilities offered by the Parole Board are available for her. "I'd sooner die in the street," Leah says.

Sandy arranges for Leah to appear on television, on a chat-show with a large viewing audience. She tells her story. She tells it well. Her viewers are deeply moved and profoundly sympathetic.

Leah concludes her interview with these words: "I love Alan, and I'm going to fight for him. I'll never stop until he's out."

The next day Leah is walking down the street. A middle-aged woman, coming from the opposite direction, recognizes her. "You're Leah Brady," the woman says excitedly. "I saw you on television last night. You were wonderful." She throws her arms around Leah. "My God, what they've done to you!"

Leah hugs the woman back. Her concern, her sympathy, feel so good. A perfect stranger out there really cares.

Holding Leah by the hand, the woman cries out to passers-by, "This is Leah Brady. She was on television last night. She was in prison. She's Alan Brady's wife – the man who saved Israel!"

The passers-by know, and they stop, too, and they cry out, Leah Brady, and more people are there, and more still. Some just look and stand there in awe, and some hug her, and hardly anyone has dry eyes. More people gather. They hug her. They touch her.

"Leah, we want to fight for Alan," someone says.

"It's our fight, too," someone else says.

Leah is standing in front of a fruit store. The proprietor brings out a box for Leah on which to stand, says, "Tell us what to do, Leah, and we'll do it."

By now a very large crowd has gathered. The faces are not all Jewish faces – but they are the faces of people who are concerned, who want justice.

The fruit store man helps Leah onto the box. "Talk to us, Leah. We want to help. We owe you. We owe Alan."

Leah stands on the box. The tears are small rivers riding down her face. "I'm sorry," she says to the crowd, between sobs. "I can't help it. I'm so overwhelmed. I never thought there was this kind of support. I appreciate it so much. It makes up for so many things."

We support you, the crowd tells her. You are the queen. The Jewish Queen. A modern-day Queen Esther. You are marvelous. You are a heroine. God bless you.

"What are we going to do, Leah?" the middle-aged woman who first recognized Leah asks.

"We're going to fight," Leah says.

"How?" the woman demands.

Leah takes control of herself. "We'll go to Congress," she says. "We'll fight there. Alan has a lot of sympathy there. We'll speak with every Senator and every Representative. I'll go there and talk personally to every one of them. They'll force the President to give Alan a pardon. And we will lean hard on Israel. Just remember, it was Israel who betrayed him."

We'll help, someone says. Someone else says, It takes money. Someone else, still, says, Let's take up a collection. Yeah – a collection. Money begins to pour in – not from heaven, but from men and women who know this fight is theirs. Suddenly her hands are clutching large numbers of notes. "Thank you," she keeps saying. "Thank you."

The crowd begins to disperse, but not before virtually all of them hug her and kiss her gently on the cheek.

"This is the best moment I've had," Leah says, "since we were indicted."

Leah's encounter on the street is mentioned on the news that night, and in the papers the next morning.

Jacob Ben Zvi, who heads the world-wide campaign on "behalf" of the Bradys, is near panic. Very soon after Leah finishes her television appearance, Ben Zvi gets the video to the Prime Minister, and explains the situation:

"Her appearance has created deep public sympathy. With her strength and her determination it is possible that she could sway the Congress, who might easily press for a Presidential Pardon – and get it. Further, she is making it apparent that Israel is responsible for Brady's plight, and this looks very bad for us as well. Leah Brady cannot travel more than one hundred miles from New York City, and therefore cannot reach Washington at this time. But her lawyer, Sandy Fraser Spaulding, is trying to get this rescinded so that she can visit not only Washington, but Marion as well, to see her husband Alan. Both are very determined women, and if Leah is able to see her husband in Marion, she could undue all the good work that has so far been done.

"Mrs. Fraser Spaulding, who can also be a very difficult and stubborn person, is representing Leah without pay. I have already clashed with Mrs. Fraser Spaulding, who is a relatively new convert to Judaism; she is driven by this cause, and does not hesitate to blame Israel for Brady's plight. She is the wife of Mark Spaulding, responsible for that report which puts so much of the blame for Brady's problems on Israel. As you know, Mark Spaulding's parents – Jonathan and Milada Spaulding – are regarded as hero and heroine in Israel.

"Now that Leah is out, she is doing more damage every day. What do you advise?"

The Prime Minister replies: "Stop her." He doesn't explain how. That is up to Jacob Ben Zvi. That is why they employ him. "Do whatever you have to. Spend money. Spend all that you need to spend. I don't care what you do – but do it. This is a very dangerous situation for us – for Israel. We cannot have that man Brady walking the streets. He has already done too much damage. Are you any closer to finding out who leaked the Brady Papers? It must have been somebody very high up.

"Just remember – stop Leah Brady!"

38

Jacob Ben Zvi is despondent. Leah Brady is ruining everything – destroying all his good work, making it into nothing. Maybe he can make her see sense. She obviously needs money. They can help. They are prepared to be generous. The Prime Minister said to spend money. All right, so spend money.

Except for Leah Brady, everything else is going well. Alan Brady is under his thumb. Whatever Jacob Ben Zvi says, Alan Brady does. No problem either with Dr. Morton Brady, the father, eminent molecular biologist. Both Alan Brady and his father have absolute faith in Ben Zvi. He's working behind the scenes. He tells them that all the time. And they believe it. And he gives out money. You want another team of lawyers? In addition to the ones you've already got? Sure, why not? The lawyers ask for parole. There's a hearing. But there's no parole. They even go to the Supreme Court. And what do they say in the Supreme Court? They say justice has been done. Alan J. Brady got justice. So who can argue with the Supreme Court – the Supreme Court of the United States?

Who could ask for more? Who could ask for better? Money; more lawyers; more expense. Money to pass around. Already it's over two million dollars that Israel has spent. Somebody calls it "hush money". He should bite his tongue. This isn't an easy job – especially going to Marion Prison to see Alan. For a visitor it's hard – very depressing. For two days afterwards he feels depressed. But it's what he has to do – he's doing it for Israel. He only hopes the Prime Minister appreciates all he's doing.

Now he's going to have to go back to Marion – talk to Alan – find out if any damage has been done. It's a hard trip getting to Marion. He feels the whole situation – right in his gut – maybe Alan is thinking his wife has a point. That could mean everything thrown away.

What if Alan doesn't think working behind the scenes is enough. What are they doing there – behind the scenes? he could ask. And what success are they having? And what's taking so long? All the stupid questions he could ask . . . What a job. A terrible job. Who would want it? It's for Israel, he tells himself. He's a soldier, fighting Israel's battle. And all that pain – like he's been shot, only worse.

The first thing is to see Leah Brady. Maybe he can make her see sense.

He comes to the half-way house. He is affable. Leah is ice cold.

"Leah, I'm glad you're out. We worked hard for it."

"If you had anything to do with it, I would have had a life sentence, too."

"Leah, I'm your friend. I want you to know that. I want you to believe it."

"I don't."

"We just want to help you."

"I've had your help. I don't need it."

"Of course you need help. Do you think we're going to abandon you? Of course not. We're all on your side."

"Who's the 'All'?"

"All is all. Everybody."

"It's too bad my father-in-law couldn't be bothered coming to see me in prison."

209

"Prison upsets him. He's a very sensitive man."

"Prison upsets me, too."

"Oh, Leah, you have such a remarkable spirit."

"And he hasn't come since I've been out of prison."

"He knows how much you've suffered – he can't bear to see you in this condition."

"For a man who's supposed to be intelligent – he's pretty stupid. And a coward, too. You obviously have him paid off. If you didn't, he'd be protesting at the Wall, and at the Knesset in Jerusalem – demanding that Israel get his son out of prison."

"Israel doesn't have his son in prison. He's here. And we're doing everything we can. We pay. We don't mind. We're glad to do it. We want to see justice. We paid to go to the Supreme Court. Without us paying, how could they go to the Supreme Court? We are generous. We are compassionate. We will be with you, too. You need money. We will give you money."

"That's very kind, Jacob. I'll need a lot of money for my campaign – to bring Alan's plight to the attention of Congress."

"Not for that, Leah."

"And I'll go to Israel and campaign there, too."

"Not for that, either."

"That's what I thought."

"You just leave that to us."

"On the day hell freezes over."

"You are not being very cooperative."

"You're right."

"I want something better for you, Leah. I'm concerned. We all are. Trust us. Trust me. We are working behind the scenes. We have good connections. Very good connections. Better than what you have – or can ever get. We can see the President. We already have."

"And he's going to release Alan?"

"Not just yet."

"That's what I thought."

"These things take time."

"You've already had the time."

"You have to be patient."

"Jacob, I'm long past being patient. You're a rotten liar. You know it, and I know it. The government of Israel has disgraced itself – and continues to do so. You – they – have absolutely no intention of trying to bring about Alan's release. The situation has made waves. You think that allowing Alan to remain in prison will calm things down – make the situation better between Israel and the United States. It won't happen, Jacob. You're ignoring Alan's message – those thousands of pages of classified documents Alan presented to you – that as far as the American Administration is concerned, Israel is expendable. The Administration doesn't want Israel around. And furthermore, he knows too much about you. You want him to stay right where he is – forever!"

"You misjudge us, Leah."

"Jacob, if you don't get out of my sight this minute – the next time they send me to prison – it will be for a real crime – and I'll be guilty – of murdering you."

"I don't deserve to be talked to this way. You'll be sorry, Leah – when we're trying so hard for you."

Ben Zvi comes to see Alan in Marion Prison. He embraces Alan.

"I'm so upset," Ben Zvi tells Alan. "Leah means well – but she did so much damage, so much harm to you. I can't begin to tell you how much harm – how much damage."

"Do you really think so?" Alan asks, surprised.

"I know so. I saw it with my own eyes. And so did all those people who saw her. Everybody I talked to – they all said the same thing. The man's in prison, and his wife goes on television to hurt him – to put a knife in his back."

"But I thought she was very good."

"Listen, you're in here – she comes on the television – you think it's a good thing – but nobody else does. I know it's hard for you to judge, but take my word for it, I'm out there – out there for you – and I listen to what the people tell me. You want to get public opinion on your side – because that's important. What Leah did to you on television – you lost all public opinion – all the sympathy – the support."

"Do you really think so?"

"I know it. For a fact. She got a lot of public sympathy for herself. She looks good. But she makes you look bad. She looks good at your expense. That's not what we want, Alan."

"No, of course not."

"She's out. You're still in. We have to get you out. That's what our job is. All the way to the Supreme Court we went for you."

211

"And I appreciate it, Jacob."

"I know you do. That's why I'm so upset. Just think what it costs us – money contributed for the building of Israel – we spend to try and get you out of prison. Just think of all the trees we're not going to be able to plant now – all the refugees we're not going to be able to help – because you're in here – and we're trying to get you out. Listen, Alan, there are Russian Jews who would love to come to Israel – and we would love to bring them – that is the reason for our existence. But we're not going to be able to bring them now – because we have these big expenses – trying to help you."

"I know, Jacob, and don't think I don't appreciate it."

"Of course you do, Alan. And we're not begrudging you. And now we're going to have to be helping Leah, too."

"That is good of you."

"We look after our people, Alan. That is the reason for Israel's existence. And that is the reason why I am so upset. With Leah destroying your chances – you could expect to stay in prison for the rest of your life. With that television appearance of hers, it looks to everybody like she just took the key to your cell and threw it out of the window."

"My god, Jacob, I had no idea. I guess sitting in here, it's hard to make a reasonable judgement. Thanks for telling me. I don't know what got into her. I suppose she has to think about herself – and what's good for her. She's suffered too, you know."

"I know it. But that isn't any excuse for what she's doing to you."

"I suppose not."

"Of course not. We do good. She does harm. Terrible harm."

Sandy arranges for Leah to speak with Alan on the telephone in Marion Prison. "What are you doing to me?" Alan demands.

"What are you talking about, Alan?"

"Your appearance on television. It was terrible."

"Did you see it?"

"Of course I saw it."

"But everybody said how good it was."

"For you. Not for me. It was a stab in the back. You had the key to my prison cell and you threw it away."

"Alan, you don't know what you're saying!"

"That's the trouble. I do know. Everybody knows. You're angry because we didn't listen to you – we didn't plea bargain. Now you want to get back at us – at me. It's no good, Leah. It's not going to work. I see right through you."

"Alan, I can't believe what I'm hearing."

"You better believe it."

"You've been talking with Jacob Ben Zvi."

"At least I have one friend."

"He's not your friend. He's not anybody's friend. He's despicable. Don't believe what he tells you."

"I do believe it. I don't believe what you tell me. You harbor this grudge. Don't think I don't know. I was ashamed to tell Jacob. But it's been there, all this time, burning in me. You think it's my fault you went to prison. You have this deep resentment."

"Alan, I love you."

"Don't say that. I don't want to hear it. It's a travesty. It's a mockery. Love. You don't have any love. You have hate. Of course you're not there helping me. You're helping yourself – at my expense. I know why you're doing this to me. Thank God I have Jacob. Thank God . . ."

Leah puts the phone down. There is no point to this conversation. She feels numb. She just sits there, hardly able to comprehend that this has happened. He is obviously affected by his life in prison. It has to affect people. Especially people like Alan. People like Alan don't go to spend their lives in prison, locked in a cage like an animal – only worse. Alan lives below the ground. A part of the window, just above the ground, lets in a bit of light, if he stretches upward, toward the ceiling, to see it. People like Alan don't go to Marion Prison – except as a political prisoner, a reminder to all the rest.

Stir-crazy. Stir-crazy, she says to herself. She does not love him less because of it. It means she has to fight harder – fight harder to get him out. She knows what it's like. First hand. She's been there. Nobody has to tell her. The nightmares are still there. They are there almost every night. Then she wakes up in a cold sweat. It feels so good not to be in prison. She's out. She can walk down the street.

Alan can't. Maybe Alan never will. It's up to her. She has to make it happen. THE CAMPAIGN FOR ALAN BRADY, she thinks. That's a good name – direct – to the point. She'll never stop fighting. THE CAMPAIGN FOR ALAN BRADY. Make everybody aware of him.

The people will fight for him. She'll work at it – night and day. She'll never give up until he's out.

If only she could see him. If only she could get to Marion. She could explain everything to him. If only he could take her in his arms. They're such nice arms. She remembers what they feel like. He'd understand, if only they could meet and talk. Alan, I'm here for you. I'll never stop fighting for you – until you're out. I can bring that day closer. I'm good at fighting for you, Alan – you'll see. . . . One day, soon, I hope, my darling, you'll be out. I'll be there at the gate. You'll put your arms around me. And I'll put my arms around you. And we'll just hold each other. We won't speak. Not for the longest time. And it will be all right. And when you wake up – in a cold sweat – having a nightmare – I'll be there for you, I'll tell you you're free. You're not in prison any more. But I'll be there for you. Always.

Leah is in the Catskills, at a Jewish hotel, where she has been invited to speak, to tell the guests about Alan, about herself, about what Alan did for Israel. The guests are very sympathetic. She is raising money. Her listeners are prepared to be generous. They know what this fight is all about. They want to join in this CAMPAIGN FOR ALAN BRADY.

Then, in front of her audience, close to the end of her talk, she collapses, and lays motionless on the floor. It takes a moment for the audience to react, to realize that Leah Brady, who a moment ago was standing before them, telling them of her and Alan's ordeal, is now lying on the floor before them.

39

Leah is in the hospital. She is in need of long term treatment. Sandy comes to see her.

Leah asks, "How are we doing with the Parole Board? Are they going to let me see Alan?"

"There are no new developments. But even if they gave permission – you're in no condition to make a trip like that."

"Sandy, I'd crawl there, on my hands and knees."

"The spirit could. But the body can't."

"He's a different Alan. I don't know this one. But if I could go there, and see him, and talk to him. I could make it all right. I could make him understand."

"We're still locked in battle with the Parole Board."

"I know this is Alan without a will – without any judgement. You go stir-crazy. You can't tell your friends from your enemies. This is what's happened to Alan. I can't believe he's so far gone that I wouldn't be able to bring him back."

Sandy informs Leah that Israel is prepared to pay for Leah's stay in the hospital. Ben Zvi has been in touch with her to say so. "But they won't agree to pay for long term treatment in the United States."

"I don't need their favors. How soon can I get out of here?"

"A week. Maybe two. It depends on your progress."

"I'll go on a speaking tour. I'll raise the money."

"Not for a very long time, Leah."

"Am I really as sick as that?"

"I'm afraid you are. I spoke with the doctors. There isn't any question."

"The Israelis are very eager to silence me. They must see me as being important – important enough that they want to get rid of me. All right, they can pay for this. But then I'll go on a speaking tour. Maybe not right away – but soon. In the beginning, I'll just speak locally. I won't do anything too strenuous. I'm sure I'll be able to manage that."

Still in the hospital, Leah is presented with divorce papers from Alan.

Sandy returns to her bedside.

"Ben Zvi made him do it," Leah says, trembling. "He has no will of his own."

"They want to get you out of the way."

"They won't succeed. I'm not going anywhere. I'm going to go on fighting this fight for Alan's release. This divorce isn't real. It's pretend. This isn't my Alan divorcing me."

A short time later Leah is presented with an injunction that prevents her from using the name Brady where it also concerns Alan. It has been issued by Dr. Morton Brady, Alan's father.

Suddenly there is no CAMPAIGN FOR ALAN BRADY.

The name Alan has to be erased from her lips – unless she speaks his name in silence. They are frightened of her. Frightened of her power. She cannot allow them to take control. They are throwing this man away, murdering his soul, his spirit, but only keeping the body alive to be abused and tormented.

They have his mind, to manipulate and maneuver, while the State of Illinois keeps his body in their prison. What is left for her? There must be something left for which she can fight. The body, obviously, as long as she does not mention his name in the process – not out loud. How do you fight for somebody whose name you are forbidden to mention?

40

Mark is at Dario's. Dario takes Mark aside. He has a message for Mark. "It is the man with the brief case – the Israeli – he gave it to me – and I gave it to you. He would like to arrange a meeting with you and your wife. Whenever it is convenient for you both."

Mark tries not to show his excitement. "Where?"

"Here. In my office – upstairs. It's safe. No bugs. I test it every day. Nobody will see you together. You arrive separately – leave separately."

At the appointed day and hour, Mark and Sandy come to Dario's. He directs them upstairs, to his office. Amos Bar Lev is already there – former Haganah section commander in Jerusalem, one-time Minister of Agriculture, close friend of the Spaulding family.

They embrace each other warmly.

There is a bottle of wine waiting for them, provided by Dario.

"Surprised?" Amos Bar Lev asks.

"Very," Mark replies.

They take seats around Dario's big desk.

"I wanted to talk to you both," Amos Bar Lev says. "I thought it only right to let you know from where the Brady papers came. You did an outstanding job with your report."

"With your help, Amos."

"With my help. Yes. You are so like your father. Being here with you now – it's like a continuation of the times we were together, fighting for Jerusalem. Now it is another war – and he isn't here. I'm grateful that you are. We have been able to fight it together. Your father would approve. This is a different kind of war – a war in which Israel may very well disappear – not from enemy action – but because the government is bowing to the requirements and demands of its enemies – compelled to do so by those who hold the real power in the United States. At least you have made the dangers apparent. But that isn't the whole story. There's more. A lot more. And I don't know it. I had access to only some of it. It isn't likely that America has many secrets left, but we know that Mossad is deeply disturbed by what Alan Brady has done. They feel that it has hurt relations with the United States."

"Theirs, Israel's, or both?" Mark asks.

Amos Bar Lev looks at Mark with satisfaction.

"There is a separation then." Sandy says it as a statement rather than as a question.

"At least on this issue," Bar Lev replies. "Mossad is deeply involved with American intelligence – as a kind of hand-maiden, doing America's dirty work – and taking the responsibility for it when it goes wrong, and when the press gets hold of it."

"Like Iran-Contra," Sandy says knowingly.

"And like Mena – in Arkansas," Bar Lev continues. "As you know, they have been bringing in drugs – cocaine, heroin – to pay for arms meant for the Contras in Nicaragua. The Arkansas state governor knows about it. But he's been told by the Federal Government not to interfere."

"How does this help Israel?" Sandy asks.

"It doesn't," Bar Lev says.

"These are actions Mossad is taking on its own," Mark says.

"It would appear that way."

"It's a kind of coup," Mark observes.

"I would hesitate to use that word," Bar Lev replies more in fear than in conviction. "But, yes. A kind of coup. I suppose we have to call it that. Alan Brady is sitting in prison because Mossad wants him there. The Government of Israel is powerless to do anything about it."

"Even if they wanted to?" Sandy asks.

"Even if they wanted to. They don't. But with all the agitation that has been going on – both here and in Israel – and by the way, Sandy, you have been doing an excellent job. They have taken note of it in Israel – and the authorities aren't very pleased. But the people are."

"It's what I have to do, Amos."

"I know. I understand. And I'm glad. For the Government of Israel – getting him out would be a popular move. But they don't have the power. Mossad has it. And Mossad says no. We have given them responsibility for our security – and now they have taken over – in areas that do not concern them, and where they should never have become involved. It is a government inside of a government, responsible to nobody, answerable to nobody, elected by nobody. Because of them – because they have the power – they can keep this man locked up forever."

"Will they?" Mark asks.

"I'm sure that's their intention."

"How do we fight them?" Sandy asks.

Amos Bar Lev shrugs. "How do you fight shadows? But then I know we must – somehow."

"You are absolutely certain that Mossad has taken over?" Mark asks.

"As certain as I can be. It is what I have been given to understand – by someone very close to the center. I notice that you take my bit of news with a considerable amount of equanimity."

"I have been thinking something similar for quite a while now. Putting the facts together – it seems to add up to this Mossad takeover. But until now, it has only been conjecture."

"Unfortunately, Mark, it's more than that."

They are all quiet for a time, digesting what has been said. Then Sandy speaks at last.

"Amos, I'm under no illusions. We're further than ever from getting Alan out of prison."

Amos nods sadly. "Yes, I'm afraid you are right – particularly since Ben Zvi pushed Alan Brady into divorcing Leah. Alan, as you assume, is completely and totally under Ben Zvi's influence. And so is Dr. Brady."

"They have won this battle," Sandy says.

"But not necessarily the war. It is essential to keep fighting, Mossad notwithstanding. That is one of the reasons why I asked you both to come here today – to tell you how important this fight is – Alan Brady, and his plight, is irrevocably tied in with the continued existence of Israel. The two are inseparable. When you fight for Alan Brady, you fight for Israel. When you stop, you let that element prevail who are prepared to sell Israel out to the United States. They think that this policy of appeasement will save them – that they can create an Israel acceptable to the United States, and the rest of the developed world. But America and the rest need the Arabs far more than they need Israel. It is a naive approach, and a stupid one. It will never work. In the final analysis, Israel may well use her nuclear weaponry – in one last grand gesture. While Israel will have struck back very hard – in the end – there will be no viable Israel."

"Not a very nice picture," Sandy says. "And not very encouraging."

"Not a very nice picture at all," Amos Bar Lev agrees. "Its root lies in the appeasement of the Arabs. We in Israel will never live with them – because they do not want to live with us. A place called Israel is not acceptable to them. They are not concerned about our plight – about our return to the land of Israel. It is therefore a question of either us or them. So far they are winning – and we are losing. We could wipe them out in a matter of days. But instead, we take prisoners who have our blood on their hands, keep them alive and then return them – thousands of them for one or two or three Israelis. We turn them back into the Arab terrorist community, where they return once again, to commit terrorist acts against us. This makes no sense. Israel has no death penalty – which may be all right for Israelis within Israel – perhaps it is the humane way. But what has that got to do with Arab terrorists?"

"I fully agree," Mark says. "Nobody can tell us what we must or must not do in order to survive. We know what to do – we're just not doing it."

"Do you look for a time when Israelis themselves will demand a show of strength vis à vis the Arabs?" Sandy asks.

"Many do. Israelis are war-weary. Most have lost somebody in their family. Israel's continued existence has been at a very high cost – because we chose not to win decisively – one victory that would put an end to Arab hostility forever. We could have done it then, we can do it now – and now, better than ever before.

"You know about the American spy ship Liberty. It was picking up our battle orders, and conveying the information to the British listening post in Cyprus, who in turn supplied the Arabs with the information. So we bombed the ship. We did it selectively – to put out their communications capacity, but to hold down the loss of life. Supposedly Israel agreed to pay compensation for the lives lost aboard the Liberty. But, in fact, the money Israel paid out was secretly reimbursed by the United States. Israel was prepared to go along with this bluff, this American hoax, which suggested Israel was at least partly culpable. But that was a mistake, too. They should have disabled the ship more thoroughly than they did, forced its surrender, and exacted confessions from all those responsible who were spying on Israel. The United States could have been required to pay a high price for such an action – the admission, for example, that they were aiding and abetting an enemy during time of war. The Israelis would have seen a very different picture then of the United States, whom they confuse as their benefactor. For most Israelis it is difficult to make the distinction between American Jews, who are devoted to Israel, and the American Administration, who isn't, and is doing its best to destroy Israel."

Amos Bar Lev falls silent for a time. There is so much that needs saying – so much that is a manifestation of his frustration, of his anxiety. He knows that the nation for which he fought, and which he and a few others created, is gradually slipping into oblivion.

They sip their wine.

"Is there any danger that they will find out who supplied me with the Brady Papers?" Mark asks.

"A very considerable amount of danger," Amos Bar Lev replies. "The Prime Minister ordered Ben Zvi to find out."

"And has he?"

"He has his suspicions. Mossad has been working on it."

"And if they confirm those suspicions?" Sandy asks.

"It will be interesting to find out. That was another reason why I wanted to meet with the two of you – so that if anything happens – if it looks like an accident – it probably isn't."

"You're very calm about it, Amos," Sandy says.

"I feel calm – as if I'm watching it all on television. I'll be going back to Israel soon."

"Wouldn't it be better to stay here?" Mark asks.

"If they're looking for me – they'll know where to find me – whether I'm here, or in Israel. I fought the good fight. My conscience is clear. It's just that I'm sorry things have turned out the way they have. It isn't what we wanted."

41

Sandy goes to the Israeli Embassy in Washington where she meets with Jacob Ben Zvi. He shakes her hand enthusiastically. He is bubbling over with triumph, with success. He projects an air of victory, which he is eager to make apparent, and which no one could miss. It is not necessary to speak the words; his whole demeanor says them with eloquence.

"It is nice to see you again, Mrs. Spaulding," he says with condescension. "You are looking more lovely than ever."

He seats her in the big chair near his desk.

"The divorce between Alan and Leah was very unfortunate," Ben Zvi says, trying to sound sad, but sounding so happy he appears about to burst with it.

"You arranged it, Mr. Ben Zvi."

"Not at all, " he says, meaning, I certainly did, and it's obvious how pleased I am. "It was Alan's own decision," he adds grandly, to make it apparent that he, Jacob Ben Zvi, was behind that decision.

Sandy says, "I want to send my client to Israel for the long term medical treatment she needs desperately . . ."

"We're ready to help."

"Good."

"Under certain conditions. What about the Parole Board?"

"They're prepared to let her go."

"Why not? They save the money, and the American Government saves the trouble she might make if she stays in the United States."

"And the trouble she might make for Israel."

"That would be minimal. But there are conditions, Mrs. Spaulding."

"Which are?"

"No agitation. She must not demonstrate. She must not talk about Alan Brady in public. She must not talk about Leah Brady who served three and a half years in prison as an accessory because she was married to Alan Brady. She would come to Israel as a normal human being who nobody has ever heard of – or cares about. We have enough problems without making more. Those are the terms, Mrs. Spaulding."

"They are very harsh."

"But those are the terms. As a matter of fact they are not harsh at all. I would say they were very easy."

"I'm not sure my client will accept them."

"Then she can stay here – and have the treatment the public health service is prepared to offer. I understand that most people would sooner choose a place on the pavement and die on it, rather than subject themselves to the public health system this county has to offer."

"It does have certain shortcomings."

"We are being very generous, Mrs. Spaulding. We are accepting a measure of responsibility in this matter. We don't have to. It's compassion. Pure compassion. I don't think you appreciate that fully, Mrs. Spaulding. Further, she is the divorced wife. She lacks credibility now. He repudiated her. Whatever it is she might want to say, it is without much meaning. And then of course there is the injunction – so what is there left for her to say?"

It is hard to argue with Ben Zvi on these points. They have obviously won, and everybody else has lost.

"And if my client should wish to remain on in Israel?"

"She can be a normal immigrant. It's her right."

"And the Government of Israel will continue to look after her."

"Hopefully she'll integrate. And then she won't need any looking after."

"Until she does?"

"If she doesn't make any trouble."

"I'll put it to my client."

"Do." He says it as if it is a forgone conclusion, as if, what else is there to discuss? Her options are limited. She has no real choice. Perhaps she does not like what they are prepared to give – but then the alternatives are worse.

There is nothing further that needs being said. Sandy stands up to go. She shakes hands with Ben Zvi again. He says, "Thank you for coming to see me, Mrs. Spaulding."

She cannot bring herself to say, 'thank you'. For what has she, or Leah, or Alan got to say 'thank you'? Thank you for what? But she knows that she has probably made the best arrangement she could under the circumstances.

Sandy leaves.

Jacob Ben Zvi remains seated at his desk, revelling in his triumph.

Later, in his office, he speaks with a Mossad operative.

"You're sure?" he asks the operative, who is in his late twenties, muscular, with a confident demeanor – some call it arrogance.

"Absolutely."

"You know who we're talking about – this man who has been close to all of the Prime Ministers – who fought in all of Israel's wars – who was a high-up officer. Who has been in the Cabinet much of the time."

"There isn't any question. He came in alone. He went upstairs to Dario's office. The Spauldings came in later. They too went up to Dario's office. That's where they met and talked. Then they left separately."

"You know they were in the office together?"

"Of course. I saw them. I climbed up on the roof of the building next to Dario's restaurant. And I recorded their conversation."

The Mossad operative takes a cassette from his pocket and puts it down on Ben Zvi's desk. "Listen for yourself. You'll find it very interesting."

"I'm sure I will. Well done."

"All in a day's work."

The Mossad operative leaves.

"All in a day's work," he says, repeating the Mossad operative's words. He, Ben Zvi, has dealt with the Brady situation, and now here is the proof that Amos Bar Lev is the one who leaked the Brady Papers. He's glad it's Amos Bar Lev. He never liked Amos. He was never really a party man – not all the way. He had gone far – Amos Bar Lev – while he, Jacob Ben Zvi, had stayed in the shadow.

Sandy tells Leah that she is to be allowed to go to Israel for medical treatment, and the terms.

Leah says, "I don't want to go."

Sandy frowns.

"I want to stay here and fight."

"For whom? Why? And how?"

"I'll find a way."

"They don't want you, Leah. They made it pretty clear."

"Ben Zvi made it clear."

"You have to start thinking about yourself."

"Alan needs me – now more than ever."

"You've been gagged, Leah. This part of the fight is over. You have to accept it. If there was any chance, I would encourage you to stay. But there is nothing you can do here. Perhaps, once you get to Israel, you will find a way. You know how much sympathy there is for Alan there – and for you, too."

Leah nods, reluctantly accepting the truth of Sandy's words.

"Of course you can speak privately – to members of the Knesset. Nobody can stop you from doing that. Guela Cohen has been very helpful – and Edna Salidar. There will be a lot of people you can talk to in influential positions. The fight isn't over, Leah. Just see it as a new beginning."

"You're very persuasive, Sandy."

"I'm just being logical. There is no fundamental disagreement here."

"All right, " Leah says, resigned. "I'm ready to go."

42

Sandy accompanies Leah to Israel. They are escorted by two men from the Mossad.

Leah, now alone in Tel Aviv, is installed in a small apartment off Dizengoff. She does not want to be here. She feels like a non-person; they have stripped her of her personality, of her soul, of her very reason for existing. She is in exile, amidst the animated throngs who are eager to get wherever it is they appear to be going, and just as eager to return from wherever it was that they had been. There's falafal to eat, an inviting Mediterranean Sea, a broad sandy beach that plays host to some of the most beautiful people on earth.

But Leah does not like falafal, is indifferent to the invitations of the Mediterranean, is not tempted by the broad sandy beach, and feels completely alone, even amongst the most beautiful people on earth. If Alan were here, then it would be different; they would eat falafal – walk down the street eating it, laughing and holding hands, walking on the beach, barefooted, the gentle waves engulfing their feet. The thought of it makes her cringe with something close to physical pain, because she knows it is never likely to happen.

The anguish runs parallel to the actual physical pain that is a part of her everyday life. She goes for tests. They are looking after her. She has no complaints there. But she wonders if it wouldn't have been better to die on the street – fighting. Then she would still have her personality, the reality of who she is. Here, that reality seems to be non-existent.

That she once had a personality, that there are those who think part of one still remains, is manifested by her telephone: it is tapped. It is not necessary to be a telephone engineer to be aware of this, but merely to phone Leah Brady, and hear the apparatus clicking into action. Probably they want her to know – to make it apparent that while she appears to be living in isolation – it is a myth. They are here – watching her, listening to her.

The watching – that is there. Was there. May still be there. A girl phoned. A reporter, from Ma'ariv, she said. She wanted to interview Leah. The girl came. They talked. She was a nice person, seemed like a nice person. Leah liked her. The girl was very sympathetic. She was eager to hear about Leah's plans, Leah's future, how she would still fight for her husband.

They became friends. Leah confided in her. It was nice to have someone with whom to talk, someone eager to listen, someone who made her feel a little less alone. Then the girl came to her, and broke down, and said she had been sent to spy on Leah. "But I can't do it anymore," she said. "You thought I was your friend. Meanwhile I was just putting a knife in your back."

So whom do you trust? Leah feels so betrayed, so vulnerable. If you talked to someone, would he or she wind up informing on you? She thought about all the support she'd had in America. Here, that support was supposed to be so overwhelming. Even the Knesset had a committee to offer support for Alan Brady. They took it very seriously here – in theory. Here nobody knew her;

nobody seemed to care. That was yesterday's problem. Today there are hundreds of new ones. Should she go to Jerusalem and demonstrate before the Wall, carry a sign that says, I AM FIGHTING FOR MY HUSBAND, ALAN BRADY. But he is not her husband. Then how about a sign that says I AM FIGHTING FOR MY EX-HUSBAND, ALAN BRADY. Or just, FIGHTING FOR ALAN BRADY.

Then of course she is in violation of the terms of her agreement. What would they do, put her in prison? She'd already been there. Maybe she should go to Jerusalem and demonstrate at the Wall, carry a sign that says. I AM FIGHTING FOR ME. I AM FIGHTING FOR LEAH BRADY. I WAS IN PRISON FOR THREE AND A HALF YEARS, IN AN AMERICAN CONCENTRATION CAMP. America doesn't have concentration camps? Then you have never been where I have been, where Alan Brady is now. He is a political prisoner. I was a political prisoner.

Maybe she should go to the Knesset, picket there. There is all sorts of sympathy there. There is Guela Cohen. She spoke with Guela Cohen, the right-wing member of the Knesset. Guela Cohen threw her arms around Leah. She was genuinely sympathetic. And Edna Salidar, from Labor – two opposite ends of the earth, dis-agree on everything – but on this, on the Bradys, they could agree.

They were doing everything they could for Alan.

Ben Zvi is doing a marvelous job for Alan in America, they tell her.

Leah is stunned. Jacob Ben Zvi is doing a marvelous job for Alan in America? They believe this? Of course. Jacob Ben Zvi speaks to them in the Knesset, to the whole Knesset, virtually all of whom support Alan Brady – and, it goes without saying, Leah Brady. And he speaks to them separately, privately, tells them that he is working behind the scenes. And they understand this. He reveals a little of what he is doing behind the scenes – talking to the President – don't breathe a word of this.

And they are working behind the scenes, too. They are in touch with Lawrence Eagleburger – the Assistant Secretary of State. They sent him two letters already – neither of which he answered. They said they would like to bring about the release of Alan Brady. They thought they were telling it to the right man. Not quite. He and his department are those most eager to insure that Alan J. Brady is put away for a long time. Forever isn't too long.

Leah feels alone. The falafal does not beckon, nor the white sandy beach, nor the calm Mediterranean Sea.

43

Iraq, as Alan Brady had pointed out, was fully equipped – by France, Germany, the United States, Britain, and others. They were fully prepared to eliminate Israel. Iraq had been provided with nuclear, biological and chemical weaponry as well as the technology to produce it. There is some disagreement as to how close Iraq was to having a nuclear weapon – weeks, months – certainly much less than a year. They had poison gas in abundance. The facilities for producing it had been supplied by Germany. It was the same poison gas, virtually, that the Germans had used before – in the concentration camps. The Germans were very good at producing poison gas. They had been so good that fifty years later the same type could be just as efficient. And the objective was the same – the elimination of Jews.

The biological weaponry, the guided missile systems – the Scuds – they were ostensibly meant for defense, presumably against Iran, and against Iraq's Arab enemies. But most of all they were meant to eliminate Israel. Those who supplied Iraq with the equipment and the know-how for producing it, were fully aware of Saddam Hussein's intentions. Saddam proclaimed them often enough.

The United States, under George Bush, had established excellent relations with Iraq, provided Iraq with five billion dollars in aid. George Bush wrote to President Hussein and called him My Dear Saddam. "Dear Saddam" thought that his fellow president, George Bush, was giving him permission to move in on Kuwait. Saddam got the signals wrong. Bush's enthusiasm was for Saddam's pending action against Israel – not Kuwait. Saddam had it in mind to get Kuwait first – then Israel second, with nuclear weapons.

The United States wanted the military action against Iraq to have the support of America's Arab allies. In order to insure this, Israel was not to be a participant, and was ordered to stay out of the conflict. Israel complied, hoped for some sort of material gain from the U.S., while the Scuds rained down upon her. Tel Aviv was the main target – there were more Jews there, more heavily concentrated.

The Scuds poured down and Israelis were told to "be brave." There were shelters in which people could cower, and wait until the all-clear. Meanwhile, issued with gas masks, they hoped to be able to endure. They were also provided with atropine and an antidote to mustard gas, in powder form.

Apartment blocks were shattered in Tel Aviv. Civilians died. Israel did nothing, stood by and let it happen.

Mark and Sandy and David, and Jews everywhere, watch the events with growing anxiety. Mark, seated at the dinner table with Sandy and David, is unusually quiet. David wants to discuss the events, the implications, the possible outcome for Israel. Sandy, too, is quiet. Would there be an Israel in the morning?

Mark has something he wants to say. He isn't quite sure how to say it. He looks at Sandy, then at David. They sense the urgency of his need to speak and they wait in anticipation.

Then Mark says, "I want to go to Israel." He speaks deliberately; he has thought about this for some time, turned it over in his mind, and reached a decision. But saying it in words, out loud, to your wife and to your son, is harder than saying it in your head, to yourself. "It's the only way I can say what I feel. I also want to be there with Leah. I don't like her having to be alone through this."

Sandy exhales slowly. She is almost relieved by Mark's words, almost exuberant. "Where you go, I go," she says. "That has been the way of our life together. It won't be any different now. If anything happens, it will happen to us both. We'll show our solidarity with Israel the way we always have – together."

"You know the dangers."

"I do. Did you think it could be any other way – for us?"

"No."

"Good. It's settled then."

Mark nods.

David, getting to be almost as big as his father, hearing his parents' words, looking from one to the other, feels a measure of surprise, of exhilaration.

"Not quite settled," he says to his parents. "I'm not going to stay here all alone while the two of you go off to Israel to get Scudded. Or do you expect me to stay with Aaron Haliday and his folks while I wait to become an orphan? I think I should be consulted in this."

Sandy says, "All right, David, we're consulting you."

"Thanks," David says, sarcasm in his voice. He says simply, but with resolve, "I'm coming, too."

Mark and Sandy look at each other. He could die before he has lived. Should they expose him to this? Has he got a right to make such a decision? And do they have the right to let him make it?

Sandy nods, almost imperceptibly, to Mark.

Mark says to David, "All right. Then it really is settled. Do you want to consider the implications? Do you want to discuss them?"

"There's nothing to discuss. It's my duty, too. I said so in front of the Wall. That's why I had a Bar Mitzvah."

Mark says, "I'm proud of you, David."

David says, "I'm proud of you, Dad. I always have been. And I always will be. And you, too, Mom. I love you both. Very much."

44

Mark, Sandy and David board the El Al airliner bound for Ben Gurion Airport, Tel Aviv. El Al is the only line flying in and out of Israel. The rest have decided that the element of risk is too great and that they will resume services to Israel after the war – if Israel is still there.

El Al is also carrying large numbers of Israelis out of Israel, those not convinced that there will be an Israel for much longer – or even if there is, there won't be a lot left to inhabit. Many who, for economic reasons, can't escape the country, make their way to Jerusalem, considered, generally, to be relatively more safe.

The El Al jet puts down at Ben Gurion Airport. Mark, Sandy and David clear Customs quickly – there aren't many arrivals – and are directed to the gas mask distribution point where they are issued with gas masks, and given a demonstration on how they are to be used. A cardboard box, with a shoulder strap, is provided for the gas mask, also containing mustard gas antidote and a vial of atropine, to be injected in the event of exposure to poison gas. There are also leaflets with more detailed instructions, in Hebrew and in English, beginning with: *Remember! immediately upon receipt, fit the mask to your face in accordance with the detailed procedure below. Pre-fitting will ensure immediate and correct donning during a gas alarm.*

The instructions conclude with the reassuring message: *A voicemitter assembly has been installed in the mask, enabling the wearer's voice to be transmitted clearly.*

Mark, Sandy and David, in their gas masks, look at each other, grotesque, conscious of the deadly implications of wearing these abominations. At the same time, they are profoundly aware that this is why they have come: they will suffer the same fate as the rest of the nation, whose government has decided – wrongly in their view – to remain passive, and allow the Scuds to fall upon a defenseless civilian population, wherever they may.

Sandy, David and Mark take a cab to the Moriah Plaza Hotel in Tel Aviv, located on the sea front. It is one of the few hotels in Tel Aviv to remain open. It is virtually empty. Do they want rooms on the third floor or the fourteenth? If you're worried about ordinary explosives you want the third, but if you're worried about gas, you choose the fourteenth.

It's a difficult decision to have to make, since it involves seeing into Saddam's mind and determining just exactly what he intends putting in his Scuds. So far he has limited himself to conventional explosives. But tonight – tomorrow night – who can tell? In Israel they know four minutes in advance – enough time to put on your gas mask. Almost enough time to get to the shelter. News of the pending attack comes over the television – keep watching. And the radio. Keep listening. In Tel Aviv more nights are spent in the shelter than out.

Sandy suggests the third floor – it's closer to the shelter in the basement than the fourteenth, easier to make one's way down the back stairway in a blackout.

They have a two room suite, with a big window, and a balcony, overlooking the sea. Military helicopters fly just off the beach. Israeli jets streak across the sky. In five minutes they could finish this war – finish off Saddam. He has a bomb shelter made just for such an eventuality. But let him see how useful it will be in the event of an Israeli reprisal.

In Tel Aviv everyone strains his and her ears – listening for the alarm. There are alarms for everything – ambulances, police, fire engines, Scud attacks. You have to identify the correct one, and respond accordingly. Tel Avivians are experts at it now. The police are busy. The fire department is busy. Scudded buildings burn quickly. And the ambulances – they carry the injured to the

hospitals, among them those who had mistakenly injected themselves with atropine, thinking they had come under poison gas
attack.

Israelis are not accustomed to this kind of war. They do not
want to sit back and take it. They want to give it back – ten times
over – a hundred times over. They can do it, too. The Government swears revenge, swears retaliation. But America has said,
keep out of this one, and, as usual, Israel complies.

Mark, Sandy and David stop for a falafal in a little place they
know on Ben Yehuda. They are unusually quiet, watching, looking, listening, trying to adjust to being in a country at war. Night is
when it happens. Night is when war comes. Night is when the
Scuds begin to fall. But not necessarily every night.

There are not many people about. Mostly they have hurried
home – to be near their families, to be close to the shelter. Mark
does not feel fear so much as anger – that Israel has remained so
passive.

David looks at his cardboard gas mask box hanging from the
back of the chair next to him. Over his falafal, which he holds in
both hands, he watches his father, then his mother, neither of
whom show any outward signs of anxiety.

"Thank you for letting me come," David says.

"I hope we did right," Mark replies.

"I couldn't have stood it – if you were both here – and I stayed
back. I got butterflies in my stomach – but it would've been a lot
worse on my own."

"I think we've all got butterflies," Sandy says.

They finish their falafal. Now it is time to go and see Leah. She
is in the Asuta Hospital, not far away, undergoing tests for her
intestinal problems which persist. Normally it would be a pleasant
walk there, on a nice evening in Tel Aviv. But not this evening,
when the Scuds might come bearing down.

They find a taxi. It is not difficult. Nobody is traveling much
now.

The Asuta Hospital is a private hospital, not a part of the sick fund
that Labor Zionism had created, but failed to run properly. One of
the problems was that the prestigious profession of doctoring, to
which Jewish parents aspired for their children, had not carried
much prestige with Labor Zionism, that said cleaning out the cow
barn was the height to which all decent Jews should aspire.

231

So Leah is in the Asuta Hospital. She hasn't got any complaints. It's a very well-run institution.

The taxi pulls up in front of the hospital, and Mark and family emerge. There is a guard at the entrance, a young man with an Australian accent, and a Jericho, Mark notes, in a holster attached to his waist.

Who have they come to see, the Australian with the Jericho asks politely.

Leah Brady.

You're friends?

Yes.

"Give her my best. She's a wonderful lady."

They find Leah in her room, sitting up in bed and watching television.

They all embrace her simultaneously. She clings to them, reluctant to let them go.

"I'm so glad you came," Leah keeps saying. "I'm so happy."

Leah is very pale. But that is why she is here. Hopefully they will be able to help her. At least they are trying. It is much better than dying on the street in New York.

Hospital patients are not evacuated to shelters here during Scud attacks. For protection, sheets of plastic have been taped over the windows, in case of gas attack.

Leah has been through a number of attacks by now. She is rather casual about Scud missiles. She explains what the procedure is during an attack. And, as she explains, Saddam Hussein has decided to send his greetings. The message comes across on the television set playing in the background.

Sandy and Mark and David put on their gas masks, carefully fitted as per the instruction leaflet. Leah puts on hers more slowly, as if in defiance of Saddam Hussein.

Leah sits cross-legged on her bed. Sandy sits on the bed near her. David and Mark are on chairs near the bed.

Saddam sends over his first missile of the evening. It hits the ground somewhere off in the distance with a dull thud. The Patriots – the anti-missile device America has sent over to placate Israel, and pretend they were offering some sort of defense – is not very effective. Proof of that comes when Saddam sends over another one, almost as audible as the first. There are more to come. Thud. Thud. Dull thuds – some louder than others, some closer than others. May they not be killing Jews. May they miss Tel Aviv. May they land in a field, harmlessly. How vulnerable this city is. The enemy had been ten miles away – but now, with the inclusion of Judea and Samaria, Tel Aviv is considerably further away. But certainly not out of rocket range, not with all that marvelous equipment supplied by Israel's "good friends", the United States, Germany, France, Britain, and most of the rest of Europe.

David watches his parents. They are completely calm. Through the plastic-covered eye-holes of their gas masks, their eyes meet. The eyes of Mark and Sandy convey reassurance. David feels a measure of fear, and, at the same time, he feels a sense of exhilaration. He could die. He has never been so close to death. He is glad he is here. It is his bond with Israel. He understands what the people here are forced to live through; even when there are no missiles falling, there is always the threat that they soon will be.

David looks at Leah. Their eyes meet. Her eyes are smiling eyes. He lets his eyes smile back at her. It's hard to smile in a gas mask.

Then there is another thud. David thinks he has counted seven.

Saddam's greetings end for the night. Take off your gas masks, at least for now. This confrontation with death, shared equally amongst them, creates a closeness that everyday life could never provide.

Leah takes Sandy's hands in hers. "Thanks for coming," she says. "Thanks for sharing the Scuds with me. I love you all very much."

"I sent you into this," Sandy says. "It's all my fault."

"Isn't Israel meant as a 'refuge' for the Jewish people?" Leah speaks with irony. "I'm sure Alan would sooner be here, with the Scuds raining down on his head – than where he is now . . . Tell me, do you think he's any closer to getting out?"

Sandy shakes her head.

"That's how I read the situation. It's more difficult from here. The government has imposed its own form of censorship on the situation – on the name 'Brady'. It's in the same category as military intelligence – it has to be approved by the censor before it can appear in print, or on the radio or television."

"They obviously take your presence here very seriously," Mark says.

"So much so that I've been made into a non-person. Of course those are the terms under which I was allowed to come here. They keep putting out these lies that they're working behind the scenes. And people believe them. What choice do they have? There is no other point of view allowed to circulate. But this situation – the Brady situation – it goes very deep. Deeper than most people realize."

"What do you mean?" Sandy asks.

"I don't know for sure. It's more what I sense. I've got a 'handler' – a government 'handler' – who looks after me – watches me, but also sees that I get most of what I need. He's frightened. I get the feeling that this is more than just the government – I don't know how to put it – I can't nail it down exactly. It's somebody telling the government what it has to do."

"Somebody like Mossad?" Mark says.

Leah considers for a moment. "Yeah. Somebody like Mossad. I don't know if it's Mossad – or somebody else – or if it's not just my imagination running wild. In this place anything is possible."

"It's not imagination, Leah."

"Then somebody else has taken over the government – somebody like Mossad?"

"It would seem that way."

"To me, too."

45

AFTERMATH

Mark brings his report up to date. A new edition is to appear.

EXCERPTS

George Bush ended the Gulf War before it was over, because his Arab allies told him to stop. They explained that it wasn't nice to humiliate Saddam Hussein, though they were not overly fond of him, themselves – at least at this moment in time. It would be bad for a Westerner to humiliate an Arab, even an Arab who was an enemy. George Bush complied.

The United States held a Victory Celebration, though there was no victory, and certainly nothing to celebrate. The American people knew that they had been cheated out of a genuine victory against Iraq, and when they could, got rid of George Bush; it wasn't so much a vote for Bill Clinton, as a vote against George Bush. It felt good, taking revenge, but the result was a Bill Clinton, another disaster.

Israel had once again succumbed to American requirements, this time staying out of the hostilities because the other Arabs refused to let them participate. Saddam had failed to use chemical weaponry against Israel, which was not an expression of humanity, but because Israel had made it abundantly clear that if Iraq did so, Israel would retaliate with a nuclear response. But Israel was prepared to endure conventional missile attacks, and merely shrug, which showed a shocking indifference towards its own population, and gave a signal to all the rest that it was all right to send conventional missiles to plunder Israel, and that Israel wouldn't do anything about it.

It was thought that a new president – though very little was actually expected from him – untainted by the events surrounding Reagan and Bush, would grant a presidential pardon to Alan Brady. Mrs. Sandy Fraser Spaulding, a leader in the struggle to bring about Brady's release, met with the President and discussed the case with him at length. Clinton claimed he had an open mind on the subject, and would hear the views of all concerned.

The views of at least some of those concerned were those of the State Department, the Department of Defense, and the Department of Justice, all of whom had put Brady where he is in the first place. And despite the appearance of a new president – a weak one – they showed no inclination to alter their views. President Clinton announced, after what he called 'due deliberations', that, in light of Alan Brady's heinous crimes against the United States, Brady should stay where he is. The sentence, he explained, was right and just (considering all that the U.S. Government was trying to conceal).

The key to Alan Brady's cell, it was felt, was actually in the hands of the Israelis, who, if they wanted to, could persuade the United States to bring about Brady's release. Mrs. Sandy Fraser Spaulding met with Prime Minister Rabin in order to express the wish of the American Jewish – and non-Jewish – communities that Alan J. Brady should be released without further delay.

While Rabin agreed to bring the matter to the attention of Bill Clinton, the request, if it was actually made, was subsequently turned down. The request was seen as disingenuous.

Rabin was regarded as essentially unstable, vacillating frequently between what needed to be done, and what the world, who looked forward to Israel's demise, thought should be done. One day he gave orders to resist the *Intifada*, and the next, prosecuted those who had done so. The *Intifada* could easily have been put down, as the Egyptians had done when confronted by disgruntled Arab youth on their side of the Gaza Strip: they eliminated them. The problem was instantly and permanently removed.

Rabin's assassination solved very little, created a wave of sympathy for him and the Labor Party, which they might not have had otherwise. It put additional power in the hands of the man who was even less qualified for the role, and more prepared to sell out Israel, more programmed to make those concessions which would jeopardize Israel's continued existence.

During this period Amos Bar Lev, who fought shoulder to shoulder with my father in an effort to create a free and independent Israel as a homeland for the Jewish people, and who subsequently provided us with the Brady Papers that proved to be so revealing, was found dead, as a result of a single gunshot wound to his head. His death was reported as a suicide. But there was no suicide note. And, according to his family, there was no reason why he would have taken his own life. Further, no shot had been fired from his own gun, a fact that government sources have tried to conceal.

The verdict of suicide is a highly dubious one. We regard Amos Bar Lev's death as murder.

We accuse Mossad of that murder.

This secret organization, with a very high profile, has assumed powers meant to be reserved for an elected government.

By virtue of its involvement with security, succeeding Israeli governments have allowed it to become more powerful than the government itself, and is now unable to make policy where it is in disagreement with Mossad. This is exemplified by the case of Alan J. Brady, whom, Mossad contends, spoiled their relations with U.S. Intelligence. Consequently, Mossad does not want Brady to be released – fearful that he would reveal more U.S. secrets – and more of Mossad's. These revelations, Mossad fears, would also expose the extent to which Mossad does America's bidding, doing the dirty work for America, which the U.S. Government wishes to conceal. The U.S. finds Israel a convenient and useful garbage dump, hiding its own involvement and its own duplicity.

More recently, Vince Foster, close to the then-Governor Clinton, who made his way to Washington, was supposed to have commited suicide, but the reality could very well be something different. It could be murder – and it was assumed by some that Mossad could be involved.

Individual Mossad agents no doubt benefit financially. They no longer serve Israel, but only themselves, and the U.S. whose aim is the elimination of Israel.

Mossad is profoundly cognizant of CIA hostility directed toward itself. There is a history of CIA support for the Arab cause reflecting the American Administration's own position. Wherever and whenever it could, the CIA has betrayed Mossad agents to the CIA's Arab partners; the Mossad agents were subsequently eliminated.

The case of Alan J. Brady has the same status as military intelligence – in Israel it is subject to the strictest censorship. It is censored because Mossad and the Government of Israel want it that way. Succeeding Israeli governments have concurred in this censorship, frightened that its own involvement will become apparent. As a consequence, the Government of Israel has spent millions of dollars attempting to divert the ire and the efforts of Brady campaigners from itself, who is culpable, to that of the United States, cynically aware that in this quarter, no release will occur without prior Mossad approval.

In an effort to insure his election, on the wave of Rabin's demise, Peres brought the election date forward. The Arabs, aware that they could do virtually as they wished, made terrorism a part of everyday life in Israel.

But by a small majority Israelis voted against national suicide, elected a man who said he was against it, too. The world's press, reflecting their governments, went into a state of shock when the people of Israel chose the man who represented life over the one who represented death. By a very slim majority the people of Israel had thwarted the aims and ambitions of the rest of the world that expressed indignation and disapproval.

The American Administration was panicked by the Peres defeat, no longer able to mold the extremely malleable puppet who had always been so accommodating. America had long since surrendered to the PLO, and part of the terms had been to exact Israel's surrender as well. The Pan Am incident, which the American Government had long tried to obscure by deliberately concealing the facts, was more than likely perpetrated by the PLO. They – the PLO – were hired by the Iranians, who sought revenge for the shooting down of their own civilian plane by the U.S. Military.

Now, faced with a new leadership in Israel, the American Government considered how intransigent that leadership might be, and prepared to bring as much pressure to bear as might be required in order to prevail.

Mark writes his concluding observations:

Regarding who owns Israel, a thousand years after the destruction of Israel, there were fifty Jewish communities throughout the land. In the 1500s, the Ottoman Turks were extremely benign, and Jewish life flourished in Israel. Safed was of special importance; it was here from where the Cabalah evolved. By the end of the 1500s there were 30,000 Jews in Safed. But successive invasions took their toll, and the Turks were not always benevolent. The Catholic Church, then as now, thought that God wanted the Jews prevented from returning to Israel.

But in Britain, during one period of the Victorian era, prominent Protestants, including members of the nobility, proclaimed that it was a Christian act to help the Jewish people return to its homeland. There were even those in Britain who thought that the British Government should buy Palestine from the Turks and present it to the Jews.

'Never once,' Samuel Katz, the noted historian tells us, 'was it suggested, openly or covertly, that the Holy Land could not, or should not, be restored to the Jews because it had become the property of others . . . The claim of historic association, of historic right, of historic ownership by the Arab people or by a Palestinian entity is a fiction fabricated in our own day . . . There never was a Palestine Arab nation. To the Arab people as a whole, no such entity as Palestine existed . . . The Arabs did, however, play a significant and specific role in one aspect of Palestine's life: They contributed effectively to its devastation.'

Then, as now, Arabs were good at trying to take over what others have created. In this era, when Israel's strength parallels that of the strongest of nations, she is in greater danger than at any time since her emergence as an independent entity. Her disappearance would signal the end of the Jewish people.

Too often in the past, Israel has manifested weakness when a show of strength was required. This has been amply demonstrated by the betrayal of Alan J. Brady, an open wound on what could otherwise be the beautiful face of Israel.

May the time be short when Israel takes a strong and dutiful stand, and brings Alan J. Brady home.